Fallen Empire

KEITH MCARDLE

NATIONAL
LIBRARY
OF AUSTRALIA

A catalogue record for this book is available from the National Library of Australia

DEDICATION

To David Gemmell and Stan Nicholls, two of the finest authors to ever place pen to paper. Not only great writers, but they are the people who instilled in me a deep hunger to create stories, characters and worlds.

Sadly, David passed away on the 28th of July 2006. A date that is burned in my mind forever. When the Big Man died, I was away overseas in an area where we had limited internet access and almost no contact with the outside world. I returned home in August of the same year eager for the new Gemmell novel to drop, only to find out the news. That day, the world for me at least, grew just a touch darker.

Stan and David, thank you.

ACKNOWLEDGMENTS

It takes many people to create a novel. I'll try to keep this short, but there are so many people who have helped and pushed me, not only with this book, but my overall career as an author.

Simone, my beautiful wife and driving force. She is the only person in my life that believed in me from the day we met. Thanks to her talent as an artist, she designed the map of the continent upon which Vyder walks.

I want to thank the patience, incredible knowledge and guiding hand of both Lee Murray and Devin Madson. These ladies, and skilful authors, perused the early draft of the book and gave their feedback. The advice they provided in itself, has taught me so much about the craft and structure of storytelling. I'll forever be indebted to you both. Thank you.

My editor, Tim Marquitz, you're tougher than nails man. Not even the small problem of open-heart surgery could keep him down. Salute!

My cover designer, Pen Astridge. Her deft skill in graphic design brought Fallen Empire's cover to life. In my view, she is one of the finest graphic designers in the world.

Dean Samed of Neotsock for providing the photograph of Karlos Moir.

Last but definitely not least, to my Street Team. These men and women are a small group of people from varying professions all over the world. They have agreed to read my early drafts and provide feedback as to what they think as a reader. My thanks to you all, you are worth your weight in gold.

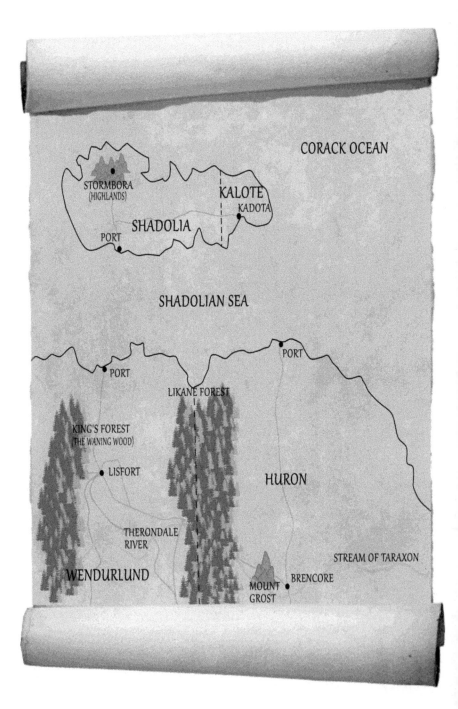

KEITH MCARDLE

Part I

Death and Decay

I

King George, ruler of the kingdom of Wendurlund stood at one of the huge windows facing east, hands clasped behind his back.

"Lisfort is beautiful this time of morning."

Jad, the king's most senior adviser, untied the leather bound scroll and unrolled it. "It is, sire." He ironed the paper flat with his palms.

The monarch glanced at him, the rising sun painting the skin of his face a deep orange. "Anything of interest there for me, Jad?"

Boring as dog shit. Not a skerrick of anything interesting really.

"Not a lot, my lord, no. Only one item that's noteworthy. Reports suggest an altercation occurred overnight at one of the taverns, involving the foresters. But, the foresters have returned to town. The lopping season is at an end." He spread his hands. "It's to be expected."

"Any of them known to the Watch?"

"Yes, my lord. One forester by the name of Brokk. He was causing trouble last season as well."

"Have the Watch find him, put him on trial and if he's found guilty, hang him from the balcony of the city hall. You shall run the trial, Jad."

"Yes sire."

"Is that all you have for me?"

Jad removed his hands from the scroll, allowing it to roll itself back into its original shape. He tied the leather thong in place. "Yes, sire. An uneventful evening."

He stood, but paused. "Sire?"

King George looked at him, eyebrows rising to

meet his hairline. "What is it, Jad?"

"Sire." Jad pursed his lips. "Following our discussion yesterday, do you think it prudent to have a highlander sent on such a high profile mission?"

"You have doubts?"

The king gestured at the chair behind him. Jad sat again. "Sire, he's not a professional soldier, and to put it bluntly, he's not of Wendurlund stock. He's highland born, a man of Shadolia, a kingdom which has, in the past, been at war with us."

King George sat beside him. "He is all you say, Jad. But he is an assassin and one that comes very highly recommended. If someone is going to creep into the heart of the enemy stronghold to free my son and bring him safely home, then it is a man whose profession is to carry out a task undetected."

"I understand, sire. However, the soldiers of your King's Own are the finest warriors in this world. Can one of their subunits be tasked?"

"No Jad, my household troops are, as you say, very skilled, but even they couldn't go undetected into the heart of the Huronian capital."

"With all respect due, I think you underestimate them, my liege."

"One assassin is more difficult to trace than five King's Own soldiers. And as you said, Vyder Ironstone is a Shadolian Highlander."

Jad's eyebrows drew together. "I don't take your meaning, sire."

"The highlanders are a warrior race. They are born to fight. Their children bred to the sword and spear not long after they can walk. I've not ever seen a highlander who was a coward. My mind is made, Jad. Vyder Ironstone is the man for this mission."

"Aye, my lord. And if he fails?"

"I'll tell you what I told the highlander when I tasked him with the mission. If he fails, I invade Huron, burn their kingdom to the ground and take my son back by force."

* * *

"We got unfinished business, Shadolian." Brokk's lips peeled apart to reveal yellowed teeth.

Vyder Ironstone seemed unconcerned, returning the man's glare. "Aye." The assassin smiled. He dismounted, tying Storm to a lemon tree growing near the house. He stroked her neck, talking gently to the horse before turning back to Brokk. "We do."

There were about fifteen men stood before him, all foresters judging by their garb. And as at the tavern, Brokk appeared to be the leader of the group. Three at the rear looked nervous, constantly licking their lips, eyes wide. The others seemed grim and determined, but the two closest to Brokk were killers. He could see it in their eyes. They were the ones to drop first if the fight became out of hand.

Brokk reached down to his belt, his fingers curling around the haft of a knife. He drew the blade. "Knives only."

Vyder left his shield, blunderbuss, and sword on the ground near Storm before unsheathing his knife. Grinning, he advanced towards the foresters. They were all armed.

Watching the group, the highlander approached slowly. One of the assailants mistook his hesitance for fear and darted forward, feigning a blow, hoping it would scare the Shadolian. But before he could withdraw to the safety of his comrades, Vyder had a hold of his shirt. Pulling the forester to him, he slashed open the man's throat and threw him to the cobbled road before him.

"Careful, lads," muttered Brokk. "This one's dangerous."

Within moments, the man's gurgling breaths were rendered silent as the last of his life-blood glistened upon the cobbled road.

Vyder held his hands out. "We can re-schedule? I am rather busy at the moment. What say you?"

Another two ran forward, one either side of him. He kicked the knee out from the one on the right and blocked a blow from the forester on the left. Twisting the man's arm savagely, he allowed his opponent's knife to clatter uselessly upon the ground. Kicking the weapon behind him, Vyder slammed his knife deep into the man's back, then pushed him towards the diminishing group of foresters from which he charged.

The forester with the wounded knee remained on the ground, holding his leg and howling like a hurt animal.

Vyder smiled at the injured man. "Keep your teeth together. It isn't that bad, surely?"

The group charged towards him as one. Vyder had expected the move but hoped honour might have prevailed. He should have known better.

Slamming an elbow into another man's face, the highlander backed away. Blocking a blow, he disarmed another before slamming his knife deep into his bowels, leaving the forester screaming and writhing upon the street, dying, clothes wet with his own blood and shit.

"Oh, that truly is terrible." Vyder retreated from the dying man as the stink of his open bowels washed over the area.

Punching a man in the face, the assassin was barely fast enough to stop a blade slashing open his throat. He was outnumbered and there was a real threat of death. He continued to block, parry, stab, and slash, all the while taking slow steps backwards towards his blunderbuss. If only he could reach the weapon, he would end the fight within moments. Honour had failed. Although Brokk had suggested knives were the only weapons to be used, Vyder also assumed the fight would be one-on-one.

Never assume! He slammed an open palm into an assailant's throat, simultaneously slashing his knife across another forester's face, the blade biting to the bone. The man dropped his weapon and ran away from the fight, clasping both hands to his face, blood streaming between his fingers.

Slowly, blow-by-blow, Vyder was winning. He knew it, and they knew it. Outnumbered as he was, those arrayed against the assassin were dwindling with each passing moment. A dying forester left upon the cold cobbled street, another fleeing in terror with some minor wound, which undoubtedly, would claim his life in the coming weeks as infection set in. Several more backing away, uninjured, but losing the will to fight, their bowels turning to water. Each tiny victory edged the highlander to triumph.

Brokk's eyes narrowed, one side of his mouth curling upward in a sneer. He dropped his blade and withdrew a small pistol tucked into the belt at the small of his back. Vyder didn't see the move until too late.

"Coward!" Vyder bellowed.

Fear curled its long, sticky fingers around his gut. He ran straight for Brokk, fast as his legs could carry him. The gunshot was deafening. Vyder wasn't fast enough to dodge the small, round piece of lead that lodged in his guts. He almost dropped his knife as pain washed over him. The foresters moved in as one.

The first knife plunged into his shoulder. Roaring, the Shadolian slammed his knife deep into his attacker's abdomen, lifting the man from his feet. Two more foresters died before another knife slid between Vyder's ribs, agony spreading across his chest like a wave. He coughed blood, blocked a knife thrust that would have ended him instantly, then sent another attacker upon the road to death. Three remained standing, but with weakness enveloping him, the highlander knew he had no way to beat them.

Vyder spat blood upon the street, then grinned, his teeth stained red. "It seems you win, Brokk."

"That's right, you piece of shit. Best served cold as they say," replied the forester, still holding the smoking pistol.

Brokk was about to mutter something else as he gloated in his victory but didn't have a chance as Vyder lunged for him. The forester's eyebrows ascended, his mouth dropped open, and before he could react, Brokk had been dragged into a sickening head-butt, which smashed his nose. Clamping a broad hand around Brokk's throat, Vyder held him at arm's length before hammering his knife into the man's midriff. Brokk's eyes widened in surprise and pain but lost the light of life as Vyder cut his abdomen open, the blade grinding to a halt against the lowest rib. The highlander kicked the man from his blade, but wasn't fast enough to block the remaining attackers. Knives plunged into his back, chest, neck, and stomach.

The remaining foresters fled before Vyder hit the

ground. Agony swept his being. Blood oozed from multiple wounds. Each racking cough filled his mouth with the acrid taste of blood.

I'm dying. Keeping a firm grip upon his dagger, he attempted to push himself into a kneeling position, but there was no power left in his arms. Resting his cheek upon the cold, cobbled street, Vyder's eyes slowly closed and blackness took him.

* * *

Drying the utensils Miriam had used to cook dinner, she placed them away, then wiped a kitchen counter down, ensuring it was spotless. Vyder had departed on his mission and would be absent for some months. Miriam had been Vyder's slave for near ten years.

He'd always treated her with respect, in fact she often berated him like an unruly son, as he was young enough to be so. Slaves were murdered by their masters for far less on a daily basis. Miriam knew she would always be safe as long as she lived under Vyder's roof. She would want for nothing and never again would she be hurt or violated.

The sharp retort of a gunshot snapped Miriam out of her reverie. The sound issued from outside the front of the house. Panic crept through her as she rushed to the main entrance.

Swinging the mighty door open, she took in the scene. Bodies lay strewn across the street, the cobblestones slick with blood. Vyder was lying face down. At least his chest was rising and falling. She screamed and flew down the front steps towards her master. His horse nearby, and his blunderbuss on the ground near the animal, she picked up the heavy weapon. Running after the several fleeing aggressors, she shrieked and fired from the hip. The hammer clunked onto the flash pan. The mighty weapon roared, smoke and sparks blasting from the muzzle.

Most of the shot missed their target, but one tiny round ricocheted off the street and lodged itself into a man's right arse cheek. He wailed in pain, holding a hand to the wound limped away, casting a fear-filled glance over his shoulder. Miriam allowed the weapon to fall from numb fingers. Turning back to Vyder, she knelt by him and a passed a hand through his hair.

"You're going to be fine," she whispered, holding back a sob. He was critically injured. Using all her strength, she rolled the assassin onto his back. He grunted, jaw clenched, eyes tight shut.

Miriam sat back on her haunches, holding a hand over her mouth, tears filling her eyes. Blood oozed from the corner of his mouth. He looked at Miriam through half-closed eyes and tried to smile but, instead, winced in pain.

"Shhh," said Miriam, clasping one of his hands and squeezing. He was going to die. She knew it. "I'm going to get a doctor."

"Miriam," whispered Vyder, a racking cough silenced him, blood flowing over his chin and down his neck. "I'm…dying, lass, too…late."

"It's never too late," she said, a fierce determination glinting through teary eyes. "You told me that yourself!"

Giving his hand one last squeeze, she stood and ran to the closest mansion. Slipping on the cobbles slick with blood, she righted herself and ran on. Slaves weren't usually allowed out past sundown, and if they were, should never be unaccompanied by their master. Certain death would be the result if a slave was found to be in breach of the law. Miriam was willing to take the risk. Vyder's life depended upon it. The wrought iron gate leading into the beautifully tended garden, creaked open. She walked along the smooth, tiled footpath leading to the mansion's front door and padded up several steps. Breathless, she hammered open palms against the oak.

Creaking the door open a crack, a young woman stared out at her. "What is it?" the woman asked, looking Miriam up and down.

"My master—" began Miriam.

"This better be a bloody good reason!" came a stern voice from behind the young woman. With a soft groan, the door opened wide and the master of the house stood glowering at Miriam. "Run along," he commanded the young woman, who promptly departed with half a curtsey. As long as she had known Vyder, he hadn't expected any such formality as a curtsey, bow, or any other such acknowledgement of his authority.

"What the bloody hell are you doing out by yourself?"

"My master, he's been stabbed—"

"You know the law don't you?" the man interrupted.

"Of course, sir, yes, but I am desperate!" Miriam pleaded.

"What has happened?" the man asked in a bored tone.

If you'll let me finish my sentence I'll tell you! Miriam was careful to keep her face neutral.

"My master has been stabbed and shot, he's dying, sir! I need help, do you know of a doctor in the area?"

"Stabbed." Suspicion entered his eyes. "Shot you say?" he asked, looking at Miriam with doubt.

"Yes, sir, *please* help!"

"You had nothing to do with his...affliction?" he asked, looking down his nose at Miriam.

"What? No!"

"Who's your master?"

She explained quickly.

"Uh," he muttered, distaste clear in his voice. "The highlander?"

"Aye, sir."

"Couldn't have happened to a nicer gentleman. Can't help you I'm afraid." He sneered, slamming the door in Miriam's face.

She stood frozen for a moment, eyes wide, jaw clenched and knuckles whitening as her fists tightened.

"My master is *dying!*" she shouted at the door.

Gathering her skirt and hitching it away from the ground to prevent her from tripping, she tapped down the few steps, ran out along the footpath and slammed the iron gate closed behind her. Miriam ran along he cobbled street to the next mansion, some three storeys tall. A marble fence at chest height denoted the boundary of the property. She opened the thick, wooden gate, negotiated around a small bathing pool, ran along the footpath and slammed her hands onto the mighty front door, trying to regain her breath. She battered on the thick wood, her fists red and painful. There was no answer. Miriam pushed herself into a standing position, clenched her teeth, and slammed her hand against the door.

She took a deep breath. "Open up! Open up now!"

There was a *click*, and the door inched open to reveal the frightened eyes of a servant. Miriam barged through the door, forcing the man to stumble backward.

"Fetch your master," she said, standing before the tall, wiry man.

"And just who do you think you are?" the words might have been challenging had they been spoken with more confidence, but the fear hadn't left the servant's eyes.

Miriam took a step forward, fists clenched. "I said fetch your master. *Now!*"

"But of course, ma'am. But of course." He bowed once and fled the foyer.

Please don't die, Vyder. She placed her face in her hands. *What were you bloody thinking?*

Standing tall, she wiped the tears from her eyes, took a breath, and let it out slowly.

The dull thud of footsteps approached. "What is the meaning of this?" The voice was muffled.

The foyer's far door swung open and a large man waddled in. "I say, you there!" the massive man stopped, wheezing for breath. He appraised Miriam with an incredulous look. "Just what in hell are you doing out and about after curfew, and without your master at that?"

The rotund man turned to his servant. "Did you not realise she's a slave, you idiot?" He punched his servant in the face. "Away with you!"

The male slave scuttled from the room, holding a hand to his bleeding nose.

"What do you want?" he approached her.

She wiped clammy palms against her skirt and ignored the thundering of her heart. Miriam stood as tall as she could and maintained a look of calm. "I come on behalf of my master, sir."

His lip curled. "I did not ask on whose behalf you

served. Are you fucking deaf as well as stupid?"

I've forgotten how cruel the ruling class truly are. Vyder has spoiled me all these years. She held back tears.

"My master has been mortally wounded. He is dying, sir! I need your help, *please!*"

The fat man took a step back, eyes narrowing. He looked at her hands as if expecting to see a hidden knife there. She held out her empty palms. "I'll have the Watch called, you bitch! You've murdered your master!"

"Sir, I've done no such thing!"

The rotund man pointed at Miriam. "Seize her! Take her prisoner, she's a murderer! *Murderer!*"

The far door creaked open and the tall slave appeared, a cloth held to his nose.

"I said seize her! She is a criminal!"

Miriam pulled up her skirt, and ran into the night, ducking down side alleys, along streets and across a small pedestrian bridge. When she could carry on no longer, she stopped, breathless, against the brickwork of a mighty mansion.

Distant shouts rent the night. Miriam ducked into the shadows. Her lungs ached and her legs burned.

She looked at the dark, early morning sky. "Gulgon, I call upon you for help." She passed a hand over her chest. "Lord of Hope, I call upon you." Slowly, she gained control of her breathing, her lungs hurting a little less. Hope returned to her.

The shouting grew louder and was accompanied by the clatter of shod horses galloping across the cobbled roads. In the dull glow of a street lantern hanging from a post on the far side of the bridge, a group of riders galloped into view.

The Watch.

Miriam's breath caught in her throat, and she

pushed farther into the shadows, wedging into a corner and sliding down the wall into a sitting position.

But are they after me? Or have they heard the shot of Vyder's blunderbuss? Surely they couldn't have responded so quickly.

As quickly as they'd ridden into view, they were gone, heading in the rough direction of Vyder's home.

Miriam needed to get a hold. Her master needed her help. She pushed to her feet, straightened her dress, and walked briskly out onto the street. She rapped on the door of the mansion with a fist. Sucking a breath in through clenched teeth, she ignored the pain in her knuckles as best as she could. A window was unlatched high above her and the dark shadow of a person appeared, leaning out of the opening. She was unable to see a face in the darkness.

"Wait there!" a voice called. "I shall be down presently." The window slammed closed and the latch dropped into place.

She wrung her hands and sent a silent prayer to Gulgon that this household wouldn't be as cold and heartless as the others.

The front door was unbolted and swung open with a soft groan. A short, plain looking man shuffled out to stand in front of Miriam.

"What?"

Miriam bowed her head and clasped her hands in a tight ball before her. "I'm terribly sorry to bother you, sir. It's my master."

He took a deep breath and let it out in a rush. "What, does he beat you? Rape you? Call you names? I'm sorry, my love, but that is the life of slavery, I'm afraid. There is nothing I can do to help you." He stepped back over the threshold and began closing the door. "Goodbye."

Miriam flinched at the words, *my love.*

Maybe he can *help me.*

"Wait, sir. No, it's nothing like that. My master's been stabbed. I need a doctor or a healer...or *anything!* I'm at my wit's end." Tears slid down her cheeks. "He's probably already dead."

The man heaved the door back open and stepped towards Miriam. "I see." His voice sounded interested. "I *may* be able to help."

"Oh, thank Gulgon!" She stared up at the early morning sky. "Thank you."

"Stay here, I shall return in a few moments." The door slammed shut.

Miriam rubbed her hands together, turned her back to the door, and leaned against a wall. In the dark, vacant street, moonlight shone with a gentle, opaque sheen upon the cobbled road. The neighbourhood was silent. Well, it was until a shutter on the upper level of a house opposite swung open. Miriam looked at the dark square beyond the open shutter, but could see no one. "Just what the *bloody* hell is going on down there?" a voice hissed.

"Everything is fine, sorry to bother you!" Miriam was surprised her voice sounded confident.

She squeezed her eyes shut and fell silent.

"Is that you, Doctor Smythe? Are you helping someone?"

She pressed her lips together in a tight line.

"I say, I'm going to have my man summon the Watch. You see if I don't!"

Miriam remained frozen in place, breathing softly. She still couldn't see anyone.

The door next to Miriam swung open making her

jump, heart leaping into her throat.

"Right, let's go," the man said.

She turned to him. "Are you a doctor?"

"Yes. Well I—"

"I say, Doctor Smythe? Is that you?"

The doctor swung towards the house opposite. "Yes, Mister Flang. Nothing to fear. I have a late caller needing help."

"Oh jolly good. I thought miscreants were up to no good."

The shutter slammed closed, the sharp sound reverberating down the street.

"Nosey old bastard," the doctor said with a growl. He glanced at Miriam. "You understand I will require payment after I heal him, though?"

"Of course, sir. Yes."

"Two gold coins."

"My master can pay, sir."

"Come let us go, then." He held a small black bag in his hand. "You lead the way, miss."

She did, walking towards the bridge. She looked at him over her shoulder. "It's Miriam."

"Doctor Smythe at your service." He touched his chest. "Well, just call me Griff."

They walked over the bridge and turned down the street the Watch had taken. Griff sidestepped a pile of horseshit, and he tutted under his breath.

"How long have you been a doctor?"

Griff chuckled. "Oh, I'm not a fully-fledged doctor. Sorry to mislead you. I almost finished the last year of study, but dropped out due to lack of funds. Studying to be a doctor is a rich man's game."

Miriam cleared her throat but remained silent. *You're richer than I'll ever be.*

"Not that I'm poor, you understand."

She nodded and smiled. "Oh I understand, sir."

"Please, call me Griff, Miriam. I promise I won't bite." He nudged her elbow. "Much."

She looked across at him to see his teeth flash in the darkness. Miriam looked away and rolled her eyes.

"I do," she said.

"What?"

She looked at him again. "Bite."

He sniffed, then coughed, but did not reply.

They turned a corner and moved to the side of the road as two riders thundered past.

The Watch again. I hope they catch whoever injured Vyder.

A third horseman reined in beside them, the horse's hooves clattering on the cobbles as it moved around on the spot, agitated to be galloping again. The mighty animal mouthed the bit and stamped a hoof. "You there, have you seen a group of men come this way?"

Miriam bowed her head, allowing Griff to answer.

"No, I can't say that I have, young man."

You're about the same age if not younger. Miriam refrained from speaking, although it was an effort.

"Thanks to you, sire."

Miriam caught what might have been a sneer, then he slammed his heels into the horse's flanks and galloped away.

Miriam increased her pace, her legs burning worse than before, but she ignored the pain. Griff, still quiet, matched her pace.

Short of breath, she turned to Griff. "It's just 'round the next corner."

As they passed the large brick home where Miriam had first sought help, the scene of the fight came into view. Vyder lay still and silent upon the cobbled street, the dark stain of blood pooled beneath him.

* * *

Griff rushed towards his patient. He waved his arm at the small crowd clustered around the fallen man. "Make way, I say, make way, there's a doctor coming through!"

The men and women stepped aside, but Griff still made sure he shouldered aside a man, ignoring his curse. "I said make way!"

He knelt by the wounded man, swallowed hard, and opened his bag. He reached in and fumbled around for a moment before his fingers grasped the clean gauze.

Knife wounds. He cursed under his breath. *Knife wounds to the gut. The worst kind.*

Stem the bleeding.

Griff licked his lips and shoved the thick gauze into one of the more prominent knife wounds. His fingers disappeared up to his third knuckles. Pulling out more of the material, he pushed it into the gruesome wound.

The blood was a dark stain in the poor light. It was impossible to tell whether the blood was bright red or dark red. He placed a hand on the man's chest and leaned down so his ear was inches from his patient's mouth.

He's still breathing, so it can't be arterial blood, otherwise he'd have bled out long before now.

"Is he going to die?" a voice asked.

The question went unanswered. He looked around at the closest bystander. He pointed at the man.

"You! Help me."

The bystander turned away. "He's as good as dead."

Miriam knelt beside Griff. She wiped her eyes. "What do you need?"

"We need to get his shirt off. There could be other knife wounds underneath"

She nodded.

"I'm going to keep plugging the wounds I *can* see." He passed a small knife to Miriam. "You cut away his shirt and expose his chest and belly."

"I'll do my best, Griff." She sniffed and wiped her cheeks.

He touched her shoulder. "Miriam. I need you to take a deep breath and concentrate on the task at hand. You can do this."

She nodded and started work.

Griff reached bloody hands into his bag and brought out more clean gauze. He pushed it into the largest wounds, his hand disappearing up to the second knuckles. Pushing in more gauze, he didn't stop until the horrific wound was completely plugged. He knelt back as Miriam carefully cut through the thick shirt.

Dragging his medicine bag closer to him, he dug a hand into the dark depths and rummaged around until his fingers touched the cold glass of the alcohol bottle. He pulled it clear, brought it to his mouth, and clenched his teeth around the cork. The cork came free with a soft *pop*. He poured the liquid over the plugged wound.

That should stave off infection.

He recorked the bottle and placed it away in his bag as Miriam finished the final cut.

She's doing well. This must be hard on her, yet she's giving it her all.

He took the knife from her shaking hands. "Thank

you for your help."

Let's see how bad this really is.

Griff peeled the shirt clear to reveal the patient's chest and abdomen. A dark stain covered the skin, making it impossible to see any other wounds. With deft hands, he pulled clear the bottle of alcohol and a gauze swab. Dousing the swab with alcohol, he wiped the patient's skin clean. Stab wounds!

Six of them. This man is going to die. He forced the thought to the back of his mind. "He's not going to die, is he?" Miriam asked.

Griff ignored her. *Better to stay silent than offer false hope.* The wounds oozed, so he cleaned them again, then began dressing them. Leaning down close to the patient's mouth and nose, he made sure the man was still breathing.

"Griff?"

Ignore her!

The patient was still breathing, although more slowly than before. Griff frowned as the scent wafted to his nose, but it was gone as fast as it had arrived.

Smelled like faeces.

He leaned down over his patient and smelled the wounds. All he could detect was the acrid aroma of fresh blood. The last wound, just below the belly button, was much smaller than the others. Griff sniffed the wound and flinched back, holding back a dry retch.

He's been stabbed through the bowels.

Resting his weight upon his haunches, he sighed.

Without emergency surgery, he'd be dead by sundown.

"Griff, please, will he survive?"

"If I can help it, yes." He pointed at a short, burly man standing nearby. "You, sir, help me carry this man to his house."

He saw the relief in Miriam's eyes. "Where does he live?" he asked her.

She gestured towards a large, nearby building.

"Do you have a lantern?"

Miriam rushed away to get it.

He delved into the bag. "Stupid bloody thing!"

He upended it, the contents —tubes, bottles, clothes, small trays, bandages, implements, and scalpels — spilling on the table. With a gentle *thump*, an old medical book slid out last. . "Ah, *there* it is! He picked the pocket-sized book up and flicked through the ancient pages. He grunted and placed it back down.

Miriam walked into the kitchen, holding a glass lantern.

"Hold the lantern over your master's belly"

"His name is Vyder."

A highlander name.

Griff picked up a nearby metal tray and emptied some alcohol into it. Rubbing his hands with alcohol, he leaned over Vyder and pulled open the wound holding his breath. One of the intestines had been nicked and faeces seeped into the surrounding cavity. He whispered a curse.

"I need to clean and suture the intestine," he muttered. Soaking a gauze swab with alcohol, he opened the wound as wide as possible, pushed the material in and allowing time for it to soak up blood and shit. Pulling it clear, he cast it aside and washed his hands in the tray of alcohol. Three more times he pushed gauze into the wound, cleaning the cavity. When he was satisfied, he took a length of bovine sinew, threaded it through a needle, and then soaked them both in a fresh tray of alcohol.

He looked at Miriam still holding the lantern. "Are you okay?"

She gave a slight smile. "Fine, thank you. If I swap hands every little while, I can keep doing this for hours."

Sterilising a spreader, he pushed the implement into the wound and opened it. The knife gash yawned open, allowing him the use of both hands. Reaching into Vyder's abdomen, he began suturing the nicked intestine. The bowel was tougher than it looked. He held the intestine with his left hand and sutured with his right. But with each stitch, his fingers lost grip on the slippery surface. The lantern helped, but the light it cast was still dull.

Better than nothing, though.

Clenching his jaw, he grasped the slippery intestine and, using the curved needle, formed another stitch. Vyder grunted, but remained unconscious. *One more suture should do it.* He ignored the sweat beading on his brow. When he'd finished, he carefully cut the excess bovine sinew away and dropped it in the alcohol filled tray. He soaked another swab with alcohol and cleaned the wound. He repeated the process several times until he was sure the wound was clean. He inspected the sutured bowel in the dull light cast by the lantern for long enough to be confident that the intestine was no longer oozing faeces into the abdominal cavity.

He cleaned the other wounds and sutured them closed but left the wound below Vyder's belly button open.

"Now, we wait for morning."

* * *

Miriam's arm ached and she changed hands,

holding the lantern over her wounded master. She frowned at Griff. "But don't you need to close that last wound?"

He turned to her and smiled. "No, not yet. When morning comes, I want to double check that no more faecal matter is being exuded by the wound."

"Whatever you think best."

She placed the lantern upon the table and breathed a sigh of relief.

"You're welcome to sleep in one of the guest bedrooms."

"No," Griff replied. "I'll sleep on the floor beside my patient. I'll need to check on him during the night."

"As you please." Miriam tried to smile but forced away tears instead. "Can I bring you anything? A drink? Food? Blankets?"

He held out his hands. "No, I'm fine."

Miriam sniffed and nodded. "I shall retire to my quarters. It is only on the other side of the kitchen." She pointed the direction. "So please wake me if you have news."

"Fear not, Miriam. I shall."

She stood for a moment, hands clasped before her. She nodded, staring at her master lying still upon the table they'd eaten so many meals together. She supressed a sob and cleared her throat instead. Nodding again, she looked at Griff. "Very well, Griff. Thank you for your help." She turned and walked away.

When she reached her room, she did not change into her bedclothes. *I may be needed during the night.* She lay on her bed, even keeping her shoes on. She stared up at the dark ceiling. *If Griff needs my assistance, I can be there in moments.*

A tear slid from the corner of an eye, down her

cheek, and dripped into her ear. She wiped her nose and sniffed.

Don't you bloody die, Vyder! Miriam closed her eyes and sobbed.

Exhaustion washed over her, causing lethargy to wash over her. Sleep took her in moments.

A loud bang on her door broke her from sleep. She sat up and rubbed her eyes. Blinking in the dim light, her eyes struggled, until Griff morphed from a dark blur and back into focus.

"Do you need me to hold the lantern again?"

"No, Miriam. No, nothing like that." His voice was soft, distant.

"Griff?" she whispered, her voice quivering.

She swung her legs off the bed and stood.

"I'm sorry, Miriam. I'm so sorry." He leaned against the doorframe and looked at his feet, breathing out in a long sigh. "He's all but dead. There's nothing more I can do."

II

"It can't be," she whispered. "Gulgon, help me."

She staggered, her legs losing their strength. Griff grasped her before she could fall. She buried her head into his chest and wept.

"Let me take you to him," Griff said.

But Miriam held fast to him, crying. "It can't be true. *Vyder is unstoppable.*

"There is one option."

Miriam took a step back and disengaged from Griff. She looked up at him with red-rimmed eyes. "What do you mean?"

"I know of someone who may be able to help." He paused, looked at the ceiling and then at his feet. "Although it is a last resort."

"Another doctor?"

"No, not quite." Griff licked his lips.

Miriam grabbed his shoulders, shaking him. "Tell me, for Gulgon's sake! Tell me now!"

"She's a Wiccan! Alright?" Griff closed his eyes as if he felt dirty for having said the word. "Yes, she's a bloody Wiccan."

"She's a witch?"

Griff swallowed, eyes still closed. "Yes."

"And you think she can help Vyder?"

He took a deep breath and let it out slowly, his eyes finally opening. "Despite what my colleagues say of the Wiccan craft, I've seen her work what can only be described as miracles."

Miriam hurried into the kitchen and halted as she looked at Vyder. Her master's skin was ashen grey, his chest barely moving. Griff stopped beside her.

"He'll make the journey to the other side soon."

Miriam sniffed. "Well, we must hurry then. How do you propose we move him?"

"I have a cart. I'll take Vyder's horse and ride home, attach the cart, and be back as soon as I can."

She nodded. "Thank you. But please hurry."

"I'll be back before you know it." He strode from the room.

She stepped forward and rested an open palm upon Vyder's chest. She could barely feel his chest move. Miriam leaned over him and looked down at his face. Tears dripped from her cheeks and landed upon Vyder's grey skin in wet splotches.

Vyder hadn't purchased her in the slaver's market held in the main square each Sunday. The assassin had stolen her.

The memory was painful as the face of her previous master came to mind. A cruel old man who beat or whipped her if he found even one piece of furniture wasn't cleaned to his liking. Occasionally he forced her to perform sexual favours, usually when he was drunk.

Sexual favours? She screwed shut her eyes and bared her teeth. *No, he raped me! Say it Miriam!* She sobbed. *He fucking raped me!*

Miriam leaned against the kitchen table, closed her eyes, and tried to fend of the memories. She was raped the night her master had died.

He'd gagged her, tied her hands in front of her, and commenced the business of violating her. Biting down on the gag and sobbing, trying to ignore his animal-like grunting, the weight of his body, previously pinning her down, suddenly disappeared, followed by a loud crash in the corner.

"You bastard!" a voice growled in a highland accent.

The newcomer, a much younger man, all but cut her master's head from his body.

"It's alright, lass, it's alright. You're safe now." The tall stranger sliced the fibrous rope binding her hands. He'd pulled the gag free of her mouth and thrown a blanket over her naked form.

"My name's Vyder, and your master's dead."

And that had been Miriam's introduction to Vyder Ironstone.

"Don't you die." She cupped his face in her hands and felt how cool his skin had become.

At least he's still breathing. She wiped her eyes with a handkerchief, and then blew her nose. *That's still something.*

"You can pull through this, Vyder." Miriam tapped his face with a hand. "You hear me?"

His mouth twitched. Or had she imagined it? She pushed the handkerchief up one of her sleeves and frowned. "You're not dying today, Vyder. You're more stubborn than that!" She tapped his cheek again. But he remained silent and still.

Miriam squeezed her eyes shut. *Gulgon, stay with me. Don't abandon me now.* A sudden gust of wind tugged at her skirt.

She walked to the closest window and looked out upon the street. The sun was kissing the eastern horizon and daylight threatened to break. Turning, she made her way back to the kitchen table and looked upon her master once again. She held her breath, staring at his chest until she saw it finally move. Exhaling in relief, she wrung her hands and looked back at the window.

"Come on, Griff. Please hurry."

A gentle noise brought Miriam back to the present and she looked around the room. The noise, softer than before, came again, and she realised it was coming from Vyder.

"Vyder!" she rushed to his side, cupped his face.

He groaned, I'm sure of it!

Her master lay silent, breathing once for every six of hers.

Did I imagine it? She pulled the handkerchief out of the sleeve and blew her nose again. *No, I didn't. I can't have.*

The *clip clop* of horse hooves grew in volume and Miriam looked out the window. Griff pulled the horse to a stop. With a creak, the wagon came to a halt behind the animal. The doctor engaged the handbrake and jumped from the wagon. Sweat beaded his brow, and he looked short of breath.

She touched a finger to one of her master's cheeks. "We're getting you out of here, Vyder! We're going to get someone to help you."

The front door crashed open and Griff strode into the kitchen. "I'll need your help to carry him off the table and outside." Griff wiped his brow with a hand.

They dragged Vyder off the table, Miriam's legs almost buckled under the weight. She swore under her breath "I'm sorry, Vyder," she said through clenched teeth.

They worked well together, pulling Vyder's limp form across the kitchen, his boots leaving narrow, parallel smears of dirt on the floor.

Her arms burned and her breath came in rapid gasps.

"Griff." She stumbled and almost dropped her

master. "I need a rest!"

But there was nothing for it but to continue. Anything less and Vyder would make the journey across the Frost River to the Veil, to live with the dead.

If you see the Frost River, you turn around and walk away. You hear me? Walk away!

* * *

Vyder crouched upon the ice, trying to gain his bearings. Behind him lay a thick, snow-covered forest of tall pines. Above him threatened thick, dark clouds, and ahead lay a welcoming open expanse of green, luscious meadows. A beautiful, warm, bright sun beamed down upon the thriving fields of grass. He brushed a hand through an ice-covered beard and shivered as the freezing cold ebbed into his being and soaked into his bones. The warm pastures beckoned. Warmth was life.

If I am to survive, I must warm myself. He pushed himself to his feet and slipped, falling face first upon the hard, unforgiving ice. Pain lanced through his nose.

Warmth is life, Vyder old son. Now get up!

He pushed himself to his feet and slid sideways but managed to maintain his balance. Blood streamed from his nostrils but froze to his skin before it reached his chin. Looking at his feet, he noticed he was standing upon a frozen river.

The Frost River? He shivered against the cold, his teeth chattering as a gust of icy wind clawed at his clothes and worked its way into his skin and beyond. *Am I dying?*

Ignoring the throbbing pain from his nose, he took a step towards the sun-swept fertile land in the near distance. *You soon will be if you don't get moving.* He took another stride and his boot lost traction. He fell backwards onto his arse and grunted.

"If you see the Frost River, you turn around and walk away," the whisper echoed across the sky. He looked up at the looming clouds.

He frowned as recognition dawned upon his frozen face. "Miriam?"

"You turn around and walk away. You hear me? Walk away!"

"Miriam! Is that you?"

He stood with care, holding his arms out to keep his balance. His question was left unanswered, and the clouds, descending ever closer to his position, remained silent.

"Am I on the Frost River, Miriam?"

He cupped his hands to his mouth and took a deep breath. "Miriam! Can you hear me?"

A cold wind, blasting against his face was the only response. Gritting his teeth together, he began moving, placing one foot in front of the other.

I must be imagining things. The ice is affecting my mind. Keep your balance and move. This is not the Frost River.

Vyder looked at his feet and flinched, cold air rushing into his lungs, fear breaching his body colder than the ice and snow assaulting his body. Beneath the ice-encrusted river, he noticed corpses sliding underneath him, their wide, dead eyes staring at him.

A trick of the mind, damn you! Ignore them! Ignore the cold and bloody well concentrate on the warmth!

He swallowed and looked up at the bright green, welcoming fields before him. Vyder ached for the heat of the sun upon his ice-encrusted skin. He stumbled forward another few steps and relief began to defeat the fear.

Two more steps, Vyder. He clenched his fists and snarled. *Two more strides and you'll be warm again.*

He attempted to control his body from shivering and failed. *But if this really is the Frost River, you'll cross it into the realms of death, never to return.*

He squeezed shut his eyes as confusion took hold. *If I stay here, I'll freeze to death.* His hands unclenched. *Not much of a choice. But it's the better of two options.* He nodded. *You can do this, son.*

Raising a boot off the surface of the frozen river, he walked forward with confidence.

* * *

Vyder's body slipped and fell to the ground.

Miriam, short of breath, wiped her brow and stepped back. "I'm sorry," she puffed. "He's so heavy."

Griff held up his hands. "It's fine Miriam, we'll just keep trying." She noticed he looked as exhausted as she felt.

Miriam looked around, but the street was empty. Gone were the onlookers who'd stood idly by in recent hours. They'd probably retired to their soft, warm beds. Her breathing began to slow, and the burning and aching, which assaulted her, began to ease just a little.

She caught Griff's eye. "Are you ready?" she asked.

He nodded.

"Let's try again."

"Just what the bloody hell's goin' on here?"

Miriam froze, fear sweeping through her. She turned to see a man of the Watch sitting astride a large horse, watching them.

Griff looked as frightened as she. When he remained silent, his mouth a tight line, Miriam decided she would have to speak.

"He's wounded, we're trying to lift him up onto the wagon."

The guard leaned forward in the saddle, forearms resting on the pommel. "Ah yes, the highlander. I thought he'd have died by now."

"He's crossing the Frost River as we—"

Miriam shot Griff a withering glare, and the would-be doctor cleared his throat and returned to silence.

Miriam held the guard's stare. "He's not dead. We're trying to take him to a—"

"A doctor," Griff blurted. "She lives just outside the city and wagon is the only way to bring him."

"I see." The guardsman nodded. "Would you like some help?"

Relief washed over Miriam.

Oh thank you, Gulgon!

"Much appreciated," Griff replied.

The guard shrugged and swung out of the saddle, jumping to the cobbled street. "It's the least I can do."

Striding towards the wagon, the guard leapt up onto the tray with lithe speed and turned to them. He crouched down. "If you can lift him into a sitting position, I can lift him from under the arms and up onto the wagon."

Miriam nodded and grasped Vyder under one arm while Griff took the opposite side.

"Are you ready?" she asked.

Griff took a deep breath. "Ready," he muttered.

They lifted Vyder's dead weight as best they could. Miriam felt like her face was going to explode. The guard leaned down. "Just a little more!"

One last effort, Miriam.

She lifted with all her strength and felt rough hands

brush her arms away from Vyder. "I have him."

Miriam stepped back, breathing hard, and watched the guard. The Watchman had a firm grip underneath Vyder's armpits, his arms encircling her master's chest. With a grunt, the guard lifted the big man up onto the tray of the wagon like he was a child.

The Watchman jumped down, wiping his blood covered hands upon his trousers. "Easy!" He grinned.

"Our sincere thanks," said Miriam. "Thank you so much."

He placed a boot in a stirrup and stepped up into the saddle. "You're welcome. Luck to you!"

With a tug of the reins, he swung the horse away and trotted past.

Miriam watched Griff climb onto the seat at the front of the four-wheeled wagon and drape the reins across his knees. He leaned down and offered her his hand. She grasped ahold and felt Griff's grip enclose upon her forearm.

He's stronger than he looks! She tried not to wince as Griff tightened his hold. She stepped up onto the wagon and sat down.

She looked at the doctor. "Thank you."

His lips formed a tight smile as he took the reins up in one hand. "You're welcome." In his other hand, he held a long whip. He disengaged the hand brake and touched the horse's rump with the whip. Finally, they were underway, trundling along the empty cobbled street.

Miriam looked over her shoulder at Vyder lying supine. She attempted to focus upon his chest to ensure he was still breathing, but the wagon's movement prohibited her from properly seeing. They rattled over bumps, slewed across uneven cobbled sections, and ignored bleary-eyed residents who pushed curtains aside to watch them pass. Dawn was breaking, and with it, the city began awakening.

"How far away does this Wiccan live?"

Griff, who seemed to have been busy with his own thoughts, cleared his throat and shrugged. "We'll probably reach her by mid-morning."

"Mid-morning?" Miriam clenched her jaw against the abject fear spreading through her body like a disease. "But Vyder might be dead by then!"

Griff shifted in his seat and looked at her. "I know," he said. "I know, Miriam, but it's the best I can do." He sighed. "I'm sorry."

At least he's helping.

"No need to apologise, Griff. But it's time we sped up."

Miriam snatched the whip off the near doctor and gave the horse's rump a sharp slap.

Vyder's horse broke into a powerful canter, and the wagon accelerated, the wooden wheels rumbling along the street.

"Apparently, we can go faster!" Griff yelled, a wide grin adorning his face.

Miriam nodded. "Of course we can." She slapped the whip against the horses arse once again, and the animal accelerated into a gallop.

Griff's grin vanished, knuckles turning white as they gripped the reins.

He threw a panicked glance at her. "Miriam, do you think this wise? I'm losing control of the steering!"

They rounded a tight corner and missed a man by a fingerbreadth. "We're perfectly safe, Griff. Trust me!"

She ignored the incomprehensible shouts of the man who'd almost gone under the wagon's wheels.

"My master's dying!" she shouted over one shoulder. "We're in a rush."

"Sorry!" Griff hollered.

She turned to Griff. "Would you like me to steer?"

"What?" he glanced at her. "No!" He chuckled. "I know exactly what I'm doing, thank you very much!" He remained silent for a moment before looking at her again. "Besides, have you ever driven a wagon before?"

"Many times," she said under her breath.

"Excuse me?"

"Yes, many times."

They missed another man by mere inches. He shouted something at them, holding up his fist, but the words were lost to Miriam as they roared past. The horse opened up its gait, seeming to enjoy the experience and the cobbled street started to become a blur.

"Do you think we should slow down?" Griff shouted, fear glinting in his eyes.

She whipped the horse's arse again, ensuring it maintained a good pace. "No!"

"Are you sure?"

She grasped the reins and pulled them out of his hands. "I'm sure, Griff, for Gulgon's sake! I'm sure. Shift over, I'll steer."

"Right you are!"

She slid across the seat so she was sitting directly behind Vyder's steed, holding a firm grip of both the reins and whip. Looking at the space between the animal's ears, she saw a slight right-hand bend approaching in the street. She gently tugged on the right rein. When they continued straight, she tugged harder and the beast snorted, tossing its head and obeying, pulling the wagon around the bend.

When the horse began breathing hard, Miriam

slowed it to a rapid walk.

She brushed the whip against the animals flank. "Well done, girl. Well done!"

"I say, lass, yes, well done."

She brought them to a halt at an intersection and allowed several coaches to trot past before proceeding.

Miriam felt Griff lean into her. "We need to head towards the western gate of the city."

She looked at him, but the doctor was staring off towards some glamourous, multi-storey building.

"Griff!"

"Hmm?"

"I'm a servant, Griff. A slave! Do you think I have any idea where the western gate lies?"

"Oh of course! I apologise, Miriam. I shall steer from here on in." He grabbed the reins.

"I'd prefer not, Griff, please trust me." She pulled the reins free from his hands. "Just tell me where to turn and we'll get there much faster."

The skin of his face began turning a faint claret colour. He cleared his throat. "Of course."

"You'll notice a large arterial road in the far distance." He pointed.

She frowned. "No."

"Well trust me, Miriam, it's approaching. You'll know when you see it. Turn left onto it and that'll take us out towards the western gate."

The horse's breathing had settled and the sweat had dried upon its flanks and between the rear legs, leaving a light layer of salt upon its fur. Tempted as she was to break the animal into a canter again, the line of coaches and wagons in front of them precluded her from doing so. A thick stream of traffic was pacing past in the opposite direction, making overtaking impossible. The wide, cobbled street was littered with horse dung and urine. Miriam wrinkled her nose at the aroma.

Seeing movement in her peripheral vision, she glanced across at Griff, who was holding a hand to his nose, pinching closed his nostrils.

* * *

Vyder yearned for the sunlight and warmth.

It's so damn close! Yet so far.

A cold wind blustered through his ice-encrusted clothes to assault his frozen skin. He squeezed shut his eyes and clenched his teeth together to stop them from chattering.

"Vyder! Come to me, my love!"

His eyes snapped open, and there, standing on the far band of the Frost River, stood Verone, his beautiful wife.

She smiled, her eyes sparkling in the sunlight. "I've waited so long for you, Vyder!"

He tried to say her name, but his lips wouldn't move and he grunted instead. He reached for her, lost his balance, and fell face first to the frozen river. Pain lanced through his nose, but it helped him focus.

So close!

He pushed himself onto his knees and stood with a clumsy lack of efficiency, his boots slipping on the ice-covered river. He almost tumbled backwards but managed to maintain his balance.

"Vyder, a few more steps my love! A few more steps."

Verone was standing on the very edge of the river, her arms outstretched towards him, their fingers mere inches apart.

So very close!

* * *

Miriam swivelled in her seat to look at the motionless Vyder lying supine in the wagon. We need to hurry," said Griff. "He'll cross to the other side soon."

Her smile vanished.

Oh, Vyder, hold on! We're bringing you to help, just hold on for Gulgon's sake!

She frowned and was tempted to overtake, but with the flow of traffic in the opposite direction, it would be impossible.

One of the coach's doors was flung open and a man in pristine clothes stepped down, turned, and held out his hand. A woman wearing a flamboyant dress took his hand and stepped down beside him with care.

Griff jumped back onto the bench seat beside Miriam. He sat down and cursed. "I say! You two!"

The pair looked back at them.

"Move off the road!"

The man raised an eyebrow. "Oh? And who might you be young man?"

"I'm a doctor and I'm in the care of a dying patient, now get the bloody hell out of my way!"

The woman smirked and made as if to speak.

"*Now!*" roared Griff, standing.

They closed the door of the coach and waved the driver on before turning away to walk off the road.

Miriam flicked the reins, and they began to trundle forward again, but not before she cast the pompous pair a death glare as they passed.

They swept along the road and within what seemed mere moments, were presented with the western gates.

40

Mighty wooden doors some twenty feet high and five feet thick were swung wide open, allowing traffic to leave and arrive. It seemed a constant stream in both directions. Families arriving in small, over-packed wagons, groups of scouts trotting out to relieve soldiers, who'd more than likely been posted out in the field for the past several weeks. Lovers walking hand in hand towards the nearby forests, merchants arriving in dual and, sometimes, triple axel wagons, stocked full of wares from every corner of the world. And the Watch; always the Watch, moving in both directions, keeping a close eye on the traffic. If any kind of disturbance were to erupt, they'd be upon it faster than an enormously oversized man on a cake.

Miriam watched a group of Watchmen canter past their wagon, heading towards the approaching western gate. A chill spike of fear lodged in her belly. *What if they don't let us pass? Or worse?*

"Good boy, you're doing well." Miriam brushed the whip against the flank of Vyder's horse. They passed beneath the great western gate. Miriam looked up at the huge doors. Built above the gates stood the western wall, upon which she could see the tiny figures of soldiers, looking out towards the horizon.

"Archers," said Griff, following her gaze.

She felt overwhelmed by the she enormity of the city's power. *And this is but one of four gates!*

"The place is impenetrable! I had no idea Lisfort was so heavily defended."

"She is a mighty city, that is for certain."

Before she knew it, the wagon was clear of the massive gates, and she saw groups of soldiers standing idly beside both the exit and entrance to Lisfort. *They look bored. Can you blame them, though? What else is there to do, but stand around talking or sit playing cards?*

Griff tapped her shoulder. "Okay, we follow the same road for a little time, at which point the road splits into five directions. We call it Five Ways." He chuckled. "For obvious reasons, of course." His smile vanished. "You want to take the middle road, which goes straight ahead. I can almost guarantee we'll be by ourselves once we hit Five Ways." He looked out at the forest in the near distance. "No one travels the third road."

Miriam frowned. "Why? Is it dangerous?"

Griff remained silent.

"Griff, is it dangerous?"

"Huh?" He swung to her. "No, of course not, Miriam. No, not dangerous at all. "The safest road of them all." He cleared his throat again, nodded, and swallowed. "Yes, a very safe road indeed." He breathed out through pursed lips.

She shifted in her seat. "Not a very good liar are you?"

"No, not really."

Miriam flicked the whip against the horse's flank and the wagon lurched, picking up speed. She overtook slower coaches, wagons, and riders. When traffic approached in the opposite direction, she ducked back into the endless convoy winding its way out of Lisfort.

They remained silent for some time, Miriam occasionally looking back at Vyder, but she couldn't see any signs of life. The constant movement of the wagon made it impossible.

"Keep your eyes on the road." Griff pointed forward. "I'll check on him."

Miriam nodded, waiting for a particularly slow coach to pass before she steered onto the opposite side of the road and overtaking the few wagons in front of them.

"What's the rush?" one driver yelled as they trotted past.

"He's still breathing, Miriam."

Relief washed over her. *Hold on, Vyder.*

"But very slowly. He's not long for this life, I'm afraid."

She felt a jolt and dull thud as Griff sat down beside her again. "He has but minutes, Miriam."

* * *

Their fingers touched. Verone grasped Vyder's hand. "Come to me, my love."

She pulled him forward, and he lost his balance, boots slipping on the thick ice. He fell onto the frozen river, the tips of his fingers thawing as warm sunlight soaked into his skin. Just a little further. Soon, his entire body could soak in the sun's rays. Verone reached for him.

"Give me your hands, Vyder, and I'll pull you to me. I've waited so long for you."

"I, too, my love," he mumbled through his ice-caked beard.

The warm skin of her hands encircled his wrists, and he was dragged across the ice towards the waiting sunlight and his beautiful wife.

* * *

Miriam cursed as the traffic slowed to a slow walk.

"We're approaching Five Ways."

She nodded. "Good. I hope we can pick up speed then."

"Oh, trust me, we'll be the only wagon heading

down that road."

She turned to him. "How can you be so sure?"

He chuckled, his eyebrows disappearing into his fringe. "Trust me."

Miriam watched the traffic in front of them, some diverting to the left, others to the two roads parting towards the right. But Griff pointed to the road directly before them. "Down here."

The road was covered in thick leaf litter and it was obvious nothing and no one had passed down the road in some months.

Perhaps even years.

"You're sure this is the way?"

Griff smiled tightly and nodded. "I'm sure." His voice was almost a whisper.

"Are you alright?"

He looks pale. Sickly.

"Who, me?" he looked at her. "I'm fine! Just fine, Miriam. No need to worry about me."

The forest closed in around the road, mighty trees crowding in. The canopy of the forest became thicker as they trundled along the abandoned road, mighty boughs intertwining high above them, blocking out the sun. The fresh, mid-morning sky was soon gone, to be replaced by a light Miriam had only seen at late dusk. The horse threw its head and snorted, the wagon slowing to a stop. The animal was nervous.

Rightly so! I'm not so comfortable myself.

"It's alright, girl," she cooed, gently sliding the whip along the horse's flanks. She struggled to keep her voice low and calm. "On we go. Everything's fine. You hear me?" She brushed the whip over the animal's rump. "It's okay, we're safe. Now walk on." She clicked her tongue and slowly tapped the whip to the horse's side.

"Walk on."

The wagon lurched, and they were once again underway.

"I say, I wasn't sure we were going any further. Well done, Miriam." Griff's voice sounded a little disappointed. He turned in the seat and looked back the way they had travelled.

"There's nothing back there for us, Griff." She clicked the horse on. "There is only one direction now."

And that's down this damn road!

"How far do we have to travel?"

He looked at the thickening forest around them. "I can't quite see the sun," he said with boisterous attitude, although Miriam was not oblivious to the quiver in his voice. "But I'd say another half an hour."

"What do they call these parts?" She glanced at the doctor.

Small talk should help calm the atmosphere and keep the fear at bay.

She clenched her hands around the reins and felt how clammy her skin had become.

"It's still part of the King's Forest," Griff replied. "Although this section of forest has an unofficial name. They call it, The Waning Wood."

The Waning Wood? Great, Miriam. So much for small talk!

She wanted to ask why it had been dubbed with such a depressing name but refrained. As the wagon rolled onward, it was obvious. The ambient light dimmed further, and if she didn't know it was daylight yonder the forest's canopy, she could be forgiven for thinking it was evening. A clicking noise came from their left, and Miriam flinched. She swung on the bench seat and saw a spider scuttling up a tree trunk away from them. The arachnid's abdomen was the size of a grown man's head. She screamed, her eyes glued to the spider's ascending journey before it finally disappeared.

Terror swelled in her as she returned her attention to the road before them. "Onwards, boy, onwards." She tapped the horse's flank and encouraged it into a trot.

Griff's breath was coming in shallow gasps and sweat glistened upon his forehead, Miriam noticed. "We're okay," he whispered, more to himself it seemed than anyone else. "We're okay."

"Have you been into this forest before?"

Griff remained silent, sitting bolt upright, eyes wide, staring straight down the road before him.

He flinched and glanced at her, terror glazing his eyes.

"I've been into the Waning Wood once as a younger man, yes. It's just as frightening now as it was then."

"Apart from giant spiders, are there any other creatures I should know about?"

The horse snorted and threw its head again. Miriam brushed its flank with the whip and whispered soothing words.

"I don't know," he said. "I've heard stories of a giant spider named Barbaron, but that's just stories to scare kids."

She jerked her thumb over her shoulder. "We just passed a massive spider. I've never seen one that big before."

Griff chuckled. "Barbaron is said to the size of a house, if what I've heard is true, and I doubt it is. *That* spider we saw was a baby."

A baby? Where the bloody hell are you taking us, Griff?

Fear bathed her being, almost forcing her body

into shutdown, but she threw a glance over her shoulder and saw Vyder lying there, motionless, pale, and for all the world, looking as if he'd crossed the Frost River.

No! He's still alive. He's stronger than that.

The road ascended, forcing the poor animal to slow as it worked to pull the heavy wagon up the incline.

"Like I said, Barbaron is just a folk's tale to scare unruly children." Griff grinned, trying to look confident but failing.

A loud crash echoed through the forest, and one of the trees nearby swayed as whatever had caused the ruckus barged past the trunk. Griff screamed, sounding for all the world like a ten year old girl.

Miriam reached across and patted the doctor's leg. "It's okay, Griff. We're okay."

Griff flinched at her touch and screamed again.

The mighty creature moved away from them through the forest at a great rate of knots. Miriam looked in the direction of the fading noise.

It's more scared of us than we are of it. She looked at Griff. *Well, me anyway.*

"I think we're almost there," blurted Griff.

Thank the gods!

The incline lessened and, before long, they were travelling on flat ground again. Miriam held her breath as a flutter of wings exploded in the treetops above them, followed by the caw of ravens. A chill passed along the skin of her spine, and she had the distinct feeling they were being watched. She heard the scuttle of some small animal scurrying through the leaf litter away from them.

We're being watched. She looked around at the dark, silent forest around her. *I'm sure of it.*

As the wagon rounded a corner, they were presented with a mighty boulder sitting in the middle of the path, blocking their way. Miriam pulled the horse to a halt, and she looked at the doctor.

"Well?"

He returned her stare. "Well, what?"

"How far from here? Can we carry him?"

"I don't think so, no. From what I know of this Wiccan, she lives at the top of a hill, which we've just ascended. It can't be too much further. Can we go around perhaps?"

She clenched her jaw and looked around. There didn't appear to be any way around the mighty stone.

"Well? What are you idiots waiting for?"

Miriam jumped at the sudden voice from above them. An old woman was standing on top of the boulder, a staff clenched in one hand, the other holding a pipe to her mouth, upon which she puffed. She looked at them through narrowed eyes.

"It's the Wiccan!" Griff hissed at Miriam.

"Does Vyder live?" she asked, leaping down from the boulder with far more agility than she looked capable.

Miriam glared at the elderly newcomer. "How do you know his name?"

She pulled the pipe from her lips and exhaled a plume of smoke. She shrugged. "I know Vyder."

"How did you know we were approaching?"

Another shrug. Another plume of smoke drifting towards the canopy high above them. "I've been watching you." She chuckled and muttered something to herself before bursting into laughter.

"Can you help us?" Griff interjected.

"Depends."

The woman limped past the pair and stepped into the rear of the wagon. She snarled, hissed, and muttered something before leaping onto the tray beside the supine assassin.

"It depends," she muttered, touching Vyder's cheek before pressing a finger against his throat. "It all depends."

"He's dying!" Miriam shrieked. "Can you help?"

The Wiccan paused and looked up at Miriam. She smiled, showing crooked teeth. "He's not dying, child."

Relief washed over her. *Oh thank you, Gulgon! Thank you.*

"He's not?" Miriam flashed a grin.

"No," the old woman looked back at Vyder and held the back of her hand a few inches from his mouth and nose. "No." She chuckled and looked back up at Miriam. "He's already dead."

III

"He can't be dead. Surely?" Miriam stepped down from the wagon.

Griff leapt onto the rear tray and squatted beside the Wiccan. He checked for signs of life. A moment later, his shoulders slumped.

It's true!

Miriam held a hand to her mouth and began to weep. She fell to her knees, defeat enveloping her. A dull *thud* beside her and Griff's arm swept around her shoulder. He pulled her to him.

A great man has died and now all we can look forward to is war and death.

"I'm sorry I couldn't do more, Miriam."

She wiped tears from her cheeks. "There's nothing more you could have done, Griff. Thank you for your help. We did as good a job as anyone could given his…" she gestured towards the wagon and burst into tears again, "given his wounds," she managed between sobs.

* * *

Vyder scrambled to his feet, maintained his balance, and clutched hold of Verone's hand. She clenched a firm grip and dragged him to her. Sunlight and warmth beat down upon him, thawing his frozen clothes and bathing his cold skin.

He pulled Verone into his embrace. "Oh, my love, how I've missed you."

"I too, Vyder." She cupped his frozen face in her hands and kissed him. "I too."

They held each other in silence, Vyder enjoying her warmth. He smiled and began to relax in the safety of her arms.

I'm home. Finally, after all these years, I'm home. This is where I belong.

Water began to pool at his feet as the ice upon his clothes melted under the sun's power. Feeling returned to the skin of his face, and he relaxed in the arms of his love.

"Finally, we are together again," she said.

"Finally," he agreed, kissing her hair. "I've missed you every single day, Verone."

"I too, sweetheart."

* * *

"There is still time, you fools!"

Miriam sniffed and looked up at the Wiccan, glaring down at them from the wagon.

"What do you mean? He's dead."

"Oh he's dead," the Wiccan chuckled. "Well and truly."

She felt Griff burst to his feet beside her. "Stop toying with us, Witch! This man has passed across the Frost River, his time is at an end. All needs to be done is to bury him."

The older woman scoffed. "Witch, is it? I haven't heard that word for some time now. I heal and help people, yet I am a foul, evil witch? Please yourself, young man. You take this warrior away from here and entomb him to the care of the earth, it matters nothing to me."

Miriam pushed herself to her feet and wiped red-rimmed eyes with wet hands. "Are you saying you can still help him?"

The Wiccan burst into laughter and leapt down from the wagon with lithe agility. "That's exactly what I'm saying. He may be dead, but he has only recently made the journey across the Frost River. If we move with speed, there is still time. I may be able to summon him back from death."

Griff grunted but remained silent.

"Really?" asked Miriam, hope re-entering her being.

"Oh, I'm sure." The Wiccan pointed a finger at Griff. "You! Help me."

"What do you need, Witch?"

I wish you'd stop calling her that, Griff!

The old woman chuckled. "Anything I decree, young man."

"Drive the horse and wagon on through to my cave." The Wiccan gestured.

Miriam turned to follow the older woman's hand and noticed the mighty boulder, once blocking their path, was nowhere to be seen.

How is that possible?

Griff stood staring, and Miriam could only presume the same thought was drifting through his mind.

The woman stepped forward and shoved Griff. "Don't just stand there, idiot! I said drive the wagon and horse on. Time is not a luxury we have, boy."

Miriam climbed onto the wagon's seat. "I'll do it."

"Good girl." The Wiccan chuckled. "Leave the hard work to a woman, she'll get it done while the men stand idly by."

"Sorry, it's just that," Griff fell silent. "It's just that…well…"

"Shut up, boy!" The Wiccan spat. She turned and

followed the wagon trundling down the path away from them.

Miriam wiped her nose. She flicked the reigns. "Good boy," she said as the horse picked up the pace.

I hope she isn't raising false hopes in me. Gulgon, stay with me. You've been with me, now stay with me, Great One. Please!

She glanced over her shoulder, but Vyder didn't look any less dead.

When the wagon rolled past an oak tree wider than a tall man lying down, Miriam caught sight of the cave mouth yawning open in the near distance. It was massive. The wagon would easily fit inside with plenty of room to move. She craned her neck, her gaze following the oak's mighty trunk, which disappeared through the canopy of the forest.

"Geldrim is his name."

Miriam jumped at the Wiccan's voice and glanced down to see the older woman was striding along beside the wagon.

She's silent! I had no idea she was there.

"My apologies, girl, I did not intend to frighten you."

"No it's fine." Miriam smiled, or at least she tried to, but her brow creased instead. "Whose name?"

"The tree, of course!" The Wiccan pointed at the huge oak. "It's his name."

His?

Miriam nodded and looked back at the older woman walking beside the wagon. "And yours?"

"I am Endessa."

"Miriam."

"A pleasure, Miriam. What is that stupid boy's name?"

Where is Griff?

She noticed the doctor had clambered up onto the rear of the wagon. He muttered something under his breath. "It's Griff!" he called and rolled his eyes.

Miriam smirked and looked at Endessa.

"Miriam?" the Wiccan asked, she glanced up. "What's his name?"

"Oh, it's Griff. Sorry I thought you heard him."

"Griff," Endessa muttered. She tutted to herself. "Stupid, stupid name. Silly boy."

"Oh, for Gulgon's sake, I'm right here, Endessa! I can hear you, you know?"

Endessa clasped her hands behind her back as she walked and began to whistle.

Miriam chuckled, but not so loud that Griff would hear. She stroked the whip against the flank of Vyder's horse. "Good boy. You can rest soon. We're nearly there now."

The wagon rumbled inside the cave's mouth and, within moments, the dim light of the forest was replaced by almost complete darkness. However, the horse continued in a calm manner, much to Miriam's surprise. She thought she could hear Endessa whispering strange words to the animal but couldn't be sure. The area was huge. She looked at the walls, where shelves, bolted into the rock face, sagged under the weight of many hundreds of thick tomes. Dull, flickering candles were scattered about the floor, providing scant light. But as they wove their way deeper into the cave system, the light returned as they neared what must have been Endessa's main living area.

The horse snorted, flattened its ears against its skull, and threw its head. It was wary and frightened. The wagon slowed to a halt. She watched Endessa approach the animal and touch its shoulder, whispering. Miriam strained to hear what was spoken but was sure it was either gibberish or some unknown language. The animal's ears flicked forward, and the tension in the beast disappeared, flexed muscles relaxing. It nuzzled the Wiccan and plodded onward.

Incredible!

They entered a narrowing section of the cave, and after rounding a sharp bend, the area opened into a huge room. Griff whistled softly behind her. She searched for the ceiling but was presented with only fading light, and then utter darkness beyond. If there was a ceiling, it was must have been more than a hundred feet above them. Mighty flames danced within a fireplace some fifteen feet tall. But it was not the sheer size of the hearth that drew her attention, but upon that which the fire fed. The logs were tree trunks cut into lengths, each taller than Vyder and wider than a wagon wheel was round. She looked at Endessa with new light and a little fear.

How in the name of the gods does that small, frail old woman carry in trunks that size? It's impossible.

"Twenty men couldn't lift those tree trunks," Griff's whispered words broke her reverie.

Miriam's eyes narrowed as she watched the old woman whisper to the horse.

Endessa is not all that she seems. That's not a bad thing, though. She turned in her seat and looked at Vyder. His skin was more ashen than it had been the last time she checked. *Maybe this Wiccan really can bring Vyder back. There is still hope, Miriam! There's still hope, now get a hold of yourself, woman!*

She took a deep breath and jumped from the wagon, thudding onto the ground, the impact jarring her legs, but she ignored the dull ache emanating from her knees.

She whirled to see the young doctor still perched upon the rear of the wagon, leaning back, searching for the elusive ceiling.

"Griff!"

He jumped and looked at her.

"Can you please get down here and help me with Vyder?"

"Yes, of course." He leapt from the wagon.

Endessa limped past Miriam. "I'll help, you need not worry yourself."

Griff puffed out his chest. "Yes, Miriam, she and I can lift the highlander." He gestured at the Wiccan.

"Not you, idiot!" Endessa pushed the doctor out of the way. "You're weaker than a day old puppy. Miriam, help me with him."

"I am *not* weaker than a day old puppy, I'll have you know."

Even in the dull, flickering light thrown by the distant fire, Miriam could see the younger man's face flush bright red.

"In fact, I'll have *you* know—"

"Oh shut up, boy," the Wiccan snapped. "You're wasting our time. Now step out the way. There's a good boy."

Miriam heard Griff growl, his face glowing with fury.

She walked around to stand beside Endessa, the tray of the wagon reaching her chin. She had no idea how she and the old woman were going to carry her giant master down. Before she could voice her concern, the Wiccan had clambered up onto the wagon like a monkey, straddled the dead man, and dragged him to the rear edge of the tray with ease.

How in Gulgon's name? Miriam stood, staring

mesmerised at the sheer strength of the old woman.

"Don't just stand there, dear, take his legs."

Miriam snapped out of it and nodded. "Of course, yes."

She clasped a hold of each boot and helped drag Vyder out of the wagon until he was in a sitting position. Endessa crouched behind him, her arms under each armpit, and her hands clasped together over Vyder's breastbone.

Now what?

"Now, you let go of his legs is what," Endessa told her.

It was as if the Wiccan was reading her mind.

Miriam released her hold and stepped back. In the time she'd taken to move away, Endessa had leapt to the ground, taken one of Vyder's arms, and pulled him so that he slumped down across her shoulders. Endessa's legs almost buckled under the weight.

"Oh gods, are you okay, Endessa?"

"Of course, child." The Wiccan grunted.

The old woman stumbled towards the massive hearth, bearing the weight of the massive highlander. Miriam stood dumbfounded. She'd never seen such a feat of utter strength in her life.

The Wiccan stooped and allowed the corpse to flop onto the thick, woollen mat near the mighty fireplace. She stood, stretched her back, and regained her breath.

Miriam approached her and placed a hand on the woman's shoulder. The fabric of her top was sweat-soaked. "Are you okay?"

Endessa patted her hand. "Fine, Miriam, just fine. These old bones aren't what they used to be. There was a time when I could lift men twice the size of the likes of him without breaking a sweat."

I'd believe it!

Endessa pointed at the doctor. "You! Yes you, young man. No, I'm not pointing behind you. Get your backside over here and help me!"

* * *

If she treats me with disrespect one more time, I swear to the gods I'll give her a piece of my mind!

Griff stormed over to the giant hearth and knelt beside the dead assassin. He glared at the witch.

"My name is—"

"*Boy!*" She chuckled. "Is that it?" she scratched her chin and looked up in mock thought. "Or, is it..." she fell silent and held up a finger, "ah, don't tell me, I know what your name is. Is it..." she leaned towards him, her steely eyes holding fast to his glare, "idiot? It matters not, if you want my help, you'll do as I say, you hear, boy?"

"I can just as easily walk away. This man," he gestured at Vyder. "He's not my master, nor my friend. I'm doing Miriam, aye and Vyder, a large favour."

"For a handsome sum too, I'd wager."

He clenched his jaw and snarled, fists clenched, face reddening. "I'll not be treated like a common..." he stuttered, "like a common bloody fool!"

"I can see you have skill with medicine, *idiot*..." she stood over him and pointed with a gnarled finger, "but you *will* learn humility."

The anger within him burned into fury, and he pushed himself to his feet to tower over the small, old woman.

"Don't hurt me!" she held her hands up and stepped back, eyes wide. "Don't hurt me, please! I am but a frail old woman." She cackled with glee, her hands falling by her side. She advanced to within inches of him and looked up into his face, the flint like glint hardening her already cruel eyes. "I just carried that man over my back." She gestured at the dead body at her feet. "You think a scrawny little rodent like you is going to threaten me?"

Rodent?

He breathed out a sharp breath, his fists unclenching.

"Yes, that's what I said. Rodent."

Is she listening to my thoughts?

Fury was brushed aside by the cold fingers of fear.

"Now, you'll do as I say, when I say it. Do you understand, *boy?*"

He focused on the index finger hovering a hair's breadth beneath his nose. "Yes, I understand." He nodded. "Yes."

"Thank you, Griff." Her voice softened. "Humility is something that must be learned, young man. Being a good medicine man does not negate the fact you must also be a good man. Being an arrogant piece of dung will get you nowhere around here."

Fair enough.

She nodded and turned away. "Very well. Now come and help me."

Griff knelt once more, with a slightly new attitude. He hadn't decided whether he respected the witch or was frightened of her.

"I'm a Wiccan," she looked at him, "not a witch. A witch is a fictitious, evil entity you city folk burn at the stake because you don't know any better. A Wiccan is a follower of Earth Power who uses his or her knowledge to help people. I'm a healer, a helper, a caretaker for the

Great Mother. I am *not* a witch. Do you understand, Griff?"

He nodded.

"Good. Here, take this."

He took a small, clay bowl from her. It emanated warmth in his hands. Had it been any hotter, he would not have been able to handle it. It contained a dark, liquefied substance. He brought it to his nose and took a sniff.

Oh gods!

He brought a fist to his lips and dry wretched.

Endessa laughed as she watched him. "I wouldn't recommend doing that."

Griff lowered the bowl to the ground and took a deep breath of fresh air. "What is it?"

"Never you mind," she replied and limped to the hearth. "Never you mind. I'll be busy here for some time. I want you to paste what's in that bowl onto the wounds Vyder carries."

"Of course, Endessa. Consider it done."

Griff thought the Wiccan's face softened for a moment before the hard scowl returned. "Good man, Griff." She turned back to the raging flames before her.

He looked about for some kind of tool with which he could use to paste the dark substance onto the skin of the deceased assassin. Aside from bare rock, tiny pebbles, and patches of sand, there was nothing that resembled anything like what he had in mind.

Use your fingers. You can always clean them.

He heard Endessa chuckle to herself as she squatted before the fire, her back to him. It was almost as if she was laughing at his thoughts.

He sighed and dug the fingers of his right hand into the bowl. The substance was tar-like. He rubbed it over the cold skin of the dead man, covering the wounds he'd so recently sutured.

* * *

Miriam detached the harness from Vyder's horse and waved the animal forward, away from the wagon. The wooden tongue of the wagon fell to the ground, and the animal stepped over the yoke, shaking itself. It turned and nudged Miriam.

She smiled and stroked its nose. "You're welcome, great one."

She found a bucket of water nearby and allowed the beast to drink his fill. Using her hand, she rubbed its back down, the fur wet with sweat. It stood motionless, silent, allowing Miriam to groom her. Using her hand was useless, she realised. Stepping up onto the wagon close by, she saw a small pile of straw bunched in a small clump in one corner of the tray. She grabbed a fistful of the straw and used that to rub the horse down. As she worked along the animal's flank, she looked over at Vyder, lying motionless near the huge fire. Griff was kneeling over him, rubbing some kind of dark liquid upon his skin. She frowned.

What the hell's he doing?

Her eyes were drawn to the hearth, before which the Wiccan sat cross-legged, swaying back and forth. Miriam's eyes narrowed.

What the hell's she doing? How is this helping Vyder?

She clenched her jaw and returned her attention to the animal that stood before her.

I hope Griff knew what he was doing bringing us here. It might have all been for nothing.

She closed her eyes, arms dropping to her sides.

Vyder is dead and Endessa might be doing nothing more than raising false hopes.

The horse nickered.

Miriam opened her eyes and noticed the beast was looking at her. She smiled. "Alright, I haven't quite finished, have I?"

She continued rubbing the animal's fur.

* * *

Endessa stared into the fire, rocking back and forth. Her eyes drifted over the flames flickering and dancing across the wood upon which they fed. She hummed the first verse of The Calling. It had been so long since she'd been in need of the spell she almost forgot the tune. She watched the fire blaze upon the logs, flames stretching metres above her. When she reached the second verse, her lips parted and she began to sing. Squeezing her eyes shut, she struggled to remember the powerful Wiccan words, but somehow, they came to her and she moved with the song. Her eyes snapped open and she noticed the fire growing larger and hues of green and purple flitting amongst the flames. The song came to a close and she hummed the first verse of The Asking. Soon, she was singing the second verse, and before she knew it, she was humming the first verse of The Offering. The fire blazed twice the height of what it'd been, and as she reached the second verse, she sang, the words flowing easily.

What do you want, Wiccan? a sibilant voice whispered in her mind.

I need help. Who else is there Gorgoroth? I don't wish to bother you.

I'll have to do, Wiccan. No other nature spirits are nearby.

Speak quickly, before I grow bored.

Gorgoroth, I need help from another. Maybe you could summon another for me?

Laughter erupted in her mind. *Am I not good enough? Now you really do have my attention. No one else is here. I will help, if I can. What is it you need?*

The ice-cold stab of concern swamped her stomach. She hummed the first verse of The Binding. Endessa stared into the fire, flames streaking towards the ceiling hundreds of feet above her.

This man's soul returned to his body.

You know the risks. When was the last time you bound a nature spirit with a human?

Once, many, many moons ago. She fell silent, took a deep breath and closed her eyes once more.

And?

The second verse came to a close and she fell silent.

It worked, is that not enough?

I care not. I will do as you say…this time.

You do me a great service, Gorgoroth.

Silence.

Gorgoroth?

I am here, Wiccan. Show me this…human!

Endessa could feel the distaste with which the last word was whispered into her mind.

She nodded and swayed, humming the first verse of The Resurrection.

* * *

"Come," Verone said, "we have much to talk about." She smiled, took his hand and led him away from the Frost River towards the luscious green grass, deeper into the warm sunlight. He shivered as the ice melted from his beard and his clothes started steaming.

He stood still and bathed in the heat. "Gods, that's better."

Vyder closed his eyes and smiled as Verone hugged him. "It's been too long husband, I've missed you."

"And I you," he muttered, holding her close.

A hand clapped onto his shoulder and pulled him away from Verone. "We have unfinished business on the other side of the Frost River, human!"

He saw the fear in Verone's eyes as she stared over his shoulder at something much taller than he. She screamed and stepped back.

Vyder turned to the newcomer and found himself staring at a dark green mist wafting in the air before him. He followed the mist upwards focussing on the piercing, glowing blue eyes glowering down at him from high above. The thing had form. It was not just a random cloud of green mist but took the shape of a massive, humanoid, well-built tree. The legs were tree trunks, the torso a single mighty trunk, the shoulders wide and powerful, arms sprouting into large branches, fingers small, leaf-covered appendages. The being's face was a thick shrub. Bright blue eyes stared at him, waiting for a response.

"On the other side of the Frost River?" he glanced at Verone and tried to step towards her, but the powerful hand held him steadfast.

"That's what I said, little human."

"But I *am* on the other side of the Frost Fiver."

A loud, creaking, groaning and hissing sound exploded from the mist-green being before him. Vyder thought it sounded like mocking laughter.

The thing held out an arm towards the way Vyder

had travelled. The leaf-covered finger pointed towards the river and the snowstorm blustering across the surface.

"Not this side of the river." The strange, mocking laughter again. "*That* side!"

"But I'm dead!" Vyder tried to shake the hand off his shoulder.

"Vyder! Come to me!" Verone screamed, running towards him, but she stopped as if held at bay by some invisible barrier. "Vyder!"

"You come with me now."

"Verone!" He ran towards his wife, but the hand on his shoulder clenched an even firmer grip, stopping him in his tracks. "Verone!"

"Hush now, little human. You will see her again. She is eternal, forever, and she'll be waiting for you here when our time together is at an end."

The entity dragged Vyder away from Verone. She tried to follow but could not advance past the invisible barrier in front of her. Her lips formed his name, but no sound reached his ears.

"Don't do this," Vyder said as he felt a chilling blast of ice wind as they approached the Frost River.

"I have no choice, human. We are together now."

"I'll kill you!" Vyder blurted, although truth be known, he felt powerless under the force of the mist that held him prisoner.

He heard the familiar creaking and groaning. "I was alive on this earth before your monkey ancestors were swinging between treetops, bickering over a piece of fruit. You cannot kill me."

He struggled against the strength of the mighty entity but failed, his feet almost sliding out from under him as he was pulled out onto the icy surface of the river.

"Why do you struggle, little human?"

"I'm dead, I've done my time amongst the living. I want to be with my wife!"

"You will be with her before you know it, small man. Time is but a fleeting blink of the eye. But you and I are bound together now, for a little while, at least."

"My name's Vyder, not little human." The assassin growled, trying to shrug the powerful hand off his shoulder.

"Is it, little one?" He swore the thing shrugged. "That's interesting."

Vyder's teeth started to chatter as the familiar, unforgiving freezing cold worked its way through the layer of his clothes and began caressing his skin with relentless assault. Ice formed in his beard. His lips, face, and fingers went numb as the cold sunk towards his bones.

"Gods, it's cold." He stammered the words through lips that felt thrice their normal size.

"Is it?" the being pulled him on across the Frost River. "How unfortunate."

Vyder threw a glance over his shoulder as he slipped and stumbled onward to try and catch a glimpse of Verone, but the far bank upon which she stood was hidden by a thick blizzard. Wind howled in his ears, and he realised his lips were frozen shut. He could no longer speak.

"Calmly now, Vyder. Calmly, little human."

He felt the being's hand gently touch his head and experienced immediate warmth spread through his body. His lips parted, and he gasped for air.

"You might be a human monkey, but there is no need for you to suffer."

Vyder nodded, enjoying the heat spread through him, destroying the freezing cold and driving it from his skin. "Thank you."

"It has manners, too," the mist muttered to itself.

Vyder looked at the being towering over him. "What is your name?"

"My name?" It seemed to fall deep in thought, and Vyder thought it would ignore him entirely. "My name. An interesting question, and a long story. I have been called many things over the millennia." The entity's pace slowed. "I've been named Demon, Tuatha, Thoth, Legion, and Gorgoroth, which is of course, my real name."

"Gorgoroth?"

"That is what I said, Vyder. Do you doubt?"

"No of course not." He took a breath and controlled the worry ebbing through him. "Why were you dubbed Demon?"

"I am a caretaker of this world. Well, *one* of the caretakers of the world. I will always strive to protect our nature. Your Wiccans call me a nature spirit. If someone threatens to harm the order of nature, I will destroy them. For instance, several years ago, a man once tortured a dog for pleasure. He started cutting off its paws until I intervened."

"What happened?"

Silence.

"Gorgoroth?"

"Hmm? Oh, I manifested into the physical realm and ripped the human limb from limb. It takes so much power to do that it almost destroys me. But I was so angry. I've only ever been able to walk the physical realm on two occasions. I healed the little dog as best I could, then hung what remained of the puny man from the town hall of the village in which he lived as a warning to the others while the villagers slept. I imagine that instance and thousands like them are why I have been called Demon."

Thousands like them? What has this thing done?

"Oh, you don't want to know, Vyder. I have done things to people that would make you sick to the stomach."

He looked up at the piercing blue eyes. "You can read my mind?"

"We are one and the same now, human. I can read your mind as you can mine. That, I think, will become more apparent when we inhabit the same physical body."

We cannot be one and the same. Surely!

He shrugged his shoulder to rid the mighty hand from him, but when he was unsuccessful, he pulled away and felt pain lance through him. Vyder glanced at his shoulder and noticed Gorgoroth's hand had grown. The fingers were long tendrils, which had worked their way beneath his skin and intertwined themselves beneath his right armpit and down his flank.

"Oh trust me, Vyder." Gorgoroth laughed in his strange hissing way. "We are one and the same until it is done."

He felt the nature spirit grin.

How in the bloody hells can I feel it grin?

Because we are one and the same. Remember, little monkey? The sibilant voice intruding his mind made him jump.

So you can not only read my thoughts but be part of them?

Endless questions, Vyder. Endless questions. It tires me. It bores me. There will be plenty of time in the coming months, maybe years, for questions. For now, perhaps we should walk across the Frost River in silence?

"Maybe," Vyder turned to look up at the tall nature

spirit, "but what is it that you—"

It wasn't really a question, Vyder. Now shut up and walk!

***

Griff wiped his fingers on his trousers in disgust. He placed the empty bowl upon the ground and stood, a groan erupting as his knees nearly crumpled, but he managed to stand and stretch his legs. The thick, black goo now covered Vyder's wounds. He frowned as he focused on the dark liquid he'd painted on with his fingers.

Is it the light?

He squeezed his eyes shut, and then opened them, blinking rapidly. Refocusing upon Vyder's body, he noticed the dark liquid had solidified into a cream-coloured crust. He brought the hand he'd used to paint the stuff on, but his fingers were still covered in the sticky, tar-like substance.

Maybe my body warmth has kept it in liquid form. Yes, that must be it.

He noticed Endessa was still knelt before the fire, although she was now silent. No more humming or singing could be heard from the old woman. Her head was bowed as if she was praying. Griff heard a snort nearby and turned to see Miriam stroking the horse. Both of them stared at him. He smiled tightly, but no longer able to face the questioning hope in Miriam's eyes, turned away to look at the dead body at his feet, instead.

***

Vyder's foot slipped upon the icy surface of the frozen river. He braced himself in an attempt to regain his balance, but there was no need, he continued walking unimpeded by the slippery surface.

You human monkeys are such clumsy creatures.

The dark mist that was Gorgoroth seemed to point at the nearby bank.

Not far to go, Vyder. We are almost there. Now let us embark upon this journey together. The sooner we start, the sooner we can get it over and done with.

"I'd prefer to be with my wife. I've lived my life. I've died."

Vyder felt himself shoved forward.

It is not a request. Walk on human.

"Why do you hate people so much, Gorgoroth?"

Another time, monkey.

"No. Now!"

Vyder slowed and attempted to stop. He faced the dark mist but was pushed on. He heard the hissing laughter boom out from the nature spirit.

Demanding little creature, aren't you? We will talk about it later. That is the end of it. We have things to do.

He was pushed forward, one boot making contact with the bank of The Frost River.

And places to be, so no more questions, Vyder. Later, much later, we will talk.

He strode up the bank, more confident that he could feel his boots gaining traction upon the hard ground. He felt the warm bubble Gorgoroth had thrown around him disappear. The air immediately became cooler, but it was still comfortable.

"Thank you for keeping me warm."

Gorgoroth remained silent as they walked.

Vyder frowned as he began hearing a dull *thud* for every four or five of his footsteps. The noise seemed to be coming from beside him. He twisted and jumped in surprise as he saw the dark, misty vapour that was Gorgoroth had been replaced by a solid, very real tree-like being. He stared at the thing towering above him. The bright blue orbs glared back at him. The nature spirit laughed.

Steady there, Vyder. It is still I. Soon, very soon, we will be amongst the realm of the living. Then I will be able to take my revenge upon my enemies. I shall kill them, blot them from existence, ensure their destruction and complete extinction.

* * *

"That's enough now, boy. My hand is going numb!"

Miriam stopped stroking the horse and dropped the clump of straw to the ground. She clenched her hand into a fist and relaxed it. She slapped her hand against her thigh and feeling returned to the palm and fingertips. The horse nuzzled her gently.

She smiled. "No! You've had enough patting for today."

Her attention was drawn away as she saw Griff jump back from the supine body of her master at his feet. He went to his knees, holding fingers to Vyder's throat as if checking for something.

She took a step forward. "What's the matter?"

Griff ignored her.

"Griff?" she asked, tentatively walking forward, ignoring the soft nose of the horse pushing against her cheek.

"I think..." Griff pushed his fingers deeper into Vyder's throat, "I think he's alive, Miriam."

"*What?*" She hitched her skirts off the ground and ran to the doctor. "He's alive?"

Silence.

She clutched Griff's shoulders and shook him. "Is he alive, Griff?"

"I think so, yes."

Miriam held a hand to her mouth and staved off tears. "Oh, Gulgon." She fell to her knees, hands still holding onto Griff. She looked over the doctor's shoulder and stared at Vyder. She held her breath, looking at his chest and, for the briefest moment, thought she saw the skin over her master's breast bone move upward.

A trick of the mind, maybe?

A single tear slid down her cheek, and she sniffed, one hand still firmly clamped over her mouth.

Is he breathing?

His chest moved again and Miriam flinched, her eyes widening. Her hand slowly moved away from her wide-open mouth.

"He's breathing, Griff," she whispered. "I think he's breathing."

"I can feel a pulse," the near-doctor said over his shoulder.

"Is that a good thing?"

The would-be doctor laughed. "Yes, yes it is Miriam. It means his heart is beating."

What in the hells does that mean?

"Oh, he's alive alright."

The sudden voice made Miriam jump, and she looked up to see Endessa standing nearby. She crossed her arms and scowled. "He's alive, Miriam. Your master will survive this. You still have a home, my love. And perhaps we have alleviated the chance of our kingdom descending into all-out war."

The Wiccan's face softened, and she smiled.

"Oh, thank you!"

She burst to her feet and ran to Endessa, pulling the Wiccan into a tight embrace. "Although, I care for Vyder, he is like a son to me. It is not just about a roof over my head."

"I understand, my love."

"His heart beat is *very* slow, Endessa. Too slow."

Miriam pulled away from the Wiccan and turned to Griff.

"What does that mean?"

"I don't know," Griff said, holding Endessa's stare. "What *does* it mean?"

She turned back to Endessa.

The Wiccan held out her hands. "It's the only way I could bring Vyder back from the Frost River. There was only one way to do it, and now Vyder lives. Is that not what you wanted?"

"It is." Miriam smiled.

"How did you bring him back from the other side?"

"I bound his soul with that of a nature spirit. They are one and the same and, together, will inhabit the same body."

Miriam sniffed and turned to the Wiccan. "What does that mean exactly?"

"It means your master lives," Endessa snapped.

"But?" Miriam prodded, her eyebrows rising.

The old woman cursed and crossed her arms once more. "But he may not be the same man you remember. Think of it like Vyder will now have two personalities. At any moment, you might be talking to Vyder or to Gorgoroth. I'm sorry, Miriam, it's the best I could do."

"At least he's alive" She fell silent and wiped the tears from her cheeks. "Gorgoroth, you say? How could you possibly entice a nature spirit into such a…bond?"

Endessa shrugged. "He wants to take his vengeance upon his enemies for past wrongs. It means Vyder lives, and Gorgoroth is able to slay those who have wronged him. It's a win-win situation." Endessa scowled. "In a manner of speaking, anyway."

"What does that mean? Who are Gorgoroth's enemies?"

Endessa shifted from foot to foot and cleared her throat but did not speak.

"Endessa?" Miriam placed a hand upon the Wiccan's shoulder.

The old woman looked at the ground.

Miriam shook the woman. "Endessa!"

"It's the only way I could coax life back into Vyder. You must understand, Miriam. You must understand!"

"For pity's sake, Witch," Griff leapt to his feet and advanced upon the older woman. "Answer the damn question!"

"Humans!" snapped Endessa. "Us!" she gestured at the three of them. "Happy now? Gorgoroth's enemies are all people on the earth. He'd happily kill us all."

She let out a breath. "But I think I can stop him."

Griff chuckled without humour. "You *think?*"

Miriam glanced down at Vyder, and her breath caught in her throat. The assassin's eyes were open and staring at her. But that's not what caused fear to ebb and flow through her like a river of ice. It was Vyder's eyes. They were the brightest blue and his lips were creased in a way that was half-smile and half-snarl.

IV

"Vyder?" Miriam knelt beside her master and placed a hand on his shoulder. "Vyder can you hear me?"

"Yes, he can hear you."

Miriam stumbled back as she pushed herself to her feet. It looked like Vyder. *Well, except for the eyes!* But it wasn't Vyder who spoke. Gone was the thick highland accent, replaced with a deep, gravelly voice that sounded as if each word was spoken in a snarl.

Miriam jumped as a soft hand touched her shoulder.

"It is fine, Miriam," the Wiccan said. "Vyder is here with us, it'll just take some time to adjust to this new man. Vyder lives, but he now occupies the same body as Gorgoroth." Endessa gestured towards the supine body of her master, still holding her gaze. "Who is currently speaking?"

"Gorgoroth is my name, little woman." Gorgoroth exploded to his feet in one fluid movement to tower over them, bright blue eyes raking the three, analysing each for a moment before flicking to the next. "Remember it."

Endessa stepped towards Gorgoroth. "Do not seek to threaten those who helped you."

Gorgoroth darted behind Miriam and dragged her into him. A powerful arm wrapped around her throat, slowly cutting off her air supply. Miriam's eyes bulged wide, and she struggled against the constricting grip, which threatened to end her life.

Gorgoroth's lips brushed her ear. "Perhaps I should start with this one." The cruel voice sounded deafening at such close range.

She clutched at the bound muscle of the forearm, which crushed her throat, but it was useless. She could no longer breathe, and the world began to fade.

* * *

Endessa watched the nature spirit grasp hold of Miriam, and even as Endessa moved towards them, the slave's face began turning a bright shade of red.

"Perhaps I should start with this one," she heard the nature spirit say with a growl.

"Gorgoroth, you shall not!"

"Don't presume to command me, Wiccan! I'll do as I please."

With a shaking hand, Endessa untied a small leather pouch attached to the thin belt around her waist and pulled clear a fistful of black powder. She charged forward and began the Incantation of Unbinding in a wavering voice. Miriam's eyes closed, and she slumped in the arms of Gorgoroth.

Endessa threw the powder with all her strength, the dark mist clouding the air around Gorgoroth's face. The nature spirit cursed, released the woman, stepped backwards, and covered his eyes with his hands, squatting to the floor, crying out in pain.

Endessa strode forward and dropped to the ground beside Miriam.

"How is she?" Griff's terrified voice asked from a distant, dark corner of the cave.

I'd forgotten about him!

She leaned over the woman and could see she was

still breathing. Pushing fingers into the soft flesh of her throat, Endessa felt the regular throbbing, which seemed only to be a privilege of a living body.

"She lives," muttered the Wiccan.

*** * ***

The Wiccan has blinded us!

Vyder felt the pain in his eyes, but it was as if he was feeling it from a distance somehow. He'd been aware of what had happened but was powerless to stop it, try as he may.

He felt anger warm him. *Why would you try and kill someone who helped me?*

I told you. All humans are my enemy. I shall kill as many as I can before your body fails of old age.

Not if I have anything to do with it, Gorgoroth! You have my word on that, laddie.

Oh, the word of a human monkey. That's something in which I can trust!

Vyder felt the sarcasm in the venomous reply.

Let me take care of this situation, Nature Spirit.

Silence followed for several long moments.

My wife is waiting for me at the other side of the Frost River. I want to be with her. Bear in mind, I can leave at any time I want, Nature Spirit. And if I do, you cease to exist in the physical realm, where your power seems to be increased beyond measure. Now if you want to hold onto that power, you'll let me damn well deal with it.

Silence again.

Very well, little man. Have at it.

Vyder felt as if he was suddenly starved of oxygen and swimming towards the surface of a deep lake. He ascended through the depths, and as he did, felt more in control, aware of his surroundings and acutely cognisant of the torture enveloping his eyes. Vyder felt his chest expand. He grinned and rose to his feet, ignoring the blistering agony beneath his eyelids. In truth, Vyder had no idea if he could simply walk away, but it sounded like a viable threat and Gorgoroth had taken it as such.

"There's more where that came from, Gorgoroth!" a female voice shouted nearby.

Vyder rubbed his eyes and tried to open them, but apart from a dark blur, his vision remained non-existent.

His grin widened as he took a second breath, enjoying the rush of air. "It is I, Wiccan. It is Vyder. Gorgoroth is gone. Well, for the time being, anyway."

He felt a small, powerful hand clasp his arm and steer him forward.

"We need to rinse your eyes, Highlander."

After several halting steps, another hand pressed against his chest. "That's far enough. Now kneel."

Vyder did so, strangely enjoying the stone beneath his knees.

"Open your eyes as far as you can."

He obeyed, ignoring the burning sting spreading across his eyeballs. Tears streamed down his cheeks. Vyder flinched as he felt a bucket of water thrown straight onto his face. The water stung his eyes almost as much as the substance the Wiccan had used to blind Gorgoroth. But the pain soon subsided, and he blinked rapidly against the discomfort. His vision cleared faster than he expected and, within moments, he found himself looking at the Wiccan. She seemed relieved, as if she knew somehow Gorgoroth had departed.

"I am Endessa, Vyder. Miriam asked me to help bring you back. Unfortunately, this was the only way it was possible."

"Miriam! Where is she?"

"She lives." Endessa pointed behind the assassin. "She is over there."

Vyder looked over his shoulder and saw the older woman who'd served him for so long, lying supine upon the cave floor.

"What have you done, moron?"

I failed, monkey, that's what I did. I intended to kill her. And now that our eyes are clear once more, I'll try again.

"Like hell, you bastard! You can stay where you are. She has done nothing but help us! If you try one more time, I shall return to The Frost River, and my wife. I promise you, laddie, try one more time and you can return to the spirit world!"

Gorgoroth did not reply. Surging to his feet, Vyder rushed to Miriam and dropped to the ground beside her.

"Miriam!"

He held a hand to her face, and grasped her shoulder firmly with the other. He shook her.

"Miriam! Can you hear me?"

She groaned, but her eyes remained closed.

Vyder tapped her face with gentle persistence. "Miriam, it's time to wake up."

Her eyes fluttered for a few moments, then opened. Her pupils rapidly constricted as they focused on his face, and her eyes widened in fear.

"It's fine, Miriam. It is I, Vyder. You're safe."

Relief washed over her.

She sighed. "You took your bloody time," she mumbled.

* * *

Griff was not a man of combat. He'd never

partaken in the discipline of the sword, spear or axe as a young man. Medicine had always been his passion. Helping people recover from injury or disease was where his heart truly lay. Much to the disappointment of his father, a retired officer of the Watch and a veteran of several pitched battles, where more than a thousand men had perished on each occasion. He'd told Griff about it once when he'd consumed too much ale and could no longer stand, but the young, would-be doctor blocked out his father's recollection. He'd always wanted to help wounded recover, not listen to how death had claimed them. As far as he was concerned, he was death's enemy. If his skills could prolong life, he'd succeeded, although sometimes they were too far gone. He glanced at Vyder. Sometimes, conventional medicine was not enough.

Terror had filled him when Vyder had regained consciousness, however. Griff had scuttled into a dark corner of the cave. The giant assassin, with blazing blue eyes, had lifted Miriam off the floor, an arm wrapped around her throat. He'd strangled her. Griff had wanted to help. Truly. He'd wanted to dart forward and distract the highlander, punch him in the face, slap at his arms, kick him in the groin. But Griff had sunk to his haunches, instead, and placed a loose fist in his mouth as hope began to flee his being. He'd watched the woman go limp and stared, helpless, as Endessa intervened.

The highlander had crouched to the floor, clawing at his eyes, and then something inexplicable happened. The assassin somehow changed.

Had his body changed? Griff tutted to himself. *Of course not!* But the man's demeanour had altered, his body language morphing into another. Griff paused as he thought of the right word. He continued to watch Vyder crouched over Miriam. *Being? No. Man? Not necessarily.*

Personality? Yes! Personality, that's the word I was searching for.

The cruel, deep voice melted away to be replaced by a thick, highland accent and, somehow, through some unspoken law, which for some reason Griff seemed familiar, he knew he was safe from harm. The tall assassin would do him no harm.

He stepped forward out of the shadows and padded forward. Endessa turned to him as he advanced.

"Oh, so nice of you to join us, Doctor. Thanks for your help back there!"

"I'm sorry, Endessa, it's just that, well, it's just—"

"Shut up!"

He moved around the Wiccan and knelt beside Miriam. He looked up into Vyder's face. Gone were the blue orbs, replaced with dark eyes, a trait common to many highland people. The iris was almost as black as the pupil itself, giving them a piercing look, even if it was unintentional. Vyder nodded at him once, then looked away, returning his attention to the woman lying at his feet.

"Griff, it's good to see you," the soft voice was almost inaudible.

It took him a moment to realise it was Miriam who spoke. He smiled down at her.

"You too! How do you feel?"

"A bit of a sore throat." She touched her neck where the skin was red. "But otherwise fine."

"I'm sorry for that, Miriam," said Vyder, staring at the stone floor of the cave.

"It wasn't your fault," Griff replied. "I saw what happened. That thing took over your body. It wasn't you who tried to…"

He stopped talking as he juggled what he wanted to say without causing offence.

"Kill Miriam?" Vyder finished for him. "Kind words, lad, but you're wrong, it was partly my fault for losing control to Gorgoroth. It shan't happen again."

Griff nodded but remained silent. Returning his attention to Miriam, he smiled once more. "Come! Let us get you to your feet."

He took one hand and Vyder clasped the other. They helped the woman to her feet. She brushed herself off and threw herself into Vyder's arms.

* * *

"It's good to have you back!" she spoke into her master's chest. He was more like a son to her than a master.

"You died, Vyder. Endessa brought you back from the other side."

"Barely," the Wiccan said.

She pulled away from the tall highlander and looked up into his face.

"I was with Verone. She was there, waiting for me, Miriam!" His shoulders slumped and he stared at the ground, then his eyes closed. "I want to go back. I want to be with my wife." His eyelids parted and he looked up at her. "My time here is done, Miriam."

"I'm sorry, Vyder, I didn't know what else to do. I didn't want you to die. I also know the importance of your mission. My father once spoke of the war between the Wendurlund and Huronian kingdoms when he was a young man. Some of the stories he told were horrible. Such massive loss of life. I don't want that to happen ever again."

He sighed. "I know," he said finally. "I understand that." He smiled. "My thanks for your help. You too, boy." He turned to Endessa. "And to you, thank you for breathing life back into me. At least long enough for me to finish the mission."

"Gorgoroth is the one who brought you back. It is he you should thank." Endessa turned away and spat on the floor before hobbling to the fire.

Miriam gestured to the wagon only just visible from the darker recess of the cave in which it was parked. "Let's go home."

Vyder nodded and took a single faltering step. Stamping his feet upon the floor as if reacquainting himself with the physical form, he took another few steps. "That's the best idea I've heard in a long while. I feel like I could sleep for a bloody month."

"You head to the wagon, Vyder. I'll be there shortly." Miriam walked over to the fireplace in front of which Endessa, squatted, prodding a steel poker amongst the glowing coals. "What do we owe you for your services, Endessa?"

The Wiccan paused and glanced over her shoulder. "Owe me?"

"Payment. What are your charges?"

Endessa chuckled and turned back to the fire. "Money is of no use to me, child. I have all I need right here. Your doctor friend will want payment though, I suspect. I have a condition, though."

Miriam remained silent and waited for Endessa to speak.

"I will accompany you. For a time, at least, so I can school Vyder in the ways of Gorgoroth and how to live with him."

"Of course, you are welcome!"

Endessa remained staring into the fire. "I shall be with you presently."

Miriam nodded, looking into the fire. The face of a demon manifested amongst the flames. Red eyes stared at Endessa. Tusks lined each side of its mouth. The thing spoke, but Miriam heard no words. As its mouth moved, flames burst from the fang-filled maw.

She stepped back, her mouth dropped open and black tendrils of terror wrapped her in their tight embrace. *What the hell is that thing?*

Endessa chuckled to herself, muttering a few words Miriam could not hear. She turned away from the Wiccan.

I'm losing my mind.

* * *

Vyder walked to the wagon, the streams of dried blood, which had flowed down the wooden edges and onto the large wheels was not lost on him. Miriam and Griff had gone to enormous length to bring him here to the Wiccan's cave. He heard a nearby snort. There was movement from within the shadows. Taking a step back, his eyes adjusted to the darkness. A horse moving toward him. The animal's coat glistened in the dull light. It was familiar.

"Storm!" Vyder smiled wide enough that his cheeks ached. "Bloody animal!"

He took its muzzle in his hands, stroking the soft nose. He touched his forehead to the area of skin between Storm's eyes.

"You helped save me, too, lass."

The horse nuzzled his face gently, soft, warm air passing across his face as the animal sniffed him.

It has been a long while since I've seen a horse!

The voice in his mind took him by surprise, and he

suddenly felt as if he was sinking beneath the surface of a vast ocean.

Gorgoroth, stay where you are! You have no power over me!

Harsh chuckles exploded in his mind. *Oh, do I not? Watch me!*

Down Vyder sank into a dark abyss, vaguely aware of his body but no longer in control. He fought up towards the surface, but an unseen power held him at bay.

I think not, little man. My turn for a while.

Storm flinched and turned to run but seemed to relax within moments. The animal faced the man who stood before him.

"Storm, my daughter," Gorgoroth said, placing a soft hand upon the horse's head. "There is nothing to fear from me. I shall never harm you."

The woman and little doctor man have taken care of her.

He took a few steps so he was standing at Storm's shoulder and placed his palm upon the upper flank. He felt the large rib cage beneath the skin and the mighty beat of Storm's heart within.

She is healthy, well-rested, cared for. Content.

"This is good." He patted the horse's rump. "Yes this is very good. Certainly not what I expected. The human monkeys are usually such destructive creatures. It is pleasant to find an animal cared for in such a way."

Storm nuzzled his chest. He stroked the animal's face and enjoyed the warmth of Storm's breath. The horse looked at the wagon before nuzzling his chest again.

"Time to leave, you think?" Storm pushed against him gently. He chuckled. "Well, in that case, let's get your harness in place."

Do you even know how to fix the harness in place,

Gorgoroth?

Gorgoroth laughed. Storm's ears swept forward at the sudden noise. She stared at him, dark, alert eyes boring into Gorgoroth.

"Of course I do, human, I was around before the wheel was even invented."

We'll see.

"We'll see, indeed," Gorgoroth muttered. He deftly fixed the harness in place with confidence and, before long, Storm was attached to the wagon. She stamped her hoof upon the cave floor.

"Patience, my girl." Gorgoroth stroked the powerful neck, and the animal visibly relaxed.

"We're ready to go I think, Vyder," a female voice spoke from behind him.

Gorgoroth turned to the short, frumpy woman. She flinched and stumbled backward, almost losing her balance. The woman screamed before turning and running away towards Endessa in the near distance.

Gorgoroth held out his hands. "What?"

Endessa hobbled toward him. She held up both hands and began to chant. The power of the words hit him like a wall and he found himself in a seated position, glaring up at the approaching witch. He bunched his legs beneath him but all power seemed to have fled his muscles. Endessa reached into the pouch at her belt and her hand came out clutching a fistful of black powder.

"Remember this?" the witch shook her fist at him, tiny tendrils of powder sifting through her fingers to drift the ground.

Dismay spread through Gorgoroth. "Aye. I do."

He felt more constricted in the physical form than he thought possible. He was expecting to be as free as a bird, slaughtering humans when and where he saw fit.

This will be more difficult than I imagined. Especially in the presence of the little Wiccan standing before me.

"You shall not harm her, Gorgoroth! You shall harm no one in this place, not even the horse."

Gorgoroth's jaw dropped. "I would never harm an animal! I am here as their custodian. I protect them, guide them, and when I can, lead them." He fixed his eyes upon the little servant woman and doctor standing by her. "Usually from humans seeking to harm them for no other reason than their own enjoyment. Now I'm in physical form, my job will be much easier."

Endessa moved closer so that she was within inches of Gorgoroth's face. "Not all humans are evil."

His lips touched one another again and one side of his mouth widened. "Are they not?"

"No, Gorgoroth, they are not. This is something you need to learn. Surely, after all these millennia you must have seen this?"

"Not often, no." He pushed up with his legs but failed again.

"Not *often*." The Wiccan smiled. "So you agree with me."

Gorgoroth growled.

He felt a weight lift from him as if some sodden, thick woollen blanket had been cast off his shoulders. Standing, he towered over the Wiccan and appraised her.

"Perhaps you are right." He twisted and looked at the doctor and the slave woman beside him, terror still shining in her eyes. "Perhaps." He brushed past Endessa and strode to the pair in the near distance. "Perhaps not."

He heard the misplaced steps of the Wiccan as she hobbled after him. "Gorgoroth! You have no power in this place!"

He paused mid-stride and laughed. "I have power everywhere, Endessa. This is *my* world." He looked around and held his hands out. "*My* cave." The little witch stood but a foot from him. "I'm not going to hurt them."

"If you do, I shall cast you back from whence you came."

He nodded. "And if you do, war will ravage the kingdoms and even more of your precious people will be put to slaughter. Perhaps you *should* cast me back?"

Endessa crossed her arms, her brow creasing, her mouth a tight line.

"You have my word, Endessa. I shall not harm them."

He turned from her and approached the pair. The doctor remained still, frozen in place, eyes wide, mouth clamped shut. The woman, however, was visibly shaking, tears streaming down her cheeks, sucking air in through clenched teeth as she sobbed. Gorgoroth knelt before them.

He reached out and clamped a hand each side of the woman's face. She screamed and pulled away, but Gorgoroth held her firm. He closed his eyes and took a deep breath as the woman's life unfolded before his mind's eye. She had survived a harsh upbringing, surviving countless beatings, rapes and violence. But not once had she harmed an animal. That was all that interested the nature spirit. She'd even saved an old dog from drowning during a flood.

People are not as cruel as you think, Gorgoroth.

He clenched his teeth, eyes snapping open. "Shut up, Vyder, and yes, more often than not, they are. Humans are a virus, a blight upon the world. This one may not have been cruel." He released his hold of

Miriam and stared at her. *Although I could understand if she was. She's felt such hate, violence, and anger in her life.*

Miriam's a strong one, Gorgoroth. Probably one of the strongest you'll ever meet.

The nature spirit nodded and turned to the doctor. The man hadn't moved, still frozen in fear. With lightning speed, Gorgoroth's massive hands were clamped either side of the doctor's face.

"Your turn, little monkey."

The man had come from a privileged lifestyle. He was used to money and elegant surroundings, but like the woman, he'd not harmed any creature. Gorgoroth flitted through the doctor's memories. Griff was his name, he learned. Anger surged through Gorgoroth as he watched the young boy try to save a cat from his father. But the doctor's father had smashed the animal's skull in with a hammer, then threw the limp carcass out onto the street to be driven into the cobblestones by passing carriages.

Gorgoroth's lips parted to reveal clenched teeth, his eyes narrowed. He released the man and poked an index finger at the doctor. "Your father. Does he still live?"

"My father?"

"It's what I asked, yes."

"No. He died when I was a young man."

The nature spirit nodded and rose to his feet. "Good. The earth is a better place for his absence."

The skinny little man nodded.

He faced Endessa. "You might be right." He gestured at the pair behind him. "But it might be that these two are just extraordinary humans. I have walked in the physical form but twice. I haven't seen much of humankind that leads me to believe they are anything more than…" He swung to Griff, and sneered. "Well…human. A plague upon the earth."

He glared at the doctor, who folded his hands in front of him and stared at the ground. Gorgoroth heard the shuffling, limping sound as Endessa approached behind him.

"I think you'll be pleasantly surprised, Gorgoroth. As I said, people are not as cruel or evil as you seem to think."

He focused on the Wiccan and held her powerful gaze. His shoulders rose and fell, teeth shining in the dull light as his lips peeled apart in a wide grin. "We shall see, Endessa." He walked to Storm and stroked her powerful, sleek neck. "We shall see."

* * *

Miriam stared at Vyder's back as he patted the animal.

Vyder? She took a deep breath and let it out slow. *That's not Vyder. Endessa calls him Gorgoroth. What kind of name is that? It's certainly not one that originates in the highlands, or lowlands for that matter.*

An incessant tapping on her arm broke her chain of thought. Miriam felt the doctor lean into her and press his lips close to her ear.

"I don't think he likes us very much."

"Really?" She turned to Griff. "What makes you so sure?"

The doctor's eyes were wide. "Are you serious?"

She breathed a curse. "No, Griff, I'm not. It's more than dislike. It's abject hatred. We'd be dead by now if it wasn't for Endessa."

Griff's eyes grew even wider.

They're going to pop out of his skull in a minute.

"You think?" he whispered.

A dry chuckled burst from her lips. "Oh I'm more than sure, Griff. I've spent enough time around violent, murderous, or cruel men, aye, and women, to know. He'd kill us without a second thought."

"Who?"

The voice made her jump. Gorgoroth was back and standing only a mere pace or two from them. He'd moved silently. Fear stabbed her as she looked up into his eyes, but relief soon followed as Miriam noticed the bright blue, glowing eyes were gone, to be replaced with Vyder's dark, piercing gaze.

"You mean Gorgoroth?"

She nodded.

"I'll never allow him to hurt you, Miriam."

She tried to smile, but her mouth refused to move. "He's more powerful than you think, Vyder."

The assassin remained silent, and that in itself was enough for Miriam to confirm the highlander knew she spoke the truth.

"Let's go." He strode to the wagon.

She followed at a sedate pace, watching her master's wide shoulders and expecting Gorgoroth to take over at any moment. Realisation struck her. *I don't trust him anymore.* She no longer trusted the only master who'd ever treated her with respect and dignity. And Miriam hated herself for it.

* * *

Vyder ran a hand along Storm's sleek flank. Whispering soft words to the horse, he strode to her shoulder and checked the leather collar, which sat around her powerful neck. The reins were threaded through the collar exactly as they should be.

"You got that part right at least, Gorgoroth."

Oh, I got everything right, Vyder, trust me. But you go ahead and check my handiwork.

"I will, have no fear on that count."

Vyder clenched his jaw as the silent laughter thundered through his mind. He tugged on the girth to make sure it was not too tight, or loose. It was perfect. Storm was watching him, her ears forward, listening to his every move.

"We'll be on our way soon enough, girl."

The wooden trace, connecting the wagon to the collar around Storm's neck, sat exactly as it should.

"Is everything in order, Vyder?"

He appraised Endessa. The small woman, who looked so helpless and frail, was exactly the opposite. He knew it and felt damn sure Gorgoroth knew it as well.

"Everything seems to be in order."

Storm snorted, still watching Vyder.

He looked at the horse and smirked. "Patience, my lass." Vyder swung back to the Wiccan. "Are you joining us?"

"I will travel with you for a short time, yes."

Oh, joy of joys.

"Keep your teeth together, Gorgoroth. Do you need help climbing up onto the wagon?"

She did not appear concerned by his conversation with Gorgoroth.

The woman shuffled forward. "No." She leapt up onto the wagon with lithe agility that should have been impossible for someone of her demeanour. She stood on the wagon, hands on her hips.

She was glaring at Miriam and Griff. "Well?" She

gestured them to her. "Are you coming or not?"

Miriam looked uncertain, even frightened.

"Miriam, it is I," said Vyder. "I'll do you no harm."

She took a step backward. "I know *you* won't."

"He's gone and I don't think he'll return for a long while."

"Are you sure?"

He smiled. "I'm sure."

You sound so sure, human. How cute.

She looked at him sidelong and walked around, moving to the front of the wagon and using the wheel to clamber up onto the tray beside Endessa. Griff was not far behind her.

Vyder sighed and stood.

They don't like you, Vyder.

He sensed the snigger in the nature spirit's voice.

"No, they don't like you, Gorgoroth!" he muttered.

More than likely. They have good reason to dislike me, I suppose. Probably not as much as I dislike them, though.

Looking up at the trio, he opened his mouth to speak, but suddenly felt far away, as if he was slipping beneath the surface of some great lake.

No Gorgoroth, not now! Stay where you are, I command you!

"Command is it, now? No one commands me, much less a human. You'd do well to remember that, you stinking monkey."

* * *

Gorgoroth glared at the trio and grinned as he saw fear enter the eyes of the man and woman. Opening his eyes as wide as possible, he took a step towards them, placing a hand on the wagon.

"I'm back! Did you miss me?"

Neither replied. The only noise was Endessa's bored sigh. She took up the reins, and with a groan, sat on the driver's bench. She cleared her throat and spat over the side. "You're having fun aren't you, Nature Spirit?"

He threw back his head and roared in merriment. "Oh, I don't remember the last time I've had this much fun, Witch!"

Storm flinched and stepped sideways, away from the sudden noise and movement. Gorgoroth placed a hand on her flank. The horse immediately relaxed. She looked around at him, her dark eyes boring into him. He walked to the mighty animal's shoulder with care. She was a gentle beast, but even he knew how powerful horses were, not to mention how fast they could kick out when they perceived a threat.

"You are safe, my girl," he cooed, resting a hand on her head. "Nothing will hurt you here."

"Do you not want to climb up here with us?" Endessa called.

He looked around as he walked. He gestured at his legs. "We have feet for a reason. Besides, I enjoy strolling."

The look of relief on Miriam's face was almost comical. He laughed and turned away.

"You're right, Vyder, she does not like me one bit."

I'm not sure why, I doubt it'd have anything to do with you trying to bloody kill her!

Gorgoroth rubbed his chin and frowned. "You think so?"

Oh, it's just a thought, Nature Spirit. People tend not to forget about almost being murdered.

"I don't think so. I don't think she likes my charm."

Gorgoroth chuckled at Vyder's scoff.

Gorgoroth walked along a dirt track through the forest. He closed his eyes, smelling the gentle aroma of fresh grass, flowers, sprouting succulents intermingled with the pungency of rotting wood and leaf litter. Cool, soft wind kissed the skin of his cheeks and, high above, the melodious hiss of the forest's canopy teased his ears. He smiled and opened his eyes, taking in the shades of green, brown, and everything in between.

"I'm home, Vyder. I'm home."

Good for you. I'm not, so keep walking.

* * *

Endessa gently tapped the whip against the horse's rump, and the wagon began rumbling forward, swaying as they rolled across the uneven ground. Gorgoroth strode well ahead of them. He was already out of the cave and on the path leading into the thick forest. She knew it was the nature spirit. Aside from the bright blue eyes, there was subtle differences in the demeanour between the man and spirit. When Gorgoroth was in control, the shoulders were pulled back, chest thrust out in complete confidence. His movements were more fluid, and he stopped often to kneel beside a fern, or hold a hand against a trunk, as if he was somehow communicating with the tree. Storm's ears were pricked forward, the animal acutely aware of Gorgoroth, constantly watching what he was doing.

"Hey, you should be listening to me." The Wiccan flicked the whip against the horse's rump, but the beast ignored her.

She squinted against the sudden light as they exited the cave and onto the dirt path. Endessa sensed movement beside her and felt the driver's bench move slightly as Miriam sat beside her.

She clicked the horse on. "That's a good boy."

Storm increased her pace and the wagon was soon eating the path as they gained on Gorgoroth, who was now sat in the middle of the path, his back to them.

"Is that Vyder or Gorgoroth?" Miriam asked in a near whisper.

"Gorgoroth, my girl. You'll be able to tell the difference soon enough." She glanced at the woman and noted the fear in her eyes. "He means well, he just needs to learn that not all people are evil."

"Endessa, he tried to kill me."

"I know, Miriam. Trust me when I say he'll never try that again."

"How can you be so sure?"

"I just know, my girl. You and Griff are safe."

I hope.

Miriam nodded and seemed to relax.

Endessa heard a commotion above her, holding a hand over her eyes to shield them from the light of the sun spearing between the forest canopy, she searched for the origin of the noise. High above them, a flock of ravens landed amongst the branches of a particularly tall oak and glared down at them, cackling amongst themselves.

A thundering arose in the distance, growing louder. A herd of deer strode into view, surrounding Gorgoroth, sniffing his face and head. Crickets began to sing even though it was day. The cacophony almost deafened Endessa. She pulled Storm to a halt. Gorgoroth still sat in the middle of the path. He patted the deer around him, smiled at the ravens above him, and held his hands out as various animals, great and small, plodded, scuttled, leapt, and slithered to him from every corner of the forest. They were around and on him.

"What is happening, Endessa?" Miriam's voice quivered with fear.

"The creatures of the Waning Wood have never seen Gorgoroth in the flesh before. They are curious."

"Do they know who he is?"

Endessa laughed. "He is their guardian, child. Their protector, their guiding hand. They know him like a parent. No matter what physical form he took, they'd know who he was."

She heard a clicking resounding above the animals surrounding the nature spirit and knew exactly what it was.

Damn you, Gorgoroth, you've summoned her.

"Steady, lass." She brushed the whip against Storm's flank. "You are safe." This time the horse's ears flicked backwards as she listened to the Wiccan.

The giant spider pushed through a mighty fern and approached the nature spirit. The arachnid's abdomen was the size of a large man's chest. Spooked, the deer ran clear, disappearing into the forest.

"Just a hatchling," Endessa chuckled. "I thought it was Barbaron herself."

Miriam made a high-pitched noise but otherwise did not reply. Storm flinched, ears flat to her skull.

"Sshh, my lovely. You are safe."

The spider pushed itself onto Gorgoroth's lap, thin, long legs enveloping his head and back. The nature spirit rubbed the abdomen and whispered soft words to the spider, although Endessa could not hear what it was he spoke.

"It's going to kill him, Endessa, you must do something!"

"He's a nature spirit, Miriam, remember that. As I said, these creatures are like his children. They are drawn to his power. The spider would never hurt him. As for Vyder? I'm not so sure."

Endessa cleared her throat and spat a globule to the ground. "Gorgoroth! It's time to leave. Say your goodbyes, we have things to do."

He looked back, piercing blue eyes boring into the Wiccan. He sneered. "Oh, but I was only getting started." He stood, holding the spider on his hip like a baby. "Did you want to say hello to Ferofoth?"

The spider leapt clear of the nature spirit's embrace and stood on the path. It clicked towards them a few paces and stopped, as if offering them a challenge.

Endessa felt fear ebb through her. Out here amongst the forest, the nature spirit held great power. She knew with a single word of command, he could send Ferofoth charging amongst them. With fangs the length of an adult's hand, one scrape would be enough to spell a death sentence within moments. "No, thank you."

"Oh, come on!" He knelt beside the massive spider and placed a hand upon the arachnid. "He's a lovely little boy." He sniggered. "As long as you're not human."

"No, we're fine thanks Gorgoroth." Endessa dropped the reins and opened the pouch attached to her belt, grabbing a handful of black powder.

"Alright, alright!" Gorgoroth held out his hands. "I mean you no harm."

Endessa watched as he turned on the spot, arms held out beside him. "Away with you, my children. Alas, I must depart."

As if by some magic, the animals turned and

departed, the ravens taking wing and flying clear, calling out. The crickets fell silent, and Ferofoth clicked away, disappearing behind the trunk of a massive tree.

Endessa noticed the nature spirit staring at her, his bright blue eyes piercing her soul. He took a step towards her and grinned. "Shall we?"

Part II

Besieged

"The soldiers of the King's Own are a small force of mounted infantry, which exists to protect the royal family. Oddly enough, our default position is actually one of peace. But, we are trained in and masters of many forms of war. If our hand is forced, and there are no other options but to fight, then my warriors will dominate any battlefield upon which they stand, regardless of the enemy they face, the season, weather, or terrain. There is a reason we are widely regarded by all empires as the finest soldiers in the world."

Tork – Commander of the King's Own.

V

"Lord Tork, a good morning to you." The servant bowed and took a backward step.

Commander Tork slammed the door behind him and glanced at the servant bent at the waist, offering his balding head towards the Commander of the King's Own.

"A fair morning to you, Brent. I trust you enjoyed a pleasant night?"

Brent remained silent, still bent at the waist. Tork's father had always drummed into him that a powerful person was not made by gold, or a sharp blade, although those things helped, of course. The first step towards true power was not only acknowledging, but treating the least powerful person in the room with respect.

Tork strode along the wide, stone hallway. A torch had extinguished, he noticed. He stopped.

"Get this lit, Brent."

"Yes, Lord Tork. Of course, sire."

He turned, a faint headache emerging behind one eye. He stared at the unlit, cold torch. It had not carried a flame in many hours. "I don't care, Brent, it bothers me not at all, but you know what'll happen if some half-wit notices and decides to have you punished."

"Aye, my lord. Twenty lashes."

Tork nodded.

A cluster of servants padded past him, dressed in drab, brown gowns, their eyes downcast.

"A fair morning to you all, I trust you slept well?"

They offered soft, frightened greetings. One of

them nodded. "I slept well, lord, thank you."

"Good! Sounds like you slept better than me then."

The soft chuckle of the servants echoed off the stone walls as they swept past, and he grinned.

Next month, I'll be forty bloody summer's old. Forty!

In his youth, he'd spent weeks in the field, often in enemy territory, leading small scouting groups galloping across Huron roads and tracks.

The good old days.

The main doors leading to the King's Own headquarters came into view. The dull thump of the two guards coming to attention before him brought Tork out of his reverie.

"Mornin', sire," one of them offered.

"Morning, Captain Beel."

Beel was one of his junior officers. Unlike many other units, being an officer in the King's Own did not refute the fact that all must share even the most mundane of duties.

He stared at the second guard and nodded. "And you are?"

A new guard to scare. Good, it might alleviate some of the boredom!

"Private Seeg, sire!"

Tork nodded. "Private Seeg. Nice to meet you, boy."

Seeg clenched his spear tighter, his fingertips turning white. "Sire."

Tork grunted. He allowed his eyes to wander to the spear Seeg held by his side. The weapon was polished, well cared for, and sharper than sin.

But where's the fun in that?

Tork pointed at the spearhead. "Is that rust on your spear, boy?"

Seeg's mouth dropped open, eyes widened and eyebrows shot skyward, deep, horizontal lines appearing across his brow. "No, sire!"

Tork took a pace forward and glared at the terror-stricken guard. "Are you sure?"

"Yes, sire!"

"Because it damn well looks like rust to me, lad. You know what that means?"

The young guard swallowed and nodded, the helmet rattling against his forehead.

"What?"

"A thrashin', sire."

"Two hundred lashes, that's right." He held out his open hand. "Let me see that spear."

Seeg handed across the weapon.

Out of the corner of his eye, Tork could see Beel was straining to hold in laughter.

As he suspected, there was nothing wrong with it. *Bloody perfect. This man is a good soldier.* He was careful to supress the impression from his face. On the contrary, he frowned as he brought the polished steel spear tip close to his eyes.

"I've never seen a man live beyond one hundred and fifty lashes," Tork muttered in a conversational tone. With a swift movement, he shoved the beautifully sharp steel towards the guard's face. "What's *that?*"

Seeg took a breath, eyes wider than saucepans. "I'm not sure what you're referring to, me lord. I can't see any rust."

"Can you not?" Tork spoke softly.

"If I'm bein' honest. Well...no, me lord."

"Excellent!" Tork burst into laughter and slammed the spear's haft against the guard's chest. "Neither can I."

He strode past the pair and barged through the doors, Beel's laughter booming into life behind him. He squinted against the poor light and waited for his eyes to become accustomed to the gloom. Several torches lined the walls, burning with soft pops and splutters, but not in sufficient number to throw adequate light upon the area. The doors *thudded* shut behind him. *The war room* always seemed to be an over-dramatic term for a large, plain meeting space. Tork shrugged. *Mine is not to question.*

"Now that we are all here, perhaps you can take your seat, Lord Tork, so that we may begin?" a deep voice boomed through the murk. Tork'd know Jad's voice anywhere.

He nodded. "Of course." Who was he to question the king's most senior advisor? A small wave of Jad's hand and Tork would be taken to the closest street and beheaded; following a short, biased trial, little means of a defence, and a swift death. Thankfully, Jad was a fair man and of even temper.

His eyes began to win the struggle, and Tork turned his focus to the small table set at the centre of the war room, around which sat three men turned in their seats, staring at the commander of the King's Own.

"In your own time, Tork." Jad tapped fingers upon the table's surface in a slow, rhythmic staccato. "In your own time."

"Aye, my lord. Apologies."

He strode across the room and took his place, folding his hands before him on the table. He met the eyes of each man around him. Mace, commander of the Watch, a tall man with sharp blue eyes and shoulder length black hair. Tork nodded his greeting, and Mace returned a tight smile before returning his attention to Jad. Tork met Blake's dark eyes and was expecting the half snarl and roll of the eyes the diplomat usually gave him as greeting each morning. He was not disappointed. The diplomat even provided a small '*tut*.'

A tut! I feel privileged!

Tork smiled at the little blond-haired man and turned away to look at Jad.

The king's advisor scribbled upon parchment with a quill. "Shall we begin?" he asked without looking up.

Tork was astute enough to know it wasn't a question and that, as the second most senior to Jad, he would be the one to start the daily report.

"All normal, no change."

Jad sighed and stopped writing. "I suppose it is a good thing nothing ever changes with the King's Own." He commenced writing again. "Still, something different once every year or two might be nice. Next!"

Tork grinned and leaned back in his chair. Mace was always thorough with his daily reports. Usually, he reported upon the odd bar fight, which had spilled out upon the street, arson, murder, and other overnight activities of the city's miscreants. Mostly, it was boring. But a few days ago, Tork's ears had pricked as he listened to Mace's report of a large fight upon the streets of the posher quarter of the city. Something which hadn't occurred in his lifetime. Close to ten foresters had been killed.

"No criminal activity to report this morning, sire."

Jad looked up from the thick parchment. "Really?"

"No, sire, but there have been several animal attacks in the west."

Blake sniggered. "Animal attacks?" he muttered. "What, a bird pecked a girl on the nose? A dog bit his master's finger?" The diplomat sneered.

Tork turned to Blake. "You know, for a diplomat,

you're about as diplomatic as a —"

"Go on," Jad coaxed, interrupting Tork.

"Seventeen dead."

Tork's breath caught in his throat, and he leaned forward. "What? Seventeen *people?*"

Mace nodded.

Jad stopped writing and scratched his head with the reverse end of the quill. "How?"

"Sire, we're still receiving reports by the half hour, but as it stands right now, five people were mauled by a pack of dogs. Well, what is thought to be wolves, whoch barged through the western gate before it could be locked closed."

Blake chortled. "There are no wolves inside the city walls, you fool!"

Jad slammed a hand upon the table, the noise sounding like a musket. "Silence!"

Throwing a glance at Blake, Mace shifted in his chair. "Three people, as reports would have it, were killed by ravens, and a further nine were slaughtered by...by." Mace fell silent, and he looked down at the table. He took a deep breath before meeting Jad's stern glare. "A further nine were taken by giant spiders."

Blake burst into laughter. "Oh, now I've heard *everything!* Spiders?"

Tork stood and moved around behind the diplomat. He took a fistful of collar and pulled the man to his feet.

"What is this?" Blake shrieked. "Unhand me this instant!"

Tork chuckled and tightened his grip. "Come with me, Blake. You've had enough for one day, my friend."

Pulling open one of the mighty doors, he pushed the diplomat through. Tork tapped the thick armour protecting Brent's shoulder. "Keep him out, for today at least."

Brent came to attention. "Yes, sire!"

"You can't presume to tell me –"

Brent took a step forward and lowered his spear, the point hovering near the diplomat's throat. "Halt!"

"Go home, Blake. Come back tomorrow when you've had some sleep, or bedded a woman, or both. You're particularly disagreeable today."

"I demand that –"

"Don't try your luck, Blake. The guards standing outside this door are King's Own and I am their commander. Right now, they've been instructed to keep you out. If that means spilling your blood, trust me, they'll do it without a moment's thought."

Blake backed away a few steps. "I'll have you know…" The diplomat licked his lips. "I'll have you –"

"Go home, Blake." Tork closed the door and turned back to the two men still at the table. He smiled at them. "Sorry about that."

Tork returned to the table and sat.

"Shall we continue?" Jad folded his hands on the table.

Mace cleared his throat. "Of course."

Tork turned to the Commander of the Watch. "You said nine were taken by spiders?"

"Aye."

"You mean killed, or actually dragged away?"

Mace shrugged, his eyebrows disappearing into the thick hair of his fringe. "Reports my men are passing on suggest these folk were stung by these things, and then carried away."

Jad stopped scribbling. Silence overcame the room for a moment before it was broken by the tapping of quill against parchment. "Were they still alive do you think, Mace?"

"I know not if all were, my lord. I can tell you at least two lived, as the reports state town folk in that area swear they heard a couple of the people bitten, screaming for help."

Tork closed his eyes and let a sharp breath out through pursed lips. "By Gulgon, that's terrible."

"Aye, it is. If the townsfolk are telling the truth that is."

Tork looked at the Watch's commander. "You doubt them?"

Mace held his hands open but remained silent.

"What reason would they have to lie?"

Mace shifted in his chair again, one of the wooden legs scraping on the tiled surface with a sudden, loud groan. "I don't know. It just seems a little farfetched."

Tork chuckled. "I was raised on stories of giant spiders creeping out of the Waning Wood at night to steal away naughty children."

Jad nodded, a smile playing upon his lips as he scribbled. "I too."

"My point exactly." Mace leaned back in his chair. "When was the last time you heard about mighty spiders scrambling over the city's walls?"

Tork chuckled. "When I was nine."

Mace crossed his arms. "I was six, and that was more than two decades ago."

Jad finished writing, placed the quill in the small jar of ink nearby, and looked up at the commanders. "I was seven summers of age, and that was more decades ago than I care to remember. Still, this report is worth investigating. If the folk are bored and fabricating tales, then the instigators will feel the lash. But what if they're not lying? What if this actually happened?"

The commanders appraised Jad in silence.

"Best you find out, Mace. Get a group of your men onto it and report their findings to me first thing on the morrow."

"I shall investigate it myself, sire."

Jad nodded and stood. He lifted the parchment to his mouth and blew on the ink to speed its drying. "Good man. I shall see you both tomorrow." He walked towards a distant door and stopped, turning back to them, his eyes boring into Tork. "And maybe we'll see Blake tomorrow as well, perhaps?"

Tork's teeth flashed as he broke into a grin. "Perhaps, my lord, perhaps. That all depends on which side of the bed he decides to roll out from."

Jad nodded, a smirk creasing his mouth. He turned and strode away.

* * *

Tork sat astride his destrier, Might, a pitch black, seventeen hand warhorse. Not only trained to bear his rider into and away from conflict, the animal was a warrior in his own right. Were Tork to fall during battle, Might was trained to kick, stomp, and bite enemy soldiers to ensure he had a clear path to withdraw to safety.

"Thanks for the company."

Tork nodded. "No problem, my friend. I wanted to see for myself."

Mace, sitting on a much smaller mount, chuckled. "You actually believe the reports?"

"Only one way to find out for sure."

Mace remained silent.

The pair walked their horses along the main drag

towards the western quarter. It was a wearisome journey, the traffic thick and slow, made more sluggish by a four-wheeled trade wagon throwing a wheel. Tork knew little about wagons or he might have been tempted to help the merchant. The stationary wagon had created a choke point, slowing traffic down. Tork steered Might into the single line of traffic making its slow way around the wagon.

"Poor bastard," Tork said as Might clopped past the wagon, which was full nearly to overflowing with fruit and vegetables. Tork was astute enough to know the produce would begin to spoil within a day or two, and the delay was doing the merchant no favours. The sweat soaked tradesman replacing the wheel worked fast, but seemingly not fast enough for the merchant, who sat on the road nearby, head in his hands. More than likely, he was contemplating his future as a beggar. It was well past noon when the soldiers managed to weave their way through the western flowing traffic and around the partial road block the disabled wagon provided.

Tork shifted into a more comfortable position in the saddle. "Do you know where the reports originated?"

"Aye. First western quarter closest the wall."

Tork hesitated as he pictured the map of the city in his mind. He frowned. "Is that not near the western gate?"

Mace nodded. "It is. I thought being commander of the King's Own, you'd know that better than me."

Tork scratched his chin but remained silent.

"Nothing to say to that, Commander?" Mace grinned.

"Let's suppose for a moment that these reports are accurate, and these...things are real. It seems to me they are directing their attention towards the gate itself."

"Possibly. What's your meaning?"

Tork took a deep breath and let it out slowly. "These creatures could attack at any point along the wall. I mean, the western wall is eight miles long, yet the only reports are issuing from and around the western gate area. If these reports are to be believed –"

Mace laughed. "And that's a big if!"

"Still, if they are to be believed, then that indicates not only organisation, but some kind of intelligence. What if only the minority are climbing the walls? What if they do manage to breach the western gate and the majority of the attack comes flowing into the city? What then, Mace?"

Mace burst out laughing. "You're overthinking this, my friend. I'll investigate this, find the culprits, and the skin of their back will be hanging in strips around their legs at the public flogging tomorrow morning. You'll see."

Tork smiled. "I hope you're right."

"I know I am."

I'm not so sure, my friend.

Mace continued. "But for what's worth, I'll be joining the Watch tonight to see for sure."

Tork clenched his fists against the numbness sweeping across the skin of his knuckles and on into his fingers. It was a feeling with which he was familiar.

"You still doubt me, don't you?"

Tork chuckled, clenching and unclenching his hands. "Aye, I do more than ever, now."

"What's wrong?" Mace stared at Tork's hands.

"Nothing, just a sixth sense I've had since before I attempted selection for the King's Own."

"Really? How so?"

Tork shrugged. "Just a strange feeling I get in my hands when things are about to go horribly wrong."

Mace grinned. "Have you seen a head doctor for that?"

"It's served me well so far. It once saved my patrol from a Huron ambush." He fell silent, staring into the horizon, his eyes losing their focus.

"And?"

Tork flinched and took a deep breath.

"What happened?"

He let the breath out slow. "We survived. That's what happened."

Mace nodded. "Well, here we are. I'm going to ask some questions around the place and see what I can find out."

Tork appraised the distant western gate, stretching seventy feet tall and thirty feet across. It was wide open, allowing citizens and merchants to come and go at their leisure. Incoming merchants were stopped for a cursory check of their cargo and identity papers by guards of the Watch.

"Enjoy that. I'm off for a ride in the forest to smell the fresh air. The stink of the city becomes a bit wearisome after a while."

Mace nodded. "Fair enough. See you in the war room on the morrow."

He nodded. "That you shall. Good luck!" Tork nudged his heels into Might's flanks, and the destrier accelerated into a smooth canter towards the huge gate.

He weaved through the slower traffic, no longer having the patience to wait behind slower travellers. Citizens either slogged along on foot, or merchants, without the capacity for agility, bumbled along on their wagons. Tork passed them all in quick succession. In no time at all he was dwarfed before the western gate.

"Good morning to you!" he called to one of the guards.

The guard, perusing the papers of a merchant, glanced up at him, looked back at the papers, and then he paused. His head snapped back up, and the guard's eyes bulged. He dropped the papers and snapped to attention.

"Sire! Good morning, sire! My apologies, I did not expect to see you."

It wasn't every day the commander of the King's Own came wandering through the gate.

"Stand easy. Don't mind me, I'm just passing through."

"Aye, sire!" But the guard remained at attention.

Within moments, he was on the other side of the gate and felt more at ease as the huge expanse of the rolling plains opened up before him. Tork clenched his fists again as the numbness intensified through his fingers. He pushed Might into a gallop and steered him off the road so he could pass the stream of meandering traffic wandering along at a sedate pace. The warhorse snorted in satisfaction as the ground streaked below them in a blur.

Within a short time, they approached Five Ways. Tork reined the destrier in, staring at Five Ways. Two wide roads peeled off to the left, another pair to the right, but it was the road stretching before him that held his interest. It was the path to the Waning Wood, and if the reports were to be believed, more than likely where the attacks originated.

"I once ventured into the outskirts of the Waning Wood when I was a boy."

Might's ears flicked back at his master's voice.

"Scared the shit out of me."

Tork frowned as he stared at the leaf littered road.

Not much traffic has passed this way in some time that much is obvious. But someone has come this way in the last few days.

"Hold!" he commanded.

The warhorse snorted and pawed at the ground.

Tork stepped out of the saddle and landed lightly upon the ground. Might would hold his position unless threatened, at which point he would attack before returning for Tork.

The commander of the King's Own clasped the hilt of his sword and adjusted it so he could kneel comfortably without the scabbard digging into the ground. He gently pressed a gloved hand into the wagon track.

"Fresh sign." He brushed aside leaves for a better view and found a second set of tracks he'd almost missed.

Either two separate wagons, or one travelling into and out of the Waning Wood.

His frown deepened, eyebrows meeting together above the bridge of his nose. He'd often been berated by his wife, Yeshira, for just such a look. In truth, he was thinking, or simply curious, but to onlookers, it seemed as if he was a hair's breadth from violence.

"What in the hells does a merchant want in the Waning Wood?"

Has to be a merchant. He scratched his chin and stood. What other reason for a wagon to come this way?

Placing a boot into one of Might's stirrups, he swung into the saddle and pushed the warhorse forward. The horse lunged into a trot, keen to be underway again. Soon, Five Ways was behind them and the road less travelled had become decidedly darker. The forest huddled closer as Might trotted on. It wasn't long and the thick canopy blotted out the sun and what felt like the light thrown at dusk quickly became night.

"Steady there, boy." Tork pulled back on the reins, slowing the destrier to a walk. He hissed against the near unbearable numbness emanating through his hand.

"At ready!" he commanded. He immediately felt Might's powerful body tense beneath him.

Tork had let the warhorse know they may be under imminent attack and the destrier was ready to respond. Tork craned his neck and looked at the various dark trees towering above, seemingly hunched over horse and rider like giant, grizzled old people. Tork swallowed but refused to be cowed. A sudden rustle in the undergrowth to their immediate left brought the warhorse to a halt. Might turned towards the noise, mouthing the bit. He stamped his foot as if in challenge.

Without taking his eyes from the area the noise had issued, Tork reached across and slowly unsheathed his sword, the weapon sliding free with a dull hiss.

If I'd thought about it, I would have brought my damn musket, blunderbuss and spear.

Small lizards and tiny ground-dwelling birds often caused intermittent sounds amongst the forest's undergrowth, but whatever had caused the commotion was not small.

All movement ceased and Tork sat like a statue, eyes wide, staring up at the forest canopy. There, dangling from several branches was a number of adult-sized, human-shaped forms encased in thick spider's silk.

"Ho there!" he bellowed. "Can you hear me?" He stood in the stirrups, sword clasped tight in his master hand. "Is anyone alive up there?"

The cluster of humanoid shapes remained dangling. None of them moved, not even slightly. No voices replied to his urgent questions.

Tork clicked and pulled gently back on the reins. Might stepped backwards, giving them room to disengage were it necessary. Another crash exploded on the opposite side of the narrow road behind them. Tork sat down onto the saddle.

"Time to leave, boy!" Tork turned the warhorse back towards Five Ways and urged him into a canter, which didn't take much coercion. He heard a deep growl and ear-shattering bark. Venturing a glance over his shoulder, he saw two wolves, half the size of Might, explode into view and give chase. Jowls peeled back to show razor sharp teeth, strings of saliva hanging in long tendrils.

Gods, they're fast!

He kicked Might into a gallop and whipped another look over his shoulder. The wolves were even closer, snapping at the horse's heels. We're not going to make this.

Tork tilted forward in his saddle as Might released a powerful double-barrel kick. The commander heard a dull thud and one of the wolves shriek in pain.

"Good lad!"

He couldn't push the destrier on any faster. They were at full pace, and whilst it was a blistering speed, Tork knew Might would be unable to maintain it for any length of time. Keeping a low profile, he leaned over the warhorse's mane so his face was close to the animal's ears. Flicking a glance rearward, he noticed the distance between themselves and the wolves hadn't opened much. They were almost as fast as the destrier at full flight.

"We're going to have to fight, I'm afraid, my boy. There's no other way."

Might was blowing hard as the powerful animal attempted to maintain the pace. If they didn't slow and turn to fight, the warhorse would have no strength for combat at all, and Tork didn't fancy his chances facing the wolves on foot.

He slowed Might and pulled him around in a sharp turn. The wolf on the left was closest, so Tork steered towards it and tightened his grip upon the sword hilt, before urging the destrier into a counter-charge. Did that bastard wolf hesitate? Tork's teeth flashed as his lips separated and widened in a death's head grin. Probably not used to his prey running towards him.

Might accelerated into a gallop, snorting as the gap between horse and wolf rapidly diminished. At the last moment, the destrier swerved slightly away from the threat, exactly as he'd been trained.

"OBRAGARDA!" Tork roared the King's Own war cry, leaning almost horizontal in the saddle, using every muscle in his shoulder and arm to swing the sword in a powerful sweep. The steel sang through the air. He felt the razor-sharp metal bite deep and rip free, and then a moment later, the wolves were behind them. He heard the shriek of agony but was too busy slowing and turning Might.

He felt the massive hooves slipping and sliding for grip beneath him, and then they were charging back towards the wolves. One of them sprinted towards Five Ways, heading straight for a merchant's wagon loaded with wares bound for Lisfort. It was a double-axel vehicle being drawn by a mighty highland draught horse. The merchant wore a wide brimmed hat and was staring in horror at the fast approaching threat.

"Oh shit!"

The other wolf cowered on its haunches, nursing an amputated leg. Tork swung the sword, sunlight flashing from the steel as it rent the air in a mighty underhand cut. The blade sliced clean through the wolf's neck, severing the head. The beast was dead before its body came to rest upon the ground. They gave chase to the giant animal almost upon the beleaguered merchant in the near distance.

"Jump clear!" roared Tork, gesturing for the man to run.

The merchant clamped a hand onto his hat, leapt from the driver's bench and ran, his screams barely audible to Tork as wind rushed past his ears. Might's rapid strides ate the ground, but it wasn't fast enough. The harnessed horse shrieked in terror as the wolf slammed into it, and they both went to ground in a mess of flailing hooves, clumps of dirt, and noise.

Tork pulled back on the reins, and Might sat on his haunches, coming to a sliding stop. He jumped clear and sprinted towards the preoccupied wolf.

"Hold! Hold!"

Tork was almost upon the wolf when Might brushed past him in a canter, reared on his hind legs, and brought his front hooves crashing down upon the wolf with powerful strikes. The canine cried out and turned from the bleeding horse to face the new threat. In that short time, Might turned to present his rump to the huge predator. Tork ran around the fighting animals and winced as Might's rear hooves slammed into the wolf's face. Blood exploded from the massive maw, several fangs flying clear. Tork noticed the canine's powerful rear legs bunched as it prepared to leap onto Might. Launching himself, Tork landed upon the canine's back and grabbed a fistful of fur with his left hand to steady himself.

He snarled. "Nice try!"

Holding the scalpel-sharp sword in a reverse grip, he stabbed the canine, a shuddering vibration emanating up the weapon and through his hand as the steel ground along the edge of a rib. Using all his power, Tork stopped when the hilt touched the thick hide. Before he could withdraw the blade, the animal screamed in agony and turned, bucking against the fresh pain assaulting its body. Try as he might, Tork couldn't maintain a grip and found himself sailing through the air. The ground rushed to make his acquaintance and all air departed him in a rush. Then the wolf was upon him.

Pinned to the ground by the weight of the animal, Tork was helpless, watching as the mighty fang-filled maw came within inches of his face. One bite and he would be without a face. The muzzle slowly rested upon his chest, the weight of the canine's head making breathing almost impossible. Then the last vestige of life fled the wolf's eyes.

Tork looked beyond the dead beast and focused upon Might standing above him. The warhorse snorted and stamped a hoof.

"How are you, my boy?" Tork spat dirt from his mouth and grunted as he pushed the wolf's mighty head clear.

Might simply stared back at him and snorted again.

"Alright, alright, I'm getting up."

He clambered to his feet, took a hold of his sword, and pulled it loose from the wolf with a grunt. Bright red blood oozed from the mighty wound, painting the fur around the injury claret. Might took a step forward and sniffed his master's face.

"I'm uninjured, my lad."

He cleaned the sword on the wolf's hide and sheathed the weapon. Moving around Might, he checked for wounds, passing his hand along the flanks, across the rump, looking at the warhorse's legs and hooves. The destrier was uninjured.

"Not a scratch, boy!"

He patted the horse's shoulder. "Good to see."

He looked at the merchant's horse, which had managed to stand up, although it was holding its nearside rear hoof off the ground. A mighty wound ran the length of its leg, blood streaming from the injury and trickling to the ground in a puddle.

A shame the same cannot be said for that one.

Might nuzzled his chest. Tork stroked the soft nose and pushed past the warhorse.

"I'm sorry I could not be of more help."

The weeping merchant stood before his wounded horse, holding the animal's head in his hands.

"If it weren't for you, we would have been killed." The merchant sniffed, wiping his eyes with the back of his sleeve.

He recognised the accent. "You are Huronian?"

The merchant nodded.

If it wasn't for me, you'd both be fine. I led the wolves to your door.

Tork clenched his jaw and swore.

"What's that you say?" blubbered the merchant.

He stopped beside the distraught man and placed a hand on his shoulder. "I'm sorry, my friend."

The merchant nodded and gestured towards the terrible wound. "He won't survive this will he?"

"No."

No point lying.

The man burst out crying and crumbled to the ground. Tork knelt beside him.

"I'm truly sorry. I can harness my horse to your wagon and pull you back into town. I will speak to my superiors and see if the king cannot replace your horse with another."

Looking up through tear-filled eyes, the merchant's eyebrows furrowed. "Would he do that?"

"Oh, our king is one of the most generous men around. When he learns of the circumstances, he won't hesitate."

More generous than your bastard dictator.

"Who are you?"

Tork heard movement nearby and noticed a newcomer approaching with musket in hand, a merchant wagon of his own parked nearby. "I am a member of his majesty's King's Own," Tork answered.

The newcomer stopped, shrugged and nodded. He held the weapon out towards Tork. "I think you might be in need of me musket."

Tork nodded. "I think so." He stood and appraised the man. "Help me unharness the horse."

"Right y'are."

Together, they unharnessed the horse from the wagon and slowly led the injured animal away.

Tork returned to the merchant and placed a hand on his shoulder. "You might want to move away, my friend. You won't want to see this. Rest assured, your horse won't feel a thing. Hold to that thought."

The merchant burst into fresh waves of distress. He nodded and stumbled away, keeping his back to the scene.

Tork held the injured horse, and the newcomer cocked the musket and brought it to bear.

The gunshot blasted around the countryside, the noise rolling across the plain in ever-dissipating echoes, until silence once again reigned.

* * *

Jad leaned back in his chair. "Let me guess, your report is all normal, no change?"

Tork sighed and looked at his hands resting on the table. "Would that it were, sire. Sadly, no."

Jad's eyes narrowed. He licked a finger and turned a page. Dipping the quill in the small inkpot, he began scribbling. "Go on."

Tork recounted his tale. As he spoke, he became acutely aware as Blake ceased his fidgeting and turned to him, listening intently.

Jad paused, placing the quill into the inkpot and leaning back. "So the townsfolk weren't lying. Those that were taken must have been subjected to a horrible fate. As for the wolves. They don't sound like ordinary wolves at all."

"They didn't look like ordinary wolves either, sire. Let me tell you."

The king's advisor clasped his hands together and remained silent, looking beyond the men sat around the table.

Tork was wise enough not to speak when Jad was deep in thought.

Jad finally broke the silence. "Gentlemen." He rubbed his bearded chin and closed his eyes. "We have a problem. Where is this merchant located? I'll seek his majesty's approval for a replacement horse."

"The White Swan over in the third eastern quarter, one street back from the wall."

"I know the place. They brew a nice ale."

Tork smiled. "That they do, sire."

"Let me guess, you have more to add?"

Tork looked across at Mace. The commander of the Watch looked exhausted, bags under his eyes, skin pale. The splatter of dried blood painted upon his armour was not lost on Tork. Nor was the fresh dent in his chest armour.

"Aye, I do, sire," said Mace.

Jad nodded, tapped the quill on the edge of the inkpot, and began writing again.

"Sire, tonight we lost twenty-nine citizens."

Jad stopped writing. He was frozen, staring at the mostly blank page before him. "Please tell me I just misheard?"

"I'm afraid you did not, my lord. Twenty-nine citizens dead, along with seven of my own soldiers."

"This will not do." Jad snarled, teeth flashing in the dull light. He dropped the quill, his hand moving in a blur as it swept through the hair, slamming onto the table with a *crack*. "This will not bloody do!" He took a deep breath and let it out in a huff. "What the bloody hell happened?"

"Spiders again, my lord. There must have been forty of them. No wolves or ravens this time. Just a swarm of bloody spiders."

Tork stared at Blake and leaned towards him. The diplomat remained silent, his face devoid of mocking laughter.

Good!

He returned his attention to Mace.

"They took us by surprise, sire."

A dry chuckle erupted from Jad. "How? Were you not prepared?"

"We were, my lord. But these things attacked further down the wall. It was almost as if they knew we were there waiting near the gate."

Jad sighed. "Gods. I shall speak to his majesty immediately."

Tork nodded. *Time for the King's Own to step up.* Excitement swelled in his chest.

"If he is in agreeance, the King's Own will deploy in support of your soldiers this evening."

Tork was not oblivious to the relief that flickered in Mace's eyes. "Thank you, my lord."

"There is to be no more loss of life, do you understand?" Jad's glare burrowed deep into Mace.

"Aye, sire."

Jad's piercing stare flicked to hold steady upon Tork.

Tork nodded again. "Understood, my lord. If his majesty agrees to deploy my forces within the city walls, we shall end this tonight."

Jad made to stand, then paused. He looked at Blake. "Do you have anything to add?"

Blake smiled his crooked smile Tork hated so much.

"Nothing else, Blake?"

The diplomat sat in silence, smiling.

The advisor to the king shook his head. "I thought not. As for you two," he gestured at the commanders, "I shall speak to his majesty presently. You will know more by noon."

Tork stood and bowed his head. "Sire."

VI

Tork swallowed cool water and placed the steel cup upon the long table where he sat. Down the lengths of the table were his officers. It had taken less than a half hour for them to respond from every corner of Lisfort to his call for an emergency briefing at the unit headquarters in the centre of the city. After he'd finished instructing them on what had taken place, and what might occur that night, they appraised him with concerned, yet hopeful stares. Some of them whispered amongst themselves. He allowed them to converse or sit silent with their thoughts. It didn't matter. Before long, they'd know for sure exactly what would be expected of them. The tangible electricity of excitement pervaded the room. Every one of them had trained so hard to become members of the elite unit, and for the younger soldiers in particular, this would be the first opportunity to test their steel.

Figuratively and literally. He grunted at the thought and reached for the cup once more, but refrained as he felt the faint need to piss.

"You think his majesty will grant the use of the Unit?" Beel asked.

Throughout the kingdom, the two thousand strong elite force was known as the King's Own, but the soldiers referred to themselves simply as *the Unit.*

Tork shrugged. "Time will tell, Captain."

Yes is my bet, but I'm not going to let them know that. With a city under siege and the Watch on the verge of being unable to contain the threat, his majesty would be stupid not to commit his most powerful force.

"Of course he will!" called a captain further down the table.

Other voices added their chorus to the symphony of opinion until Tork held up his hands.

"Shut up!" he yelled.

Captain Beel's voice broke the silence. "What're your thoughts, sir?"

Tork sighed. "Captain, you're smart enough to know my thoughts. Our army, whilst capable and large in number, will be too cumbersome to organise and deploy inside the city walls within several short hours."

Fuck it. He lifted the cup to his lips, drank the rest of the water in several gulps, and slammed it back upon the table.

"So that leaves we few." He swept an arm around the long table and grinned.

As if on cue, the far doors paving the entrance to the King's Own headquarters were held open by two guards, allowing Jad to stride through.

Tork climbed to his feet, watching as the officers around the table fell silent and sat ramrod straight in their chairs.

Tork nodded. "Afternoon, sire."

Jad acknowledged the greeting with a tilt of his head. "Sit easy."

The officers of the King's Own relaxed in their seats, although Tork remained on his feet. "What news, sire?"

Jad smirked. "I think you already know, Commander Tork."

Tork was wise enough to remain silent, waiting for the king's advisor to continue.

"His majesty has agreed to release one hundred of

his most elite unit to assist the Watch."

Tork's jaw muscles bulged through his beard. "One hundred?"

"One hundred."

Tork placed his hands on the table and looked at his feet. "I thought he'd authorise far more than that." He sighed and supressed a curse.

"Why? You think one hundred incapable of taking care of this threat, Commander Tork?"

"No, sire, not at all." He straightened and swept his arm around the room. "Take a look at the officers sat around this table."

He watched Jad turn to take in the young men staring back at him. The king's advisor shrugged. "What of it?"

"Each of these officers commands one hundred soldiers. Only one of these nineteen men will see battle tonight."

Realisation dawned on Jad's face, but he hesitated. "Wait. Nineteen? Shouldn't there be twenty?"

"Indeed, sire. There is a patrol currently away in Huronian territory."

Jad nodded.

"Sire, welcome to the elite unit of the King's Own. These men have spent years training their bodies and minds for just this opportunity."

"Oh."

He gestured at the silent captains sitting at the long table. "They want to serve their king and their country. If it means fighting to defend their empire, believe me, sire, they'll climb over each other for the chance."

Jad nodded slowly. "I see."

"So it's not a matter of not having enough soldiers on the ground to defeat the threat. The threat itself isn't the issue. I now have to choose one man out of nineteen to serve his king and empire."

To Jad's credit, he stepped back and held out his hands. "I'm sorry, Commander Tork."

Tork smiled. "Oh, it's not your fault, sire. Both our hands are tied, and I'll certainly not question his majesty's command. You have my word that inside the hour, one hundred of the King's Own will be patrolling along the inside perimetre of the western wall."

"Thank you." Jad walked away but stopped before he reached the door. He turned back towards the table. "It may be that tomorrow, more of your soldiers will be needed."

We can only hope.

Tork smiled and nodded. "Yes, sire."

"Good day." Jad swept through the door.

"And to you, sire."

Tork slumped back onto his chair, hearing the dull *thump* as the door closed and locked in place. When he was sure he could no longer hear Jad's departing footsteps, he hammered a fist upon the tabletop.

"Fuck!" the word echoed around the room.

He clenched shut his eyes and ignored the stares he knew were boring into him. Off the cuff, he knew thirteen officers present had seen battle, albeit mostly minor skirmishes, but at least it was something.

Waert? Has he seen battle? He allowed his eyelids to part, and he sought out the young man. As he expected, the officer glared at him with impatience. *Yes! He saw battle last year. A Huronian Border Patrol from memory. Klorf saw battle earlier in the year.*

His eyes closed once more. One by one he ticked them off the list. All of the men present had seen battle as soldiers of the King's Own, but Tork was whittling down the men who had not yet led soldiers in battle. Only one newly fledged captain hadn't led troops in battle.

I'm sure of it!

Tork's eyes snapped open, he stood and leaned forward on his fists. "Captain Beel with me, everyone else, dismissed!"

* * *

Tork adjusted himself in the saddle and patted Might's powerful neck. They faced the western gate, waiting and watching as the sun kissed the horizon and the afternoon began to meld into dusk. Reds and pinks bled across the sky, mixing with the pale blue of what little remained of the afternoon light.

A small patrol of the Watch were sat just as silently upon their steeds, although their horses were decidedly more skittish than Might. The soldiers often had to pull on the reins, or touch heels to flank to try and push a horse forward that was edging away from the gate. Tork could feel the massive horse, without a care in the world, completely relaxed beneath him.

Is he dozing?

He craned his neck to see the animal's face, but from the mounted position, it was too difficult.

"Safe travels!" the distant voice of one of the guards at the gate echoed across the area.

A merchant rumbled through the gate and out into the world beyond, offering a wave and a nod in response. Then the giant gates were closed for the night. No one would be allowed in or out until dawn. The massive crossbeam locking the gates closed was craned into position.

A horse from the group of soldiers nearby broke clear, crying out in fear. Despite his master's best efforts, the animal continued to flee until another Watchman was able to ride alongside and take hold of the reins. A few quiet words of reassurance and the horse was back amongst the Watchmen, silent and waiting for what the night would bring.

Tork clicked and squeezed his legs. Might responding immediately. He walked the destrier over to the group of Watchmen. The tallest of their horses, almost sixteen hands tall, was still dwarfed by Might.

"Is everything in order, here?"

Tork directed the question to a young man in the front row. A golden epaulette was welded onto his shoulder, signifying he was an officer and more than likely in charge of the group.

"Aye, sir."

"Very well, I am going to patrol along the wall for an hour or so, but I shall return later in the evening." Tork paused before he turned Might away. "Or sooner." He smiled. "Depending on what takes place between now and then."

The officer swallowed and wiped his brow with the back of a gloved hand. "Yes, of course, sir. And, sir?"

Tork pulled gently on the reins bringing the warhorse back to the halt.

"Thank you, sir."

He nodded. Might took little urging before he was striding along the cobbled streets at a rapid pace. Captain Beel had deployed his men in twenty groups of five. He passed the first tiny group of elite soldiers mounted in a brick formation, the sub-unit commander of the small team sitting in the centre of the square the remaining four soldiers created. An elderly woman stood nearby, holding a shawl around her shoulders, talking to them.

"You won't leave us tonight, will you?" Her voice quivered with terror.

Tork passed within hearing shot and watched in his peripheral vision as the sub-unit commander turned to the old lady. He looked down at her from his mounted position. "Ma'am, the only way we're leaving tonight is dead."

Tork suppressed a grin as Might walked on. He passed the second, third, and fourth group of mounted soldiers, all keen-eyed and ready to not only fight, but defend their people, their city, and their king. They were formed up between much larger clumps of nervous Watchmen. Pride swelled within Tork. The King's Own was such a unique unit, tiny in comparison to the general army, but the ranks were made up only of the finest warriors, trained to an exceptional standard and unflappable in even the most horrendous circumstances.

Beel trotted towards him, closely followed by his bugler, and reined in alongside. "Evening, sir!"

Tork nodded in response. "Beel. Have you briefed your men?"

"Of course. Thank you for this opportunity! We'll not disappoint you."

"I have no doubt, Captain. And you're welcome." He looked at the bugler mounted on a horse beside Beel, although it was difficult to make out his face. Buglers, whilst not strictly soldiers, were still highly respected members of the unit. It was their duty to recall every command listed on the ledger of the King's Own tactics and formations and be able to play the requested command during battle without flaw. Only the senior officers were allowed personal buglers. Throughout the lower ranks, the sub-unit commanders carried their own bugles, which they used to control their soldiers during the thick of battle should their unit become separated from the main force. "And you, bugler, are you ready?"

The man nodded. "Aye, sir."

"Good." He returned his attention to Captain Beel.

"Sir, I was talking to Commander Mace of the Watch earlier, and he's noticed the townsfolk are more nervous for our presence." The captain shrugged. "I thought we'd have the opposite effect."

Tork nodded. "I understand your thinking, Beel, but think of it from a civilian's point of view. When was the last time the unit was deployed *inside* the city?"

Beel hesitated, opened his mouth, and then closed it again. "Forgive me, sir, I know not exactly. Certainly not in my career."

"Not in *my* career either, Captain. In fact, not in living memory. It has been nearly two hundred years since the King's Own were deployed in a warfighting role inside the city walls. That was during the Third Great War, when Huronian forces held the city to siege. Had the unit not been deployed, the city would have been sacked inside a day."

Silence overcame the trio as they made their way along the waiting, ragged formations of Watchmen, occasionally interspersed with tiny units of the King's Own.

"The people remember. So, while the Watch might be reassured by our presence, the fact that the king thinks it pertinent we be deployed suggests to the people who live here that things are becoming much worse."

"Ah," Beel said. It was too dark for Tork to see the realisation dawn on the young captain's face, but the tone of voice in his reply was enough to suggest he understood.

Distant shouting erupted from ahead, followed by several musket shots in quick succession. Tork brought Might to a halt, Beel following suit simultaneously. A frown creased Tork's brow.

"Obragarda!" the word cut through the faint shouting and screams.

Tork felt his heart rate increase. At least one sub-unit of the King's Own had advanced to battle. Still, the two officers waited, as did the tight brick of mounted King's Own who stood nearby. Then the bugle erupted, its song cutting through the roar of battle like a knife.

Tork's eyes closed as he concentrated on the wailing blasts. Only when the bugle faded to silence did his eyes snap open. "Seventeenth Street forward of the western gate!"

The three men kicked their warhorses from the halt into a headlong gallop.

Tork pulled back slightly to allow Beel to take the lead. Whilst he was the overall commander of the entire King's Own, this was Beel's unit and, as such, it would be up to Captain Beel to control his soldiers throughout the battle.

Have at it, Captain Beel. Let us see what you can do.

"Bugler!" Beel shouted.

"Sir?"

"Even numbered sub-units, advance to battle, odd numbered sub-units, hold position!"

The bugler brought the instrument to his lips and, at full gallop, distributed the command.

Tork grinned. After all these years, it still amazed him how skilled the buglers were.

Casting a look over his shoulder, he watched in the dim torchlight as sub-units peeled out of side streets behind them and accelerated to the gallop, and whilst maintaining speed, melded together into three neat ranks, eight deep.

Tork returned his attention to the front, the wind once again blasting into his ears. He saw King's Own soldiers streaming out of side streets before them and had formed up, advancing towards the fight. As they thundered past a mile marker, indicating they had covered two miles, Tork noticed a large group of Watchmen milling about in the middle of the road ahead. They were obviously trying to work out what to do. Even at such distance, it was easy to see they were nervous and hesitant to join the fight.

One of the soldiers, probably a sub-unit commander in the formation galloping ahead, fired a musket shot in the air. The huddle of Watchmen split asunder and made way for them to pass.

No sooner had the first group swept past, Tork, Beel, and the bugler galloped amidst the stationary Watchmen, closely followed by the formation behind them.

"Leading group, open file, at the trot!"

The bugler reacted instantly, and Tork watched as the group of King's Own before them slowed and opened apart to line each side of the street, allowing the trio to pass through to take the lead.

"Join up!"

The bugle blasted into life, and Tork glanced over his shoulder, watching as the group who'd initially led the charge became part of the formation directly behind.

Well done, Captain Beel!

He expected nothing but exceptional standards from the King's Own, but Tork constantly found himself impressed by the warriors and leaders who made up the ranks of the elite unit.

They belted around a gentle curve in the western wall and came upon the scene of battle.

"Halt!"

The bugle blasted and the group came to a stop, horses nickering to one another. The powerful animals threw their heads, snorted blasts of air, or pawed at the cobbled street, eager to join the battle.

Tork sat silent, calmly watching Captain Beel as the younger officer took the scene in, working out where the enemy were, in what numbers they had deployed, and how best to combat them. Tork looked beyond Beel and took the scene in for himself, his heart skipping a beat, although he was careful to keep the surprise from his face.

Spiders, some of them larger than Might, cluttered the lower wall, scrambling to close with the beleaguered force of King's Own fighting for survival. The sub-unit were surrounded by dead arachnids, but one soldier, as well as his horse, lay lifeless nearby. Anger warmed Tork's chest.

"Make your decision fast, Captain Beel," Tork said through clenched teeth.

Beel nodded his understanding. "Bugler."

"Sir?"

"Swine array, full charge. Forewarn those already in combat."

"My pleasure."

The notes peeled out, cutting through the night. Tork remained in place, watching in silence as the soldiers of the King's Own swept around him, accelerating to the gallop, then at full flight, forming up in one of the hardest hitting formations used in close quarters. He'd have wished them luck, but luck was for fools. Battles were won by sharp swords, good training, outstanding leadership and, above all, courage. Tork stood up in his stirrups to gain a better view and watched as the original sub-unit, aware of what was taking place, withdraw in quick order away from the wall and towards a side street, drawing the spiders in after them in a large, thick group. Then the main force impacted the flank of the arachnids, smashing clean through their ranks.

If the spiders weren't slaughtered by sword or spear, they were trampled into the street by the destriers. No sooner had the charge passed through, Beel had brought them to the halt, turned them about so that those at the rear became the front rank, and they charged back towards Tork in what looked like the arrowhead formation, slamming into the remaining arachnids, leaving them smashed and dying upon the cobbles.

Tork glanced at the top of the wall, towering high above them. It was difficult to tell, as there was no light that high, but he thought he saw the dark shadows of the spiders turn and depart, disappearing from view. He smiled.

You aren't fighting the Watch now, you bastards!

But he wasn't naïve enough to think it was over. If any of the reports were to be believed, the previous attacks suggested the creatures conducting the attacks possessed a modicum of intelligence. The arachnids might simply be regrouping to assault a different section of the wall.

Captain Beel's force reinforced the area, checking all enemy were deceased, before moving to their dead comrade and carrying him away. They placed him away from the area of battle. Both his body and that of his destrier would be removed once dawn made itself known. Tomorrow, he would be farewelled and sent on his way across the Frost River.

Distant screams rent the air behind him, and Tork turned Might about. He pushed the warhorse into a trot. The piercing wail of the bugle behind him indicated Captain Beel was aware of the new onslaught and called upon those members of the King's Own he'd ordered to stand fast earlier to advance to battle. Tork pushed the destrier into the canter. When a new host of screams and shouts peeled across the night, he allowed Might to accelerate into a gallop. The horse instinctively swerved away from a family running out of their house, towards the centre of the city and away from the wall.

Speeding around the curve in the wall and back towards the gate, he watched sub-units flowing out of streets and forming up at the gallop into a large group. He pushed Might harder until he was on the heels of the rear-most sub-unit.

"You!" Tork shouted.

The sub-unit commander threw a glance over his shoulder, and even in the dull light, Tork saw the man's eyes bulge. "Sir?" the man bellowed over the deafening thunder of hooves around them.

"You are my bugler!"

"Sir!" The sub-unit commander dropped back beside him and unclipped the bugle from his belt.

"Let Captain Beel know I now have control of this formation."

The ear-piercing blast cut the night sky like a knife, the acknowledging bugle like a whisper in comparison.

"Open file, at the trot."

As the last bugle blast faded, the formation of King's Own peeled apart and slowed, allowing Tork and his newly-acquired bugler to gallop straight up the centre to the front. The group closed up behind the pair and accelerated to maintain pace.

From the gloom appeared a battle scene that made the last look like a wedding party. A full group of Watchmen, and most of their horses, lay dead upon the road. At the outer most extremity of the group lay an entire King's Own sub-unit, lifeless. He snarled as fury took him. A massive cluster of deceased arachnids lay piled closest to the overrun sub-unit.

Tork called his group to the halt and moved away from the formation, closely followed by his bugler, to stand to one side so as to better view the battle. A second group of Watchmen fought valiantly, but they were surrounded by spiders and dying in number as the moments drew by.

"Six abreast, musket shot, fighting withdrawal."

The formation moved like lightning to carry out the bugle command. Within moments, the group had morphed six wide and seven deep. The warriors of the front rank had withdrawn muskets, brought them to their shoulders, and fired a single shot before breaking formation. Three galloped left, three right. They rejoined into their original line at the rear of the group. The new front line fired another musket barrage before galloping to the rear in a similar fashion. By the time the original front rank was back in their initial position, they had reloaded and were ready to fire once again. The rolling fighting withdrawal continued and, as Tork had hoped, the distraction drew the arachnids clear of the all but destroyed group of Watchmen. They scuttled towards the small unit of King's Own, virtually clambering over each other to be the first to engage the newcomers. The soldiers of the Watch galloped clear to avoid being hit by musket-shot, should any round not find its mark and injure them instead. But not a single shot went beyond the arachnids. Each bullet found its home, hammering through the tough carapace and lodging in the soft flesh behind.

The King's Own moved with rapid precision, their fighting withdrawal tearing the life from countless arachnids, but still more came to replace the fallen. It was a tactic to combat an infantry charge and worked with sickening efficiency. Tork and his bugler edged their horses backward to maintain their position near the retreating formation. The acrid aroma of gunpowder drifted around both man and horse but did nothing to deter the spiders closing the distance. Another barrage of muskets crackled, and another, and another, ceaseless, uncompromising, murderous. On the spiders scurried until they were almost upon the formation of King's Own.

Change of plan.

"Halt, front rank blunderbuss."

The bugler complied with the order.

Muskets disappeared into leather sheaths, and the soldiers in the front rank each pulled clear a blunderbuss, aimed in the rough direction of the fast approaching opponents and pulled the triggers. The sound that followed sounded more like an explosion than a series of gunshots. The small ball bearings, ten per weapon, hissed through the air, cutting through the ranks of the spiders.

"Swine array, charge!"

Tork pulled free his sword and urged Might into a gallop.

That one word, screamed from fifty throats boomed around the city walls, "Obragarda!"

For the second time that night, Tork witnessed the spiders hesitate as they realised hunter had become prey. When the formation covered the small area of bare cobbled stones separating man from arachnid, the King's Own had reached full gallop. They hammered through the spiders' ranks like a battering ram, the soldiers on the outer edge of the swine array cutting down with swords sharp as razors. Those in the centre stabbed down with spears, each weapon taller than a man. The warriors swept clear of the arachnids, leaving them in disarray, half of them carcasses.

"Halt, about turn!"

The haunting bugle blasts rent the air and, within moments, rear rank had become front rank. The King's Own once again faced their enemy.

"Musket shot, fighting withdrawal."

And so it began again, the muskets once more singing their ceaseless, pervasive saga of death. If spiders could feel fear, then Tork was sure he tasted it oozing along the cobbles and wafting amongst the buildings. What was left of the dwindling enemy scampered towards the wall, desperate to escape the relentless musket fire. They scuttled up the wall, some of them falling clear to smash onto the street below, riddled with lead. But a few, a scarce few, reached the top and disappeared from sight.

"Halt!"

The muskets fell silent at the same time as the bugle.

"Stand ready!"

Apart from the occasional warhorse pawing the stone, and some soldiers turning in their saddles, craning their necks to keep a watchful eye on the wall, the formation did not move. But silent and still as they were, they could react to a threat in any direction at a moment's notice. Not a word was spoken, but Tork noticed the warriors were just as keen-eyed and eager as they had been before closing with the enemy.

"By the gods, that was impressive!"

Tork turned Might to address the man who'd spoken from behind him and came face-to-face with Commander Mace. A small huddle of Watchmen was mounted behind him, in the near distance, the few survivors of the spider attack prior to the King's Own lending a hand. They looked frightened.

No, terrified would be a more apt description.

He returned his attention to Mace and noticed the fresh laceration adorning the man's forehead. Blood had streamed from the wound, painting half his face with now dried blood.

"I fear it is not yet over, my friend. How did you fair?"

"Not well, Tork," he replied, voice quivering. "Tonight, I lost more than half the force designated to guard the western wall." He cleared his throat. "That means I've now lost a full tenth of the entire Watch capability for the city."

Tork was aware of the way his comrade had spoken the last sentence. "You've lost nothing, Mace. These men died defending the city they love. They were overrun by giant spiders. You speak as if you slew these soldiers with your own hand." He cast a glance at the numerous bodies lying nearby.

"I may as well have." The commander of the Watch nodded and looked away. "It'll be dawn in a couple of hours."

"Aye." Tork was astute to know when the conversation was at an end. "Time to retrieve the dead, I think." He turned the warhorse away, walking his steed towards the still silent formation of King's Own.

He gently pulled Might to a halt near the neat ranks

and dismounted. "Hold." The destrier stamped a hoof but remained in place.

"I want ten volunteers with me!"

Men closest to him reacted instantly and, soon, twenty men stood before him in a half-circle. "I only needed ten, but many hands make light work. Help me move the bodies of our fallen from the road. There're also two horses that weren't killed in the fight and have fled. I want five of you to mount back up and find them. Understood?" Heads bobbed in reply. "Let's get to it!"

Likewise, soldiers from the Watch had commenced carrying their dead away, placing them in neat rows in the near distance. Tork strode towards the six deceased soldiers of the King's Own. He knelt beside the sub-unit commander and placed a hand upon the man's face, pushing closed the eyelids.

"Ma'am, the only way we're leaving tonight is dead."

The words, spoken so recently, echoed through Tork's memory.

Well fought, young man. Stand down, warrior.

He lifted away his hand, the eyelids remained closed, lending the lifeless face a look of peace.

King's Own soldiers moved around Tork.

"Stand down, brother," some of them muttered as they carried their comrades away.

Some simply said, "Duty done," as they lifted the deceased between them.

Six of my soldiers died tonight. Tork straightened and clenched a fist. *That's enough for one night.*

Sighing, he walked to the men of the Watch. They'd need help to carry their fallen from the scene of the battle.

* * *

Tork felt bone weary as he sat before Jad. Mace was beside him, and further down the table, crinkling his nose against the offensive body odour of the pair of soldiers, perched Blake.

"You both look exhausted."

Tork nodded. "I feel it, sire."

"Commander Mace, what losses have you to report?" Jad held the quill's tip a fraction from the page, ready to commence writing.

"Forty-eight, sire."

"No, no. My apologies for not explaining. What are your losses for last evening only? Not the total count."

Tork watched in his peripheral vision as Mace slumped in his seat and let out a long, pained sigh. "Forty-eight, sire."

"By the gods," whispered Jad. He wrote the figure down with hesitance. "This is becoming worse by the day, is it not?"

He watched Mace look at the king's chief adviser. "Aye, lord, it is. Another week with nights like that and the Watch will no longer exist."

Jad's eyes flicked across to bore into Tork. "And your losses, commander?"

"Six."

"Six, now that's a more reasonable number," Jad said, scrawling on the page.

"Begging your pardon, sire. But no it bloody isn't!"

"Do not presume to raise your–"

"Six soldiers is six too many! Now, with all due respect, I'd like you to approach the king and request another several hundred King's Own soldiers."

Jad's mouth dropped open as he glared at Tork, but before he could say anything, Tork continued. "The Watch are exceptional at maintaining the law of the city but…" he turned to Mace, "and with all due respect, they aren't trained to fight like this."

"You'll receive no argument from me," Mace muttered.

"I don't appreciate your tone, Commander Tork!"

"My apologies, sire, but my soldiers are more than…" he gestured towards the thick tome upon the table before the adviser, "they're more than numbers on a bloody page! They deserve more than that!" Realising he'd bawled his hands into fists, he relaxed his fingers and took a deep breath. "They deserve more than that."

Jad placed the quill away in the small inkpot nearby and leaned back in his chair. He appraised Tork with a piercing stare. Eventually, he spoke. "Alright." He nodded. "I shall speak to his majesty as soon as he will see me. What argument do you want to me to present for using even more of his household troops?"

"Captain Beel did a good job last night, but his forces were spread thin in order to cover several miles worth of the wall. Had we twice, or three times as many warriors on the ground, I'm confident our losses would have been more than halved."

"I shall put it to his majesty."

"Thank you, sire. We have a difficult fight on our hands here." The familiar numbness teased the skin stretched over his knuckles. "Something tells me it's only just the start."

"You think things will become even worse than they already are?"

Tork leaned back into the chair, ignoring the dull ache in his lower back. "Aye, I do, sire. I certainly think it'll become much worse before it gets better."

"I shall pass on your concerns, Commander Tork." Jad scribbled several short sentences in rapid succession before returning the quill to the inkpot. "There is every possibility his majesty may authorise the use of the army."

Tork nodded.

I respect King George, he's a great man, but what does he know about the army?

Tork stretched his back, but the dull ache remained in the same area of his spine. Wendurlund's last warrior king had been Henry the Great, King George's great-great-great-great grandfather. A tactical genius who'd led from the front, literally. King Henry had fallen during a cavalry charge against a much large formation of Huronian foot soldiers, during the Third Great War between the two kingdoms.

Tork remembered the stories his father had woven around the fire during the long winters.

King George's father, Harold, was barely out of swaddling clothes when he was crowned king of Wendurlund. He smiled as his father's voice echoed in his mind. *There ended the reign of the great warrior kings of old. He was a good king, even a great king. But like his son after him, was never a warrior.* Tork allowed his eyes to roam to the ceiling, where he noticed a tiny strand of spider's web, hanging freely. *I wonder what it would have been like to serve under a warrior king? To have the most powerful man in the empire beside you in battle?*

"Commander Tork!"

Tork flinched out of his reverie and focused on Jad, who leaned forward in his chair and fixed him with a piercing glare.

"Sorry, sire."

"Gods, man, I thought you'd taken a brain injury."

"No, sire, not quite yet." He smiled. "Still plenty of time for that, though."

Jad let out a breath in a rush. "Very well. Is there

anything else I need to pass onto his majesty?"

"Aye, sire."

I knew there was some reason I began reflecting on recent monarchical history. Our liege is no warrior.

"If he does decide to declare total martial law and employ the services of the Royal Army, it may be beneficial to remind his majesty that they will need up to two days in order to be deployed and ready to fight. We need immediate reinforcements, and to make that possible, we need more King's Own on the ground tonight."

"I understand, Tork. I'll be sure to pass on your thoughts."

Tork clenched his fists against the deepening numbness sweeping across his knuckles and into his palms. "Please do, sire. I have a feeling tonight will be much worse."

* * *

Two miles north of the city's northern gate was the military cemetery. Tens of thousands of graves lay in neat rows and columns. Each headstone indicated where a warrior who'd served his king and country had laid down his life.

At the centre of the graveyard, inside a large open square, Tork sat mounted upon Might, staring out upon the near entirety of the King's Own formed up facing him. To his right, in extended line, were ten captains, and to his left, the remaining nine. In the area of short clipped green grass between the officers and men of the King's Own lay six coffins. Beside them, and enshrouded in the Blue and White flag of Wendurlund, lay the lifeless bodies of four horses. The warhorses who'd died carrying their warriors into battle would be buried in the same grave as their human counterparts. Immediately behind each coffin stood a riderless horse, held by a bugler. Two of the horses were the steeds belonging to dead soldiers, the others being spares used especially for the ceremony.

Off to the side of the mighty formation, stood either side of the coffins, huddled a small number of family members, watching the ceremony as they dabbed already damp handkerchiefs to their eyes, hugged one another, or comforted weeping children, who'd never again be able to feel safe in the arms of their fathers. But around the family of the dead was a much larger group of family members belonging to those soldiers still living. They attended not only to show their respect but to comfort the forlorn.

A truly special unit.

Tork looked away from the men and women huddled around the group who'd lost a loved one. He returned his attention to the priest whose voice continued to boom out over the formation, entombing the dead into the care of the gods. When the priest spoke his last word, silence reigned supreme. A gentle wind flittered across the field, touching uniforms, brushing across horses' manes, and playing with the mighty Wendurlund flag, which flew high above the formation.

The buglers brought the instruments to their lips and blasted out a single command. *Stand down!* They allowed the bugles to drop to their sides. Silence ensuing once more.

Tork deliberately looked from one coffin to the next. Silently giving his respect to each soldier.

Bringing the instruments back to their mouths, the

buglers sounded a funeral call. *Your duty has ended!*

Tork stared out at the horizon and focused upon a large cloud nestled above the distant treetops, but it disappeared in a green blur. He blinked and felt the tear slide down his cheek.

Stand down, brother, stand down!

VII

Miriam lay on her bed, the top sheet pulled up to her chin. She stared into the darkness. Sleep would not come, and she'd been turning and tossing without avail since she'd retired to her bed. She knew exhaustion would take her come dawn, and the struggle to keep her eyes open throughout the day would be a chore. Miriam was envious of the muffled snores she could hear rumbling from the adjoining bedroom in which Endessa slept. She took a deep breath and let it out through pursed lips.

That seems to help.

She closed her eyes and felt the fickle call of slumber. Such a faithless beast was sleep, that no matter how close, it would dart away or melt into the shadows at the slightest movement or noise. Faint horn blasts rent the sky. She frowned. Intermittently, and in seldom the same rhythm, the horn blasts continued.

Must be some party! Hopefully the Watch will take care of them before long, I need sleep!

Miriam took a few deeper breaths and allowed herself to relax, sleep once again beginning to tease her.

It's good to be home, however. Although Vyder may have become a changed man, he was still alive. Miriam hadn't seen Gorgoroth take over Vyder's body since they departed the cave several days before.

Thank the gods. If I never see or hear from Gorgoroth again, it'll be too soon.

She heard a *crackle* roll out over the city, and her eyes snapped open. The sound came again, then again.

Slumber fled like the fickle bastard she knew it to be. An ache built in her chest, and as it increased to the point of discomfort, Miriam realised she'd been holding her breath. She exhaled in a rush and sat up. Miriam had been but a child when her father departed to hunt their dinner. She could vaguely remember the distant musket shot echoing from the forest maybe an hour later. Aside from mouth-watering memories of the juicy rabbit they'd eaten at the dinner table that night, the noise of her father's trusty musket had sounded for all the world like what she'd just heard. A mighty *boom* thundered through the night sky like some monstrous explosion. Then silence. More horn blasts, so distant she was unsure if it was her imagination.

Another *crackle* cut through the night sky from what must have been the outer western edge of Lisfort. A second musket barrage fired, a third, a fourth, then a fifth in well-timed, consistent barrages. She flung her legs out of bed, slammed bare feet against the cold ground, and stood, heart thundering within her breast. She rushed out of her room, bustled down the corridor past the living room, and opened the door leading into the kitchen.

Miriam stood by the open window of the kitchen, staring out towards the west. It was difficult to know the exact time without one of those expensive, round, timekeeping devices the pretentiously rich carried in their pockets. But she knew the sun had dipped below the horizon many hours before. Another slew of distant musket fire echoed. She thought she could hear yelling or screaming, but it was so far away she couldn't be sure. If it wasn't some stunt or military exercise, something serious was taking place in Lisfort.

She heard the front door creak open and stood on

her tip-toes to look down at the road in front of Vyder's mansion. The shadow of her master stood in the middle of the street. He clasped his blunderbuss but remained silent and still, facing west.

Padding from the kitchen, she made her way downstairs, brushed past the half-open door and out onto the street. She stopped beside Vyder.

"You heard it, too?"

He grunted.

She glanced at her master. The bright blue glowing orbs indicating Gorgoroth's presence were absent.

"It was musket fire. I've never heard that many muskets inside the city walls before."

She nodded and sighed. "I *thought* it was muskets. What's happening, Vyder?"

"I don't know."

Could it be a Huronian attack?

She voiced her concern, but it went unanswered.

They stood in the middle of the street for quite some time, but the musket fire, which had crackled consistently for such a long duration, remained silent. It was clear, whatever had occurred, the threat had been contained.

I hope.

She turned away and made her way towards the mansion. "I'm going back to bed, Vyder. I shall have breakfast ready for you at sunup."

"Thank you, Miriam."

She'd already helped him gather the few belongings he'd need to survive on his mission. She'd never travelled outside the mighty city limits of Lisfort, so it meant nothing to her when he explained the road he travelled would take him through the forests and badlands of Wendurlund. Then it would be on into

Huronian territory.

Enemy territory. A place where they'll kill a Highlander on sight, from what I've heard. You think you live among barbarians here in Lisfort until you hear something like that.

She slid back into bed and pulled the cover up to her chin. Sleep betrayed her still. She was tired, but her exhaustion belied Miriam's eyes.

Just after breakfast, she knew Vyder would depart on his mission.

Whoever, or whatever, you are, Gorgoroth, you'd better watch and keep him safe out there.

Miriam forced closed her eyes, took a deep breath ,and allowed exhaustion to sweep her being, spiriting her away into the dark blankets of slumber.

* * *

Vyder stood in the darkness, clasping the cold metal of the blunderbuss. Watching and waiting. For what, he wasn't sure, but it was clear something was amiss inside the city walls. An uprising? A bar brawl gone wrong? A Huronian scouting group venturing too close to the city? If word on the street was to be believed, small scouting patrols from the King's Own were often sent out into Huronian territory to collect information and news on the activities of their enemy. What was to stop the Huronian Army from doing something similar? And if what he'd heard was indeed a Huronian scouting patrol being engaged, would it mean all-out war?

If that's the case, will my mission be cancelled? Will I still get paid?

The front door of his mansion creaked and soft footfalls padded towards him through the darkness. One stride sounded much shorter than the other, indicating a limp.

Not Miriam then.

"How goes it?" the Wiccan's voice broke the silence.

"Not sure." He placed the butt of the weapon upon the cobbled street and held the barrel with a hand. "Something seems to have gone horribly wrong out there."

She touched his elbow. "I'm not interested in what's going on out there." She stepped in front of him and pointed at the patch of skin between his eyes. "I'm more bothered about what's going on in there!"

"You mean Gorgoroth?"

"Has he revisited you at all since I retired to my bed?"

"Not a skerrick. It's almost as if he never was."

Endessa turned away to face the direction from which the musket shots had so recently rolled across the city. "He's up to something," she muttered. "Oh, by the gods, he's up to something alright. Although, I know not what."

"What could he possibly do?"

"It's not a good idea to underestimate him, Vyder. Gorgoroth is much more powerful in physical form. More power is at his disposal now than he has ever known." She turned to Vyder and clutched his arm. "I mean no disrespect, as you seem a good boy, but I hope I don't grow to regret using him to bring you back from death's clutches."

"Thank you." He chuckled. "I think."

She grunted and released his arm.

Vyder stared out into the vast blackness. "You think he had something to do with whatever happened out there tonight?"

"I don't know."

"Do you have any way of communicating with him?"

She hawked and spat, rubbing the globule into the street with a foot.

Charming.

"Not now that he is in physical form, no. I can communicate with many of the…" she fell silent.

The assassin watched her intently. "What?"

"I'm already telling you too much, Vyder. Things you need not know. Things you *should* not know."

He grinned. "I won't tell anyone." He touched his nose and winked. "I promise."

She cursed and whispered a string of words under her breath Vyder could not understand. It sounded almost like some kind of odd chant.

"What's that you say?"

Endessa ignored him, turned away, and walked back inside, slamming the front door behind her.

Vyder shrugged. "Nice talk."

Lifting the blunderbuss from the ground, he rested it upon one shoulder and made his way towards his home. He tried the door latch.

At least the crazy old bat didn't lock the door, I suppose.

He closed the door behind him and engaged the locking mechanism. Padding upstairs without haste, he strode to the master bedroom, leaned the weapon against the wall closest to the door and collapsed upon the bed. He closed his eyes, the dark, blurry heaviness of sleep sweeping around him immediately. He allowed himself to be taken away, and as slumber settled upon him, he heard Verone's voice, clear as crystal. She called for him.

* * *

Miriam stood just outside the front door, watching her master fastening a bulging saddlebag. "Are you sure you have everything?"

He pulled tight the leather strap and allowed the steel tang of the buckle to bite into one of the holes. "I'm sure, Miriam. Worry not."

"Are you sure you don't need to take your blunderbuss? You might need it. It may save your life, Vyder!"

He held up his hands, and smiled. "I'm sure, Miriam. It's loaded with shot, and you know where the powder and rounds are. At least you can feel safe knowing you have it at your disposal if needed."

She nodded.

"I'm an assassin. If I needed to shoot that weapon, it means everything's gone to hell, anyway."

That makes me feel so much better.

Miriam nodded again. She walked out to him and gave him a brief hug. "Stay safe. You too, Endessa."

The Wiccan grunted and spat onto the street, ignoring her.

"Always." He swung up into the saddle, patting Storm's neck. "Thanks for breakfast. Delicious as always."

Miriam smiled, refusing to cry. After all, this may very well be the last time she ever saw her master. Her struggle disappeared, and she stifled a chuckle as she watched Endessa wrestle her way up into the saddle of a much smaller bay mare. Vyder had purchased the horse for the Wiccan the day before.

Endessa shouted a string of curses as she attempted to clamber into the saddle.

156

"The horse suits you," Vyder called before looking back at Miriam with a grin and winked.

Miriam held her hands over her mouth and tried not to burst out laughing.

To the horse's credit, it stood patiently in place, waiting for Endessa to mount. Eventually, red-faced, she was successful.

"It's been many-a-year since I've ridden a horse, I'll have you know."

Miriam smiled. *You don't say!*

"Gods keep you safe!" Miriam called, waving at the pair as they turned away.

Vyder swivelled in the saddle, waved once, and then disappeared around a corner in the road. Miriam walked back inside, closed the door, and locked it.

Then she allowed herself to cry.

* * *

Vyder watched the bay mare walking beside him. The animal moved well, and the muscle bulging with each step beneath the glistening coat suggested she was powerful and fit. "How is she?"

Endessa glanced up at Vyder and shrugged. "Good so far. The journey is yet young, however. Time will tell."

"You doubt my ability to choose a worthy steed?" Vyder smiled. "I think you'll be pleasantly surprised, Endessa."

They weaved their way through the streets, winding towards the eastern gate. When the sun was close to its zenith, the pair had merged onto the main arterial road leading towards the gate. They followed the flow of traffic like sheep.

Eventually they'd made their way through the great eastern gate and along the road that would, in time, lead them into Huronian territory.

* * *

Tork sat before his officers at the table within the King's Own headquarters. He'd still not slept, much less removed his armour or bathed the stink of stale blood and sweat from him. Captain Beel, further down the table, was in a similar state, bags under his eyes. The others were mostly silent, lost in their thoughts as they waited for Jad to return with orders from the king.

He felt cold fury sweep the room and saw it glint in the eyes of his officers. No one and nothing killed men of the King's Own without justice being served.

Tork looked from one man to the next, each face as grim and fierce as the last. *They'd march into the fires of Hell if required.* Nothing less would do, either. Not in the King's Own. Not now. Not ever.

The doors groaned open, held wide by two soldiers to allow Jad to stride through. Every head turned, and Tork supressed a smile as he watched Jad swallow as he approached the long table.

"Good afternoon, Commander Tork." He nodded at the others. "Officers."

"Afternoon, sire." Took climbed to his feet. "What news?"

"The king sees fit to allow four hundred soldiers of his most royal guard to fight in defence of the city this evening."

That's more bloody like it!

"Commander Tork!"

Tork placed his fists upon the table and leaning

forward. "Sire?"

"His majesty has decreed that you will not proceed to the wall this evening. If you die in battle here, the King's Own have no overall leader should the wall fall to the enemy."

"Every member of this unit is as important as the soldier beside him, thus I'm no more important than anyone else here!"

Jad held up his hands and closed his eyes. "I'm just passing on the message, Commander."

To the pit with your fucking message!

"I understand, sire."

"His highness has also declared martial law and has ordered the army be deployed in support, although it will take another day, maybe two, before they will be in a position to fight."

Tork took his seat. "Sounds like his majesty is taking it a little more seriously than before."

Jad ignored that. "As you know, most of the inhabitants of the western quarter have been evacuated and placed in temporary accommodation in the city centre. When the army is deployed properly, the last few families who've refused to move will be forcibly relocated. Once the army has taken up positions, the view is the soldiers of both the Watch and the King's Own will be pulled back."

"Until soldiers start dying in their droves," a voice muttered further down the table.

Tork did not rebuke the officer because it was his same thought.

"Questions?"

Silence greeted the king's advisor.

"No?"

Faces creased with savagery and fury returned his

questioning glance.

"Well then, Commander Tork, I'll leave it with you."

Took stood once more. "Thank you, sire."

"A good day to you all. Commander, I'll see you in the war room tomorrow morning."

"Aye, sire."

He waited for the doors to *thump* closed before he turned back to his officers.

"Captain Beel, you and your soldiers will remain at the palace with the majority of the unit. Make sure your men and horses are rested."

Tork pointed to four warriors one after the other. "Captains Terax, Dask, Thrun, and Gat, you four will move to the front this evening and hold the western wall." He deliberately chose the four most experienced and accomplished officers. "If you fear becoming overrun, call for reinforcements. As for the rest of us, tonight, we will all stand on duty at the palace in support of our brothers. Ensure your soldiers and horses are fed, rested, and ready to fight." Tork took a breath and clenched his fists as the numbness spread through his fingers. "Each night, the assault upon the western wall becomes worse. If it continues, I envisage our entire unit will soon be deployed. If these…*things* manage to somehow breach the gate itself…" he clenched his jaw, "we will need all soldiers ready to fight. You four, have your men deployed no later than sundown. The rest of you, be deployed and ready at the palace at dusk. Questions?"

Silence reigned supreme, and once again that faint feeling of excitement and purpose crackled around the room.

Tork grinned. "Then let's get to it!"

* * *

Tork stepped clear of the bath. He took the neatly folded towel laid upon a ledge nearby and shook it loose before drying himself.

That's better, I feel bloody human again!

Dressing into the soft, cloth garb he wore under his armour, he opened the door and walked into the outer section of the bathroom, where a servant girl waited.

"Thank you, Fraya. The water was the perfect temperature, as always."

"Welcome, lord." She curtsied and moved past him to empty the dirty water.

Padding through the next doorway, he walked into the massive living room of his home and grunted as a small force thundered into him.

"Papa!"

He pushed a hand through his daughter's dark curls. He knelt and held her at arm's length.

"Teeka, have you finished your school reading for the day?"

She giggled and tried to squirm clear, but he held her firm. "Yes, Papa," she said finally.

"Tell me something. What did you learn?"

Teeka's eyes widened, and she looked up at the ceiling. She opened her mouth but remained silent for a moment. "Well…" she looked back at her father, "do you know the story about the demon and the egg?"

"No, my child." He stood, took her hand, and led her towards a bench seat padded with soft fur. "Enlighten me."

He sat and listened as Teeka recounted the story. It was an ancient tale he'd heard many times, but he'd never heard his daughter tell it. He listened to every word, although he was forced to hold back laughter when she'd obviously forgotten a section and began making it up as she went. Before he knew it, the demon, a fierce evil entity called Agogathoth in the original tale, became a tiny little cute thing called Thog dressed in girl's clothes, playing with an egg.

"A wonderful tale, my daughter." He grinned and hugged her.

"Dinner's being served early this evening because papa has to work. So, go and wash your hands."

Tork released his daughter and stood, noticing his wife, Yeshira, leaning against a doorway, smiling at them.

"You have to go to work tonight, *as well,* Papa?"

"I'm afraid so, little one."

Yeshira gestured towards their daughter. "Come, Teeka, hurry along!"

The girl darted away, swept past her mother's skirts, and disappeared from sight.

Yeshira was just as beautiful as she was the day Tork laid eyes upon her. Thick, dark curls framed her face and touched her shoulders. Deep green eyes held his gaze as he approached. She did not resist when he pulled her into his embrace and held her close, enjoying the smell of apricots her hair emitted.

"Be safe out there tonight, husband."

He stroked her back. "Always, my love."

"Teeka must not know what is happening, Tork." She pulled away and looked up at him.

"Of course not, my love."

She smiled then, cupped his cheeks, and kissed him.

I haven't been entirely truthful. Even you don't know what's really going on out there, love.

* * *

Tork stood on the upper plateau of the royal palace situated in the centre of Lisfort, staring out at the waning light. Even in the gloom, the silhouette of the mighty western wall towered above the city. Captains Terax, Dask, Thrun and Gat alongside the soldiers under their command were deployed along the wall and prepared to defend their positions. If they requested reinforcement, it was possible the entire force of The Unit would advance to battle this evening.

The tiny sliver of what was left of the sun vanished behind a distant mountain range, and with it, the last natural light. Tork stepped forward and looked down at the acres of open space in front of the western side of the palace. Acres of land currently filled with the neat ranks of fifteen hundred King's Own troops. Along the edges of the open land were positioned torches in even spaces. He watched one of the mounted soldiers trotting from one torch to the next, igniting them as he went.

In stark comparison, upon the acres of open space to the north and south of the palace were spread rows upon rows of hastily erected tents, occupied by families who lived along and near the western wall. They'd obeyed the direction to evacuate more than a day before.

"It is done, we are at fifty percent stand-to. It is going to be a long night, I think, sir."

The voice snapped him from his thoughts. He didn't even hear Captain Beel approach. He glanced at the warrior standing beside him.

"Very well, Captain. And yes, another long night."

He returned his attention to his force arrayed upon the ground beneath him and watched half of the soldiers dismount and feed and water their horses prior to folding out bedrolls and lying down. Try as they might, Tork was confident many of them would not find slumber. In several hours, those resting would mount back up to allow the others to dismount and attempt sleep. Thus, they would rotate between standing duty or resting throughout the hours of darkness.

The soldier charged with the duty of igniting the torches finally trotted to his starting point and placed the torch, which he used to ignite the others, back in its bracket staked deep into the earth.

"Did you get some sleep today, Captain Beel?"

"Yes sir, plenty, thanks."

He looks rested. Good.

"Yourself, sir?"

"Yes, I did." The lie came easily enough.

"Good to hear. I'm going to check on my soldiers, sir."

"Aye, Captain, you do that, I'll be down shortly."

He took a deep breath and let it out gently, looking out across the silent, sleeping city. The booming voices of the merchants were silent and the marketplace in the near distance stood desolate. The hustle and bustle would recommence come the dawn.

If we win the night.

He clenched his fists, stretched his fingers, shook out his hands, but the tingling would not leave him.

Of course, we'll win the night. To let such thoughts gain traction is stupidity at its best.

Tork turned and commenced his descent of the innumerable steps towards the open field upon which his soldiers were stationed. Some horses lay beside their masters in an attempt to rest.

A bugle blasted from the area of the western wall, near the gate, or at least that was where Tork thought the sound had issued in the few seconds he'd taken to analyse the faint reverberation. He froze and listened. A rolling *crackle* of musket fire burst to life, interrupted only by the deep, bass *boom* of blunderbuss. The gunfire increased in intensity until the musket and blunderbuss shots were an incessant barrage of noise.

Gods, it's worse than last night.

Further bugle blasts cut through the storm of noise. He listened to each bugle and their rough location, his mind painting for him a bird's eye picture of the battle scene.

One is commanding his force into Swine Array at full charge, another two are conducting fighting withdrawals under musket shot. The fourth force?

He listened intently, but the fourth bugle remained silent.

Must still be uncommitted.

The night was only young, and for three quarters of his deployed force to be already involved in such intense fighting did not bode well. He'd expected a few minor skirmishes to commence later in the evening, which might build to a larger, more protracted battle. But this? The fighting had been ferocious from the very beginning.

They have a real chance of being overrun.

It was possible the thousands of rooftops and empty streets between the western wall and the palace might have increased the echoes or channelled certain sounds and made the fight sound more intense than it was in reality. He started his descent again.

I doubt it.

Another bugle, the missing fourth, sliced through the wall of sound, but sounding much more distant than the others. He stopped and turned towards the sound.

They must be farther down the wall, close to where we were last night.

The bugle fell silent.

Arrowhead, full charge, right flank engage with blunderbuss.

As if on cue, the mighty *boom* of the blunderbuss rolled out over Lisfort.

They're fighting an enemy in front of them and on their right flank. Gods, help us.

He jogged down the stairs, and strode towards his soldiers. The few of them who'd taken the time to try and rest were on their feet, packing away bedrolls and rechecking their weapons.

Tork felt a presence beside him and didn't need to turn to know it was his bugler, Roland.

"Advance to battle, sir?"

"Not yet, Roland, no. Hold that thought, though."

He continued until he was standing in the centre of the formation of King's Own warriors.

"All captains to me! Now!"

* * *

Vyder lay with his back to the fire, the warmth soaking through his clothes and caressing his skin. He'd no idea how long he'd been asleep, but it must have been several hours if the moon, now high in the night sky, was anything by which to gauge. He rolled onto his back, closed his eyes, and sank into the depths again. Endessa whispered softly nearby and chuckled.

She must be dreaming.

The whispering came again, louder this time. Vyder sat up, pushed away the thin blanket and looked for the Wiccan. He found her sitting on the far side of the fire, looking into the flames. A chill of fear spread spindly fingers across his soul as he focused on the area at which the Wiccan stared.

Within the flames was the face of another, not a man, not even a human. Vyder pushed himself to his feet in an explosion of movement and backed away into the darkness. The fire entity had a human-shaped head, but he could see the flaming horns that erupted from the temples.

"Fear not, Vyder. This is Agoth," Endessa gestured at the fire.

The head turned and red, glowing eyes locked onto the assassin. Tusks pushed out each side of Agoth's mouth, and when the thing spoke, flames flickered from within the fang-filled maw, but no voice was audible.

Vyder Ironstone. Your reputation precedes you. The deep, resonant voice filled his mind.

"I've heard your name, or something like it. Are you the same demon recounted in children's tales?"

Agoth laughed. *I am no demon, Vyder. I am a fire spirit. I was born in the fire, and when the Great Spirit sees fit to end my time here on earth, it will be to the flames I shall return.*

"And do you hate we humans as much as Gorgoroth?"

The fire enshrouded spirit smiled. *I have no hatred of humans, assassin. I do not control all fire at any one given time, but I have watched some of your ancestors squatting in caves, rubbing wood together in the hope of summoning me. I obliged them, too. I've been known to save the lives of many of your people over the generations.* The fire entity laughed. *Aye, and killed a few.*

Vyder nodded. "Have you seen Gorgoroth?"

Agoth cast a glance towards Endessa. *We were just discussing this. I have not, but I can feel his presence. He is close but has cloaked himself.*

The assassin frowned. With the initial shock departing his system, he walked around the fire to sit beside the Wiccan.

She patted him on the arm. "Nothing to worry about, boy. Agoth is a friend."

"Powerful friend to have."

Endessa chuckled. "Indeed."

"Why is he cloaking himself? I don't understand."

Agoth appraised him for a moment. *Lisfort is under assault from the west, more specifically from the Waning Wood. We think he is controlling the assault against the city. As you mentioned before, Gorgoroth has no love of humankind, and now that he is at his most powerful, it would be a prime opportunity to wipe one of the largest cities, being so close to the Waning Wood, from the face of the earth.*

"We must go back! What about Miriam?"

Endessa smiled into the flames. "I told you he was a good, lad."

"We must return! We can't just sit around here while people are dying. What if the city falls?"

"And you think you can make a difference, Vyder? What's one man going to do?"

"If the city falls, then my mission is for nothing! Bringing a prince back to a smoking ruin is kind of pointless, is it not?"

Then the man in your presence would no longer be a prince. But a king. And someone upon whom a new empire can be built.

Endessa threw a small log onto the fire. "But it won't come to that. The king's household soldiers are dealing with the onslaught well."

And although I cannot see Gorgoroth, I can sense his power waning. It won't be long before he must return to you, Vyder, and reenergise his strength. Although it is still possible he may mount one final all-out assault that may overrun Lisfort.

Endessa placed a hand upon his forearm. "So, continue we must, Vyder. There is no other way. Lisfort is well defended, and King George can call upon some of the finest soldiers in the world."

In addition, young man, the further we travel from Lisfort, the stronger the pull you have on Gorgoroth. Eventually, he will have no choice but to return to you. Never forget that you are both bound together.

"So why then does he not draw me back to him? Surely if I can do it, he can too?"

Although he is a spirit of immeasurable strength, it is your body and, as such, you have more power than he. Wherever you go, so must Gorgoroth.

Vyder nodded. "Then we depart at first light."

* * *

Tork closed the door behind him, exhaustion burrowing into his soul.

"Good morning, Lord Tork."

He turned to see Brent offering him a deep bow of respect.

"Morning, Brent. It seems I am late to the meeting once again. This is beginning to become a habit."

He strode towards the war room, acknowledging with a nod the pair of King's Own soldiers stood either side of the doors as they thumped to attention in unison.

"Morning, sir."

"Lads."

Emotion was devoid from the faces of both soldiers, but their eyes hid nothing. The unit had taken a hard loss during the night. Many warriors had crossed the Frost River.

Tork placed his hand on the door and paused,

looking from one soldier to the other. "Chin up, warriors. Today, we remember our brothers, and tonight, we fight. I don't care what the king decrees. Tonight, we fight. All of us. And we'll send those things back to Hell where they fucking belong."

Glistening eyes narrowed and hawk-like focus returned.

Better.

He stepped forward, barged through the door, and squinted against the dull light, waiting for his eyes to become accustomed to the gloom. Eventually, the table came into view. Seated at the head, as always, was Jad. A little further down the table was Blake, his hooded eyes watching him like a snake.

Two-faced slime-riddled piece of shit.

"So nice of you to join us, Tork, but it seems Mace has outdone you. If he's not here shortly, we'll commence without him."

Tork sat at Jad's right hand and cleared his throat. "Mace won't be coming, sire."

"What, is the man sick?"

He lay his hands upon the table and looked at the king's advisor, holding his piercing glare. "No, sire. He fell in battle last night, along with what was left of the Watch protecting the western wall."

"He fell, you say?"

"Aye, sire."

"You mean to tell me that an entire quarter of the Watch tasked with patrolling our city streets have been killed at the western wall?"

"It pleases me not at all, sire, but yes."

"Mace was a good man," Jad whispered.

"He was, sire."

Tork cast a glance at Blake and controlled the

sudden fury that swept through him as he noticed the smirk on the diplomat's face.

A scratching filled the silence as Jad wielded the quill like some tiny weapon, deft strokes painting ink upon the paper forming swift sentences. He stabbed the quill into the paper to signify the end of a sentence, closed his eyes, and sighed.

"What the bloody hell is going on here?"

Tork held out his hands. "Sire, if I didn't know any better, I'd say we were at war. I don't know with whom…or with *what*, but we are fighting to maintain the integrity of our city's walls."

The advisor nodded, placing his head in his hands, but did not reply.

"And, sire, we're fighting hard. This is the most difficult fighting some of my soldiers have ever faced. We are a skilled force, we have to be through necessity. But we are tiny in number. If enough of those things climb the wall, then… Jad, the city will fall. And this…" he gestured at the yellowing paper in front of the king's advisor, "is meaningless. The pen is only mightier than the sword when enemies aren't knocking at the gate."

The advisor raised his head and met Tork's eyes.

"What of your losses, Commander Tork?"

He chuckled, but there was no humour in the sound. He swallowed down the fury and struggled to keep the emotion from his face.

"Our single greatest loss of life in recent times I'm afraid, sire."

Jad lifted his quill from the page and dipped it in the inkpot nearby.

"Seventy-two members of King George's most royal King's Own died fighting defending the city last night."

"Dear Gulgon above." The king's advisor held the quill inches from the paper. He sat there for some time, frozen in place, before he placed the quill upon the table without haste, leaned back in his chair, and linked his fingers together, staring at the ceiling. "Gods, I'm sorry to hear that, Tork."

At least he sounds genuine.

Tork deliberately abstained from looking in Blake's direction. If he found the man smirking like he'd been earlier, he knew he'd kill him. He'd leap across the table and throttle the life from the stick-thin little weasel and watch the life flee from the snake's eyes.

Not the first time I've strangled a man.

* * *

He was high on a mountaintop, surrounded by Huronian soldiers, his small patrol fighting for their lives. Prince Henry, training to become a King's Own captain had joined the patrol deep into enemy territory. A meagre group of Huronian warriors burst through the ranks and charged towards Roland and he. All but one of them cut was down by Tork's blunderbuss. The last collided with him, and they'd gone to ground, grappling and yelling in the mud. He'd felt the knife slam into his thigh, but he ignored the pain, smashed a palm into the nose of his adversary, and then rolled on top of his enemy, clamping his hands around the man's neck and squeezed hard.

"Protect the prince," he roared over one shoulder at his men still committed to the fight behind him. "Protect the prince!"

The mud made it difficult to maintain a grip, and despite the burning from the muscles in his forearms, Tork squeezed, watching the man beneath him fight, saw his eyes bulge in terror and, in that moment, Tork knew the Huronian soldier realised he would die. Still Tork squeezed, as hard as his fatigued muscles allowed. Even after the dead eyes looked up at the sky over Tork's shoulder, he squeezed until he sensed movement around him and felt hands shaking him.

"Sir, he's dead. SIR!"

He leaned back and stood.

"Sir?"

Tork wiped sweat from his brow before turning to the soldier. "Speak."

"The prince was taken. He charged into the enemy midst like some madman. We tried fighting to him, but there were too many Huronian soldiers. Only we few survived." The soldier gestured at the few remaining warriors stood behind him.

Tork swore. "Did they kill him?" he closed his eyes, afraid of the answer.

"No sir, not that I saw. They clubbed him and dragged him onto a spare horse before withdrawing at speed."

* * *

"Commander Tork!"

Tork jumped in his seat, took a deep breath, let it out slow, and unclenched his jaw.

"Are you well, man?"

Tork nodded and cleared his throat. "My apologies, sire. Yes, I'm alright."

"Very well then." Although he didn't sound convinced. "I shall speak to the king and—"

"Sire, tonight, I lead the King's Own into battle. Tonight, we all march." Tork stood. "You let King George know, I'm sure he'll agree, and if he doesn't, you let him know the dire nature of what we face."

Jad's mouth dropped open. "But —"

"One more night like last night and we are lost, the wall will fall, the city will be ruin, and you won't have a king to advise."

Tork turned to face Blake and offered him a parting shot, as well, but the diplomat was gone. He'd departed without anyone noticing. The skin over Tork's hands began to tingle.

VIII

Orange light filtered through the thin canopy, glinted from dew-soaked leaves and drifted through the forest to caress the leaf litter below.

I love this time of morning.

Vyder finished pissing against a tree trunk and returned to the campfire in the near distance. Aside from a thin plume of smoke drifting skyward and mingling with the morning sun, the fire had long died. Endessa was chewing idly upon some kind of root.

The assassin kicked dirt upon the ashes. "Time to move."

"In a minute, boy."

"No, now! More people will likely have been killed in Lisfort. The sooner we move on, the more likely I can drag Gorgoroth away from his cowardly business."

Endessa chuckled but remained silent, chewing on the root and looking through the canopy at the rising sun beyond.

"What's funny?"

"Gorgoroth is no coward, child, despite what he's doing." She turned to look at him. "He honestly believes his purpose is pure, and in his mind, he is protecting the earth itself."

"By attacking Lisfort?"

"Oh, Lisfort is only the beginning, Vyder." She took one last bite, placed what was left of the root in a satchel, and put it in a pouch at her belt. "He means to extinguish all human life from the earth." She sighed. "I wish I'd let you die, Vyder. But I couldn't. Unlike Gorgoroth, I hold *all* life sacred. I could not stand by when there was a chance to revive you. Unfortunately, only Gorgoroth was close enough at the time to respond to my request."

"So, by bringing me back from the Frost River, you may have doomed the human race?"

She grunted as she stood and stretched. "That's a dramatic way to put it. I doubt it, but that is certainly Gorgoroth's intention, yes."

"Can we stop him?"

"We are trying, child."

"*We?*"

"Agoth and I. We can, I think, yes. But it will be a difficult journey. For now, let us drag him away from Lisfort. That is our first course of action."

Vyder stooped and lifted the saddle. "Then let us get it done."

He walked to Storm tethered nearby and laid the saddle upon the powerful horse. He tightened the girth strap and turned away to lift Endessa's saddle onto her mount.

They mounted and meandered through the forest towards the main path to the south. Vyder always set camp well away from any major road to reduce the chances of discovery by nefarious newcomers.

"Still nothing from Gorgoroth?" Endessa called from behind him.

"Not a thing."

Although it's only a matter of time, I suppose.

He spotted the main road through the foliage, turned Storm onto it, and headed towards Huron lands. By his estimate, they were still two weeks from the outermost boundary of Huronian territory.

In the far distance, he heard the soft bubble of the mighty Therondale River, the powerful body of water that ran adjacent to the road all the way into Huron. Although the Huronians called it the Stream of Taraxon, it was one and the same.

Vyder turned in his saddle, placing his hand on Storm's rump for balance. "Let's water the horses."

"A fine idea."

He only needed to gently guide Storm from the road before the horse made a beeline towards the fresh water. Storm stepped into the shallows of the river, dropped her head, and took her fill. A moment later, Endessa's horse stopped alongside and began drinking.

He watched the Wiccan, who was looking back at the forest behind them. He'd heard the rumbling of wagon wheels long before and knew it was probably a merchant on his or her long, endless journey upon the road between the two kingdoms.

"Would your presence in the Waning Wood have made any difference to Gorgoroth's actions?"

She swung back to him and smiled. "No, child. I do have some power over Gorgoroth, but I'm only human. In spirit form, other entities like Agoth, for instance, can rein him in, but now that Gorgoroth is bound to a human in the physical realm, he's a force unto himself." She sighed and patted her horse's neck. "And he's making the most of it while he can."

When the horses quenched their thirst, the pair moved back onto the road and plodded onward. The day dragged on. They passed merchants and one family who'd packed as many of their belongings as possible into leather bags bulging from either side of their horse. When Vyder asked where they were travelling, the oldest child explained, despite his parents attempting to silence him. They journeyed to their aunty, who lived on a farm in one of the outlying towns, far away from Lisfort.

"We don't want any more trouble," the husband added, his eyes wide with fear as he glanced at the weapons hanging from the assassin's belt.

Vyder held out his open palms. "You'll see no trouble from us, sir. I'm on your side."

The man didn't look convinced, but relief washed over his face as he and Endessa accelerated past them.

"That's the start," said Vyder.

"What do you mean?"

"People are like sheep. If the trouble continues at Lisfort, more families will leave. All it'll take is a few dozen families to depart before words spreads throughout the city like wildfire. Then people will begin fleeing in their thousands."

* * *

Dusk arrived fast, the sun sinking beneath the horizon silent as an assassin, and with its departure, the dark advanced, soaking into every crevice, settling upon the landscape like a rain-soaked blanket. Nothing escaped. Tork knew that the night brought with it terrors from the depths. That and death. Soon, it'd be time to fight.

Tork sat astride Might, looking at the top of the western wall high above. Massive torches placed at close intervals along the peak shone from the armour of the soldiers standing upon the parapet, looking out towards the Waning Wood. There must have been ten thousand soldiers, or more. And that was just on the western wall.

Now that's more like it!

Torches had been staked into the ground some three hundred paces from the wall, on the exterior of the city, so as to better give the men looking out forewarning as to what was approaching.

"Quite a sight," muttered Roland.

On the cobbled street running adjacent to the wall far below, stood the King's Own in its entirety. Something for which Tork had been pushing for days. Well, almost in its entirety. Tork had ordered Captain Beel to take his soldiers to watch the northern gate, Captain Dask stood with his warriors before the eastern gate, and Captain Terax stood guard over the southern gate.

Finally, we can mount an adequate defence against this onslaught.

The elite force was ready to plug a gap should a section of the wall fall to the enemy.

"Incredible to think that soldiers stand upon the entire length of the wall surrounding the city this night. All four gates are protected. At last, the reports of Commander Mace and his departed Watchmen have been taken seriously."

"In the gods' keep may they rest," Roland's deep voice cut through the still night air.

Tork nodded his agreement, offering a silent prayer for all the soldiers who'd lost their lives in the last few days.

Too many. Far too many.

He nudged Might forward a couple of steps and peered right, his eyes running along the length of seven hundred odd King's Own warriors mounted in silence, armour shining in the dull light thrown by the torches. Swivelling left, he was met by a similar sight.

"It's a quiet start to the night, sir."

Tork guided Might backward several steps to offer his bugler a glare. "Don't bring ill luck upon us, Roland."

The man held up his hands and smiled. "Just an

observation. In comparison to yesterday evening, tonight is rather different. That's all I'm saying, sir."

A commotion further up the wall drew Tork's attention, and he swept the top of the wall until he found the cause of the noise. A group of soldiers were crowded around a pair of men who were in a fistfight.

"And there's our weakness," Roland said. "There might be a lot of them up there, but they lack discipline."

One of the soldiers was knocked down and the second pulled back by several others.

Tork nodded. "Let's hope they can fight when it counts."

Roland grunted.

A distant bugle echoed across the city, giving Tork pause. He listened to the individual blasts, which when strung together formed a rudimentary situation report.

Northern gate under heavy attack. Enemy gaining upper hand. Gate may fall. Request immediate reinforcements.

"Gods, the bastards are hitting us from a completely new area."

Roland unclipped his bugle. "These things aren't stupid, it seems."

"No, they are not. No way on earth they'd be able to attack in such a formed mass if there wasn't some kind of intelligence in control of them. Right, Roland, I want three hundred soldiers heading to the northern gate. Fast as you can, please."

"Sire."

Roland brought the bugle to his lips and issued the order. Within minutes, Tork's force had dwindled, the clatter of galloping hooves fading into the night as the three hundred-strong force of King's Own rode in support of their comrades to the north. It'd take the warriors some time to reinforce the smaller force standing guard at the northern gate, as there was more than fifteen miles, as the bird flies, to cover before they arrived.

The distant bugle echoed out over the city once more. Tork closed his eyes as the notes washed over him.

Extended line. Musket shot, fire at will.

Fleeting moments later, the faraway crackle of musket fire rolled over Lisfort from the north.

Tork cursed. "I hope the reinforcements arrive in—"

Another musket blast brought him to silence.

"Oh shit," he whispered.

Eastern gate under heavy attack. Request reinforcement.

He glared at Roland. "Send three hundred east. Now!"

The bugler complied and, again, Tork's force became smaller.

Tork looked at the parapet high above them. The soldiers standing watch were relaxed, albeit throwing curious glances towards the north and east. The fistfight had stopped, too, he noticed. There seemed no attack imminent at the western gate, which was the only gate of Lisfort to have been attacked in the past.

Ironic.

"This isn't quite progressing the way I thought it might, sir," said Roland.

Tork shifted in his saddle. "That makes two of us." He looked past his bugler at the mounted King's Own nearby. "In fact, that probably makes close to a thousand of us."

Roland chuckled.

Soldiers on the wall above began shouting along the length of the western wall. Some of them waved their arms, and others even attempted to flee, but were ordered back to their posts under pain of death. One soldier, so desperate to run, misplaced his footing and fell from the parapet, smashing onto the cobbled street below, narrowly missing one of Tork's soldiers. Blood exploded from his head, splattering upon nearby horses and soldiers.

Here we go. Our turn.

A distant, familiar sound cut through the incessant shouting. A bugle. A King's Own bugle.

Southern gate under assault. Requesting immediate reinforcement.

Tork didn't take his eyes from the upper area of the wall, watching as panic gradually began to sweep the soldiers standing guard there.

"Send three hundred south, Roland."

"Sire!"

Once more, Tork's force was whittled to a fraction of what it had been less than an hour before.

Soldiers standing on the parapet the length of the wall continued shouting, the noise growing in intensity until Tork could make out the subject of their wailing.

Wolves!

He acknowledged the fear sweeping through him but refused to allow it to control his thoughts. The day he'd taken on the pair of giant wolves chasing him out of the Waning Wood had been a close thing.

How many are there out there now? Two? Ten? A hundred? Thankfully, for the sake of everyone, they can't climb walls.

Screaming erupted further down the wall, and Tork pushed Might forward so as to gain a better vantage point. Spiders cluttered the parapet, decimating the soldiers desperately trying to hold the line. Some soldiers ran towards the fray to assist their comrades, but just as many ran away in terror. The general infantry might be useful against a conventional, human force, but combating giant spiders was an entirely new experience for all involved.

Roland edged alongside his commander. "They're not fighting up there as well as I'd hoped."

That's an understatement. They'll be overrun soon.

"With me, Roland."

Tork pushed Might into a canter and steered the destrier down the line of waiting warriors, his bugler beside him. As he passed each of his soldiers, he noticed all eyes were cast upon the peak of the wall, watching chaos ensue.

They know they'll soon see battle, and once again, it'll be up to us to stop the enemy advance.

When he neared the extremity of the right flank, he stopped beside the captain responsible for the one hundred men sat astride their warhorses nearby. The man dragged his eyes from the parapet and met Tork's glare.

Shit what's his name again? Captain Groth? No, that's not right.

"Sir? Can I help you, sir?"

Groll! That's it, Captain Groll.

"Captain Groll, should those spiders push past the infantry, you are to take control of your soldiers and those of Captain Meers and protect the right flank."

"Aye, sir." Groll's eyes returned to the battle high above them. "Only a matter of time, sir. Those spiders are making short work of them."

"I will maintain control of the remainder of the King's Own. Understood?"

Groll locked eyes with his commander once more.

"Yes, sir, understood."

Tork looked at Captain Groll's bugler to ensure the man had also heard. The bugler nodded at Tork, confirming he knew what was about to take place.

He turned away from the pair, and with Roland beside him, made his way towards Captain Meers's position to pass on the order.

"Good luck, sir!" Groll shouted after him.

Tork ignored him. "Luck is for fools," he muttered.

With Captain Meers informed of proceedings, Tork trotted back to his original position. He swept the length of the wall as far as he could see in both directions, but there was only the one area being assaulted by spiders.

Movement in his peripheral vision caught his attention, and Tork turned to see several soldiers tumbling from the parapet, closely followed by a dead or dying spider. They slammed onto the cobbled street together with sickening *thuds*, none of them moving.

"They're falling in hundreds. They can't contain those bastard things."

Tork nodded agreeance but remained silent as he watched proceedings. All along the wall closest the gate, spiders dominated the space, all the soldiers in that area of the parapet having either been killed or fled in terror. He noticed the spiders did not advance, however. They stood poised as if waiting for some silent command. He felt as if the arachnids were staring down at him and his mounted soldiers.

What in blazes are they waiting for?

"Muskets at the ready."

Roland brought the bugle to his mouth and issued the command. Within moments, loaded muskets were withdrawn from sheaths, buttstocks pulled into shoulders, and determined eyes stared down metal gunsights. Waiting, silent, ready to do death's bidding. If there was any modicum of intelligence amongst the spiders, they'd know the fight against the mounted troops far below wouldn't be quite so easy. After all, they'd fought those soldiers before and failed.

Slowly, the troops along the top of the western wall fell...or ran. And before long, only spiders stood where overconfident men had been less than an hour before.

"And so it begins," muttered Tork, glaring at the arachnid-lined parapet high above them. "Well then, let's get it over and done with."

A whooshing sound swept above him, and Tork noticed a blur of movement. Giant eagles glided towards the western gate. They were mighty birds, wingspans perhaps the length of five grown men lying end to end. He was mesmerised as he watched the monstrosities grasp hold in their claws the mighty crossbeam locking the western gate closed. The dull *thump* their wings made as they flapped against the air echoed across the city, and the huge piece of wood locking shut the gate began to move upward, out of the brackets holding it in place. If the locking beam came free, the giant gates would swing open, letting in whatever was out there.

"Left flank fire!"

Roland blasted the command.

A moment later, muskets exploded, the left flank of the King's Own formation disappearing behind a cloud of gunpowder. When the smoke cleared, Tork saw the corpses of the birds lying sprawled upon the road beneath the gates. He felt the air move above his head and saw more eagles, four this time, fly towards the gate.

"Left flank fire!"

But even as Roland issued the command, he knew the soldiers were still reloading. He considered commanding the centre to fire, but knew they were out of range, and they may need their shot if the spiders descended towards them.

Several soldiers, faster than the others, finished reloading, brought weapons to bear, and fired. One eagle dropped clear, slamming onto the ground, dead. But it wasn't enough. The mighty crossbeam fell from its brackets, bouncing from the cobbles with a mighty noise. The giant gates groaned open and huge wolves, perhaps fifty, half the size of horses, came sprinting into view, ears pinned to their skulls and jowls peeled back to display fangs the size of dinner knives. They turned and charged straight towards the soldiers of the left flank.

Scuttling movement caught his eyes. The spiders descended the walls towards the formation of mounted soldiers.

"This may be a hard fight, Roland."

The bugler cleared his throat and nodded. "Seems that way, sir."

* * *

Vyder stood beside Storm, wiping sweat from the animal's fur with a soft, silk cloth. The saddle lay beside the campfire. Endessa sat still and silent before the flickering flames, eyes closed.

After he'd finished, he used a fine-toothed bone brush and swept it along Storm's back and flanks in long, practised strokes. The horse had already taken her fill of water at the nearby creek and was contently chewing on the thick, luscious grass. He'd pushed the horse hard throughout the day. Only twice had he urged Storm into a canter, and only for short durations. But it was the great distance they'd travelled that had exhausted the beasts. By Vyder's estimate, they must have covered nearly forty miles. Endessa's mount seemed to have kept pace well, but standing beside Storm, it looked even worse for wear.

A night's rest will do them good.

They'd only stopped once for a brief snack at midday. He finished brushing his horse and moved to Endessa's mount. The Wiccan had decided to call her Mia. He rubbed the animal down, drying the sweat from her fur before brushing her. The horse stopped eating and craned her neck around to nudge Vyder on the arm.

"Enjoying that, Mia?" he chuckled and stroked her nose.

He glanced over his shoulder. Endessa remained near the campfire, eyes still closed as if she was in some kind of trance or meditative state. When he'd finished, he strode to the creek-side and knelt, rinsing the cloth and brush before washing his hands clean of horse sweat, dirt, and fur. That done, he returned to the campfire and sat beside his saddle. Unclasping a leather bag, he placed away the cloth and brush before fastening closed the bag. Opening a haversack tied to the side of his saddle, he pulled clear some dried beef and began chewing on the snack.

Looking through the flickering flames, he focused on Endessa's face. She remained frozen in place, eyes closed. He stopped chewing and watched her shoulders. When they moved rhythmically, and he was sure the old woman was still breathing, he continued chewing.

Little monkey, are you there?

Vyder almost choked on the jerky. He spat clear a piece, the soggy meat hissing amongst the flames.

Can you hear me, little human? You need to head back to Lisfort. Do it now! You hear me?

He cleared his throat. "Not happening."

Vyder noticed one of Endessa's eyes snap open. She watched him intently, although she remained silent.

Stupid, tiny little monkey, who are you to disobey me? You will return to the city and you'll do it right now!

Vyder leaned back and laughed. It was a genuine sound, which echoed amongst the dark forest. Endessa continued to watch him, that one, unblinking eye boring into him.

Think it's funny, do you?

Before he could reply, Vyder felt himself sinking, a sensation he'd not felt in a long time. Had he been floating upon the ocean, it was like he was slipping beneath the waves to be consumed by the depths.

He fought and for a moment was able to regain control.

"I think it's hilarious," he spoke through clenched teeth.

But soon, he felt himself slipping away again, and resist as he may, darkness enveloped him so tight that only silence kept him company.

***

Endessa closed her eyes and took a slow, deep breath. She began humming "The Calling," aware of the heat emanating from the fire, radiating against her skin. The crackling chorus of the fire drowned out her soft voice, so that even she barely heard the notes. But she continued, her voice lilting as she commenced the second verse. The fire burned brighter and, without thinking, she shuffled slightly away from the blaze. She was halfway through the third verse when she heard Vyder's voice boom out across the small camp.

"Not happening."

Endessa forgot herself for a moment and opened an eye to watch the highlander. He sat on the opposite side of the fire.

Is he in contact with Gorgoroth?

She softly hummed the rest of the third verse whilst watching Vyder. The big assassin seemed to relax, his eyes rolled back in his head, and he went still. His eyelids snapped open a moment later, face breaking into a grin and bright blue eyes staring at Endessa.

It is *Gorgoroth!*

But before the nature spirit could speak, the assassin's body went limp once more, and the bright blue eyes disappeared to be replaced with Vyder's dark irises. The man's face looked haggard as if he was on the verge of complete exhaustion.

"I think it's hilarious," he said with a growl.

Then he was gone, to be replaced with Gorgoroth once more. The piercing, bright blue eyes gauged Endessa. His lips peeled apart in a wide grin, and he jumped to his feet in an explosion of movement. Leaping forward, he passed clean through the fire and landed on one knee beside Endessa. The unwavering death's head grin remained in place as he stared at the Wiccan.

"Hello, Endessa!"

She'd started the fourth verse when Agoth's voice pierced her consciousness.

I am here, Endessa.

The campfire exploded into life, flames stretching several metres into the air, reaching for the night sky, sparks exploding in all directions.

The face formed amongst the flickering fire.

"Oh, and I see you made it here, too, brother!" Gorgoroth spoke, although his unblinking eyes remained fixed upon Endessa.

Finally, Endessa turned to the nature spirit knelt beside her. "Greetings, Gorgoroth. Have you had plenty of fun slaughtering innocent people?"

Laughter exploded from him. "Innocent? *Innocent?*" He laughed long and hard before taking in a breath and wiping his eyes. "No human is innocent, Endessa." He pointed an index finger towards her, the digit hovering inches from her forehead. "You are all a plague, a blight upon the earth. It is high time a cleansing take place." The grin vanished from his face, his brow creasing and the bright blue eyes taking on a glint of fury. "And that time is now."

* * *

Tork edged Might forward so as to see the distant wolf charge heading for the left flank of his force. "Left flank, left face, extended line, blunderbuss!"

Roland began blasting the commands as Tork was still shouting them.

Those soldiers on the far flank, faster to react, galloped into an extended line, the width of the cobbled street, and disappeared in a cloud of gunpowder. The mighty *boom* of blunderbuss shot reached Tork's ears a moment later. The remaining left flank formed up behind the front rank.

"Left flank, charge!"

He heard the King's Own war cry echoing from the walls and watched the rear most soldiers of the left flank, swords and spears in hand, disappear into the thick cloud of gunpowder still drifting around the area. He heard shouts, screams of men, and the howl or screech of animals in pain.

"Centre and right forward face, muskets!"

He decided to add the forward face command in just to remind the soldiers of the centre and right flank that their enemy were the spiders advancing upon them down the walls. Some lesser experienced soldiers might become focused upon the wolf charge to the left.

Tork reached into the large leather holster forward of his right knee and retrieved his musket. The weapon felt good in his hands. He pulled the butt into his shoulder, rested index finger upon the cold steel of the trigger, and stared down the iron sights, keeping them centred upon one massive spider closest to him, which had descended the mighty wall and was now scuttling across the street towards them.

"Fire!"

He squeezed the trigger and heard the *clunk* as hammer slammed onto flash pan. A fraction of a moment later, he felt the musket buck in his shoulder. The heat of the blast rushed past his cheek, and his target disappeared behind a cloud of acrid gunpowder.

"Blunderbuss, fire at will!"

As Roland blasted out the order, Tork reached forward with his left hand until he touched the opening of the holster forward of his right knee. He dropped the musket into place and patted around until he felt the much shorter weapon. The acrid stink of gunpowder worked its way into his nose and mouth, making him cough. Bringing the blunderbuss clear, he pulled it into his shoulder and squeezed the trigger. The explosion that followed left his ears ringing, cheek burning, and shoulder aching. As he dropped the weapon back into the holster, the remainder of the King's Own soldiers opened fire with blunderbuss shot.

"Left, centre, and right, battle at will!"

As Roland blasted the commands, the bugle sounded muffled and faint. He reached forward and withdrew the spear from the leather sheath in front of his right knee. It would be up to individual soldiers how they fought the enemy that was almost amongst them. He sat, spear poised ready to strike for the attack that never came. Apart from some distant groaning from the left flank, where some warriors lay wounded, silence reigned supreme. Tork blinked against the thick cloud of gunpowder that assaulted his eyes.

The spiders should be amongst us by now.

Readjusting the haft of the spear in his clammy grip, he swung towards Roland.

"Centre and right, ten paces forward."

He edged Might forward as the order was being delivered and brought the warhorse to a halt when the cloud of gunpowder dissipated.

The spiders were nowhere to be seen.

The cobbled street lay bare. He heard them before he saw them, and with arched neck, looked up at the heights of the wall, which the arachnids climbed. The spiders seemed in disarray, terrified, as if they were no longer controlled by some central force. Had they pressed their attack, there would have been a real threat of Tork's force being overrun where they stood. But the creatures were hell-bent on fleeing.

"Musket shot!" Tork roared.

He dropped the spear back into the holster and withdrew his musket. He clamped the musket between his left thigh and Might's powerful flank. Opening a pouch at his belt, he felt inside and grasped one of the many small paper satchels that lay there. Tearing the small square paper packet open with his teeth, he felt for the round and clamped hold of it between index finger and thumb. Upending the torn opening of the satchel over the muzzle of the weapon, he emptied gunpowder into the barrel. As he did so, Tork pulled clear the ramrod out of its sheath beneath the barrel with his left hand. When the majority of gunpowder had been poured from the satchel, he released the small lead round, watching as it disappeared into the open maw of the musket. The ramrod followed the lead bullet. He tamped the round firmly amongst the gunpowder, withdrew the ramrod from the muzzle, placed it away, and brought the weapon into his shoulder. A musket shot blasted from Tork's right.

Damn he's fast!

Tork prided himself on being able to fire four musket shots per minute, but it seemed one of his soldiers was even quicker.

Glaring down the steel sights, he lined up a spider about to disappear over the ramparts, and squeezed the trigger, the weapon bucking and familiar heat blasting past his cheek. A moment later, the majority of King's Own soldiers had finished reloading and opened fire. He nudged Might forward and ignored the discomfort in the back of his throat, along with the need to cough.

Several spiders, which had fallen clear, lay upon the road, riddled with lead and thick dark ooze spreading out upon the cobbles beneath them. One of them twitched but was rapidly surrounded by mounted soldiers stabbing down with spears.

"Roland, with me!"

"Sire!"

He steered Might towards the left flank and pushed

the warhorse into a gallop. The destrier snorted and snaked his head against the persistent cloud of gunpowder drifting across the area. The familiar smell, one which Tork had always found comforting, would take a few days to wash out of clothes, saddle leathers, hair, and boots.

Might jumped over the deceased bodies of giant spiders, swerved around the corpses of man and horse and, before long, was dodging the carcasses of huge wolves. Although, given the thick cloud of gunpowder, the destrier had only a moment to react as the lumps of dead flesh appeared through the manmade mist. The cobbled street closest the western gate seemed painted in the blood of horse, man, and wolf. The gunpowder fuelled cloud began to dissipate, and Tork watched as the western gate was pushed closed by a group of dismounted King's Own warriors.

Good! Someone's thinking.

With large ropes tied around the massive crossbar, several Watchmen used a crane to lift the heavy piece of wood off the shattered cobbled stones upon which it lay. The mighty piece of wood swung clear of the ground amongst shouts of warning and, before long, with deft skill, the Watchmen had manoeuvred the crossbar, the giant piece of wood dropping into place and locking the gate closed once more.

"Apologies, sir!"

Tork turned to see Captain Regnak edging his horse through the light cloud of gunpowder towards him. "I thought it prudent to lock the gate as fast as possible. I considered sending a message down the line for your approval, but you were busy with the spiders at the time."

Tork held up a hand. "No need to apologise,

Captain. Good thinking."

The captain's face was blackened by burnt gunpowder.

Much like my face, I'm sure.

"Something tells me it's not quite over just yet, sir."

Tork chuckled, although it was without humour. "Agreed."

His hands began tingling, the all-too familiar feeling spreading across his fingers. "And it'll start again sooner than later, I think."

Captain Regnak nodded. "Luck, sir!"

Tork grunted and turned Might away. "Let's go, Roland."

* * *

Vyder shuddered awake and took in a sharp breath. It was the first time he'd regained consciousness while Gorgoroth retained control of his body. He lay floating supine in a place dark as night upon a thick, tar-like ocean. He tried to move, but his limbs felt heavy and sluggish.

"Verone! Can you hear me?"

His wife, if she even heard him, chose to ignore his calls.

"Verone?"

Nothing! Where am I?

He ceased struggling.

Where is she?

Anger's familiar warmth spread across his chest and weaved its way through his entire being.

I was summoned back from the Frost River and out of the arms of my love, to sit in darkness while some nature spirit takes control of my body? I think not!

He sat up and felt himself float clear of the coagulated surface trying to keep him contained. Vyder's upward travel seemed to increase in speed, and he felt like he was rising with blistering speed towards the surface of some deep sea and the relief that clean, crisp air would bring once his head broke clear of the water.

I think not!

* * *

The fire hissed and crackled.

Not all humans are evil, brother.

"I've been telling him the same thing endlessly, Agoth. Don't waste your time."

Gorgoroth sat beside the Wiccan, staring into the flames that had formed around Agoth's face.

"You truly believe that don't you, Agoth?"

A burning log split asunder, sending sparks into the night sky.

I know it!

Gorgoroth leaned towards Endessa beside him. "I bet you wished Agoth had been around when you called for help?"

She cleared her throat and spat onto the dirt.

"Pity for you that I was the only one around when you came calling."

She turned to him, her eyes locking onto his and, for a moment, he felt like he wanted to look away. "Things happen for a reason, Gorgoroth. It is what it is. But as long as you are here, you can no longer hurt innocent people. Gods know how many you have already killed."

Gorgoroth looked away from the Wiccan's searching gaze and returned his attention to Agoth. "Not enough." He smiled, teeth flashing in the orange light the campfire lent. "Nowhere near enough." He snarled as fury swept throughout him. "They've slaughtered enough of my precious children!"

Brother?

"What!"

Are you sure you've not become evil yourself?

"Me? How am I evil? I tend to all living animals, I am their custodian!"

Are humans not animals? Do you not call the host of your current body little monkey from time to time?

Gorgoroth opened his mouth, but the words would not come initially.

"Yes, I do, but humans are different."

Are they?

"Of course, they are, Agoth! I know all animals need to survive, and part of that survival requires killing. But humans..." he threw a twig into the fire and clenched his jaw against the fury, "they kill my children in their hundreds for their fur, in the hope they'll be paid a single copper coin. They leave the corpses of those I swore to protect to lie decomposing in the forests."

And those corpses left in the forests, do they not serve to feed even more of your children? Does their decomposition not serve to enrich the ground upon which their bodies lie?

Endessa's voice cut the silence. "Don't bother, Agoth."

"Do you know how many of my forest deer remain alive?"

The campfire spluttered, several sparks flying clear. *No.*

"Seventy-five." Gorgoroth slammed an open palm upon the ground beside him. "Seventy-five!" he shouted. "Three more years and the forest deer will no longer exist! So, I'll rid the world of humans first to protect my children."

But if you extinguish humans, are you not doing exactly what the humans are doing to your forest deer?

"You always have a smug reply, don't you, brother?"

Gorgoroth suddenly felt himself sinking towards the depths and fought against the powerful pull.

* * *

Endessa was not completely oblivious to Gorgoroth's plight, but killing innocent people was not the answer.

It's never the answer!

She sat in silence, listening to the conversation between the nature spirits. But when Gorgoroth fell silent for a protracted time, she looked at him and noticed his eyes rolled back in his head, mouth hanging open, a tendril of saliva hanging from one corner of his mouth.

In a blur of movement, Gorgoroth's mouth clamped shut. He leant towards the fire, and his eyes regained focus.

"No, you bloody don't!" Vyder's voice spoke.

"Try me!" Gorgoroth's sibilant tone replied.

Silence again.

What in gods is happening? Endessa reached a hand into the pouch attached to her belt and grasped hold of a fistful of Black Drassil powder.

The assassin's body sat up straight for a few seconds, and then seemed to relax. His face turned to look at her, and the breath caught in her throat.

One eye was the bright, glowing blue of

Gorgoroth, whilst the other was the dark, brooding eye of Vyder. Somehow, both nature spirit and assassin had worked out a way to inhabit Vyder's body at the same time.

Very interesting.

Part III

Against All Odds

IX

Blake pushed his horse with relentless persistence until he traversed the road up Mount Grosk.

I don't even recall the animal's name. The stableboy mentioned it, but it's no great thing, it's just a method of transport.

He dug his heels into the horse's flanks. It was the final journey before he reached the capital of Brencore. He cursed as the long, thin shroud wrapped object he had slung against his back, rubbed constantly against his clothes. He'd managed to steal the thing from near the Western Wall of Lisfort, after hacking it clear with a small hand axe. It had taken all his resolve simply to approach the dead beast, let alone cutting the appendage off. He was remiss to take it with him, the thing disgusted and frightened him simultaneously. But wrapped and tied within the thick cloth made it more palatable.

At last, I'm home.

He urged the animal past slower merchant wagons, ignoring the occasional calls of greeting. After all, he had an important message to deliver to the king. It had been almost five years since he'd set foot inside the empire of Huron.

Five long bloody years. Finally! The stink of Lisfort is behind me forever! After I deliver this news, the king will have to reward me my own small parcel of land, perhaps a nice house and maybe even a young slave woman to tend me.

He smiled at the thought and sunk his heels into the horse's flanks as he felt the animal slow with fatigue. The incline up the hill grew even steeper. His mount did not respond. He kicked his heels even harder into the animal.

"Get up there you laggard!"

Finally, the horse broke into a sluggish trot, although it was breathing hard.

"No rest for the wicked, you shit! I have an important message to deliver, now get your arse moving!" he kicked his heels as hard as his legs allowed, the animal grunting in pain attempted to quicken its pace, but almost tripped.

The diplomat pulled on the reins, snapping the horse's head back and helping the animal to regain its balance. But even through the leather reins, he felt the metal bit grinding against the mouth of his mount.

"Keep your bloody footing, damn you!"

He passed another merchant wagon.

"Steady on lad, you're going to kill your horse if you're not careful!"

Blake swivelled in his saddle to glare at the merchant sitting on the driver's bench of the wagon. "Shut your bloody mouth old man! I'm a royal diplomat. One word from me and your head will roll!"

The merchant clicked his horses onward, gently tapping the long leather reins against the skin of their rumps. He muttered something under his breath and Blake swore he rolled his eyes.

"What's that you say merchant? Like living dangerously do you?"

"I said my apologies my lord," called the merchant.

Blake turned away from the merchant becoming more distant by the moment.

That's better, you stupid old bastard.

During the minor altercation, Blake's horse had slowed to a fast walk. He snarled and sunk his heels into its flanks. The animal grunted and broke into a trot, albeit with clumsiness. Sweat glistened from every part of its coat.

He reached the apex of the road up Mount Grosk and pulled on the reins. Blake sat astride the ever-patient horse to stare down upon the distant sprawling might of Brencore below. His legs moved rhythmically in time with his mount's inhalations and exhalations. The animal regained its breath, hot air blasting from its nostrils so it could take in cool mountain air.

He smiled as he focused upon each section of the city. The Merchant Square, the Sphere of the Holy Clerics, the mighty barrack lines of the Military Quarter, the Trade Quarter, the Noble Quarter, the Quarter of the Guards and nestled in the centre of the city, the royal palace itself. Of course, on the outside of the huge city walls spreading out in all directions were the numerous suburbs where the middle and lower classes lived.

Blake urged the horse onward and began the long descent towards the city of Brencore.

It's exactly as I remember it.

As the sun neared its zenith, he'd reached the western gate of the city. The portcullis was raised and locked in place. Guardsmen leaned against the wall on either side. Some even sat, head resting against the wall, sleeping.

They'd be whipped for that in Lisfort! Maybe even put to death.

The guards who remained on their feet kept a cursory watch over those arriving. Many of them were merchants, some proceeded on foot and others, like Blake, came to the city with nothing but a few saddle bags and the horse they rode in on.

As he neared the gate, one of the guards spotted the emblem denoting him as a royal diplomat, which was fixed to the rearmost saddlebag on either rump of the horse. A white scroll upon a red background. He felt proud to wear the emblems once more.

I've kept them hidden for so long, it's good, once again, to display what my duty is to my empire.

The guard pushed himself off the wall and slapped his comrade on the arm. The second man spotted Blake and snatched his spear up from the ground at his feet. He kicked the man sat sleeping beside him. When the slumbering guard did not move, he kicked him harder. Soon all the guards of The Western Gate, close to ten in number, stood to attention, keenly aware of Blake's progress towards their position.

As he approached the mighty gate, the closest guard, probably the commander, strode towards him.

"Afternoon sire!"

Blake nodded at him, pride swelling in his chest. "Good afternoon, guard."

The guard looked at Blake's horse, his gaze sweeping the animal, eyes giving away his surprise. "Looks like you've had a long ride, sire."

He pulled the horse to a halt, keenly aware that he'd also brought the heavy traffic wanting to enter the city behind him to a stop.

"Aye, we have."

"Your horse looks like it could do with a good rest, sire. Must be an important message you carry."

"Yes, he's a good animal." He reached down and patted the sweat-soaked fur. "And yes, a very important message."

"Beggin' your pardon sire, but your horse is a mare."

"Yes of course. *She* is a good animal." He smiled, but anger warmed him.

How dare he belittle me in front of his soldiers?

Blake looked at the soldier who'd been sleeping and noticed the man was struggling to keep a straight face.

"I notice that guard there was sleeping while on duty." He nodded at the man in question and felt smug as the humour vanished from the man's face.

"Who, him?" the commander pointed towards the same guard.

"Aye...*him!*"

"Yes sire, we work long hours. Some of us take it in turns to rest."

"Well, guard, that is to stop as of right now. I want him taken out and whipped for dereliction of duty. Thirty lashes should suffice."

The commander nodded and took a backwards pace. "I'll see to it, sire."

"Make sure you do. I'll check in the following days to see if you've followed my orders. If you haven't," he raised his voice so all and sundry could hear his words, "I'll see you all put to death."

The commander nodded once more.

"Understood?"

The commander nodded, but remained silent.

"Good." He kicked the horse on and within moments past beneath the gate and into Brencore.

Blake turned down a side street, content to leave the arterial road upon which all and sundry chose to travel. The Military Quarter was the closest to the western gate and seeing as it was the gate most likely to receive an enemy attack from Wendurlund, it made sense. He allowed the horse to stroll at its leisure, content to take his time heading towards the palace. He never grew tired of the sound of the smith's hammer, or the smell of molten steel. Rounding a corner in the path, he noticed a farrier in the near distance hammering glowing steel into the rough shape of a horseshoe. An assistant worked the bellows, ensuring the fire remained ablaze and retained the correct amount of heat. The farrier stopped work for a moment to wipe his forehead with a gloved hand. The man offered a cursory glance in Blake's direction, but didn't seem interested in the progress of the royal diplomat. The hammer's song soon recommenced, accompanied by the chorus of the bellows.

Turning down another side street, he passed by a section of soldiers in formation standing to attention, their muskets being inspected by their commander. The officer spotted Blake and swivelled back to his troops.

"Present arms!"

Blake smiled and offered a clumsy salute in reply.

It's good to be recognised for my rank. Yes, it's good to be home.

He rode by rows of barracks, marching formations of soldiers, others practising with swords, or tired soldiers running through bayonet assault courses. Blake watched one red-faced, exhausted soldier, hands on knees, vomiting upon the ground. A superior standing beside him bellowed into his ear to hurry up.

One man, huge in stature, sat on the steps leading up to his barrack block running a whetstone along the length of a sword in a slow rhythm. Occasionally, he stopped to inspect the edge. The warrior noticed Blake's progress and offered the diplomat nothing more than a glare, before recommencing work on his weapon.

How dare he ignore me?

His mouth dropped open and he was about to speak when the soldier looked up again and Blake found himself looking into fury-filled eyes. Violence seemed hidden only barely beneath the surface. It was clear the soldier was angry about something.

Either that, or it's his normal state of mind. I shan't say anything, he seems to be busy enough.

Blake looked away and clamped his mouth shut, relief washing over him as he noticed in his peripheral vision the soldier return to sharpening his sword.

I wonder how long the king will take to see me? I might even have time for a slave girl to bathe me.

He smiled as he thought of warm water and soft hands caressing his skin. Reality ripped the image clear of his mind as the sudden explosion of muskets seemed to tear the sky asunder. Blake pulled on the reins, stopping the animal from fleeing away from the noise in terror. With heart thundering in his chest, he realised he'd ridden behind a musket range, where soldiers practised the art of shooting and reloading.

He glanced at the soldiers standing in extended line, facing away from him, straw targets in the near distance and behind the targets stood a tall wall of dirt to catch the musket shot. The soldiers were busy reloading their muskets.

They must be recruits.

He halted his mount and watched. One soldier dropped the ramrod, an officer standing beside him, screaming a string of insult riddled commands less than an inch from his ear as the young man stooped to pick up the implement. Another officer stood behind the line of troops and levelled a pistol between two soldiers busy reloading. He pulled the trigger, both men jumping at the sudden noise, one of them dropping his musket. The officer holstered the pistol and began yelling at the weaponless soldier who scrambled to pick up the musket. The technique of randomly firing weapons near those reloading, especially if they were inexperienced troops, was thought to desensitise them to the noise of battle.

It's called bomb proofing as I recall.

"Faster! I want two shots per minute! Sergeant, what time have you?"

A short, well-built man at the rear of the formation looked down at the round timer he held in one hand. "Fifty seconds, sir!"

"Too slow. Too...bloody...slow! Stop, stop, **STOP.**"

All movement ceased in the ranks.

"You just don't get it. Get out on the road in two ranks. We're going for a little jog, lads. Perhaps that'll clear your heads! Sergeant, take them away."

The bull of a man shoved the timer away in a pocket and grinned. "My pleasure, sir."

Blake kicked his horse forward and left the soldiers to their fate as they scrambled out onto the road closely followed by the yelling sergeant. Eventually the military quarter was behind him and he passed through The Sphere of Holy Clerics. Robed, hooded people walked, sat or knelt in small groups amongst rich, beautifully tended gardens. Silence was truly golden, it was a stark difference to The Military Quarter.

"Greetings," he offered one group of clerics as they walked along the stone footpath towards him, hands folded in front of them.

One of the clerics looked up and the light streaked through the darkness of the hood to illuminate the face of a young, attractive woman. She dipped her head, darkness reclaiming her features. She ignored him. The group bustled past the diplomat without so much as a sound. He yanked on the reins, the horse stopping, but threw its head in protest. He snarled and pulled on the reins again, this time harder. He turned in the saddle at the departing backs of the robed group.

I should stop them and put them to rights, damn them!

He then recalled that some clerics were sworn to predetermined vows of silence for various reasons, some of them under pain of horrific execution were they to break it.

I should *stop them. But I'll leave it this time.*

He sunk his boots into the flanks of his horse, the animal grunting in pain as it stumbled onward towards their final destination.

Before long, he stood before the mighty palace. A behemoth of a building, it had its own massive wall running the perimetre with one exit to the north and another to the south. Blake had navigated to the southern gate, outside which stood ten guards, five on either side of the closed entrance. They stood ramrod straight and in perfect formation.

A bit different to the demeanour of their colleagues on the western gate.

Red cloaks adorned their armour, the material fluttering in the slight breeze. Apart from one soldier, the rich blue cloak hanging almost to the stone road behind him and covering his off arm. As he approached, Blue Cloak stepped forward and held up a hand covered in a plate armour glove. "You, halt!"

What? He dares to stop a royal diplomat?

He reined in the horse and turned the animal so the seal of the royal diplomat blazoned upon the saddlebags was seen more easily by the guards.

"Who goes there?" Blue Cloak continued to advance, spear now held in both hands, the weapon diagonal across his chest.

Blake did not consider himself a naïve man and was acutely aware the soldier could bring the weapon to bear and attack in the blink of an eye.

He tapped the thick leather of the saddlebag closest to the advancing soldier. "Isn't it obvious? Now open the gate. I carry an important message for his majesty."

"No, it isn't bloody obvious! Get down off the horse, right now."

"How dare you?"

The soldier levelled his weapon, the polished, razor sharp spear tip hovering mere inches from Blake's nose.

One firm stab and that thing would easily puncture my skull. Looks like I'm dismounting.

He swung a leg over the saddle and stepped down onto the road, stretching his legs and supressing a groan. He paused as the red cloaks surrounded him. Spears levelled at him from all directions.

"What *is* obvious, is that this horse belongs to a royal diplomat. That doesn't mean *you* are a royal diplomat. Show me your papers."

"My papers?"

The soldier's eyes narrowed, his jaw bulging. "Do it right now."

Blake held his hands open before him, palms facing the sky and turned back to the saddlebag. He released the leather strap and threw open the lid, rummaging around in the bag, fingers touching cooking implements, a small haversack of what remained of his food supplies. His fingers touched a soft, pliable sac and knew immediately it was the water bladder.

No papers! Shit. I think they were on the other side.

He turned back to Blue Cloak. "Must be in the

other saddlebag."

The commander's eyes flicked over Blake's shoulder and he nodded once, then returned to bore into the diplomat. "Round the other side then, and hurry up about it. You try anything on and my soldiers will kill you. Do you understand?"

Blue Cloak's eyes, hard as flint, spoke no lie.

"I understand."

With legs weak as water, he stumbled around the rear of the horse, swallowing as he noticed the red cloak nearest him clench his hands tighter around the spear he held. Blake opened the saddlebag on the opposite side and delved into the large leather bag. Once again his fingers brushed against spare clothes, tinder and several large pieces of flint bound together with a narrow leather thong. His hand clamped onto a large paper envelope and relief flowed through him in a rush.

Thank the Gods.

He pulled it free and held it in the air, smiling. "Right here."

Blue Cloak gestured to him and as Blake neared, snatched the envelope from him. The guard commander untied the small piece of leather binding closed the envelope and pulled free the papers Blake had kept so carefully hidden during his time in Lisfort. Were his true identity to be discovered there, he'd have a noose around his neck and been hanging beside the common criminals in the city square within the hour.

Blake watched the soldier as he perused the papers. "Show me your arm with the birth mark," Blue Cloak said without looking up from the papers.

Blake sighed and rolled his eyes. "Are my papers not enough?"

"No."

The papers described the location, colour and shape of the birthmark on the inside of his left bicep. Anyone trying to imitate Blake would be doing an incredible job if they'd managed to copy his birthmark.

Blue Cloak paused and glanced up at Blake. "Show me now, or this will not go well for you."

Grinding his teeth together, he rolled up his left sleeve, pushing the bundled fabric as high up his arm as possible. Holding out his arm and rotating it outward so that the underside of his bicep was exposed, he allowed Blue Cloak to inspect the red patch of skin.

Blue Cloak nodded. "Thank you, sir."

Sir, that's bloody more like it!

"One more question, sir, in which year was your mother born?"

He still doesn't believe me!

He spoke the numbers in a growl.

"This all seems in order, sir." He folded the papers carefully and placed them back in the envelope. "My apologies, lord, but we can be none too careful. You understand?"

He snatched the envelope back from Blue Cloak and nodded. "Unfortunately, yes I do."

Thumps resounded as the soldiers came to attention around him, spear points pointing skyward instead of at his throat. Relief washed over him.

"One more thing, sir. I cannot allow you to be in the presence of the king with a weapon." He gestured at the long, thin shroud wrapped thing he wore slung across his back.

"What, this?" he pulled at the strap running diagonally across his chest which held the parcel resting against his back in place.

"Yes, sir, that."

"It's not a weapon, I assure you."

"Sir, my apologies, but you understand I can't just take your word for that. My job, nay my life, depend on me doing my duty correctly. If it's not a weapon, then may I see what it is that you carry?"

Blake swore under his breath. "I suppose so."

"With all due respect, sir, it was not a request. You cannot proceed until I am sure you are unarmed."

He sighed and nodded. "I understand."

Blake pulled the chest strap over his head, brought the parcel clear and dropped it to the ground. Kneeling beside it, he untied the bindings.

Gods, I have to look at this thing again.

He paused at the last binding and licked his lips, not oblivious to the single step the guard commander took away from him, more than likely preparing to spear him if required.

Just get it done, you fool!

The bow holding the binding in place pulled free and he flicked the thin rope away before unwrapping the thing. He lay it bear for all to see. It remained unchanged apart from a new, faint odour of rot, drifting to his nostrils. He stood and took a pace back. He looked at the guard commander. The man stood transfixed, staring at the thing lying on the road at his feet.

"Is that," his eyes widened. "Is that what I think it is?"

Blake shrugged. "I'm no seer, commander, but yes I'd say so. As I said, I carry an important message."

The guard nudged it with a boot and recoiled. "Let's get you on your way," he muttered. "Wrap it back up, sir. We had to check."

"I know." He re-tied the bindings in place and re-slung it, feeling nauseous as the weight of the thing pressed against his back. During his journey, having it wrapped away and out of sight brought a certain amount of distance between him and reality. But laying eyes upon it again brought everything rushing back to him. He'd gained an appreciation for how fearless and skilled Tork and the soldiers of the King's Own really were.

He took a deep breath and let it out through pursed lips. He nodded at the guard. "Ready."

"Please, follow me, sir. Let's get you inside so we don't keep his majesty waiting any longer than necessary."

Blake kept a tight grip of his papers and threw the reins of his horse to a nearby guard still standing to attention. "You, see my horse is watered, fed and stabled."

The guard reacted like lightning, catching the reins in one hand. "Yes, sir!"

Blue Cloak stopped by the closed gate. "Gate guards, open up."

Blake looked up at the battlements above the gate and noticed it was lined with soldiers he'd previously not seen. But it seemed they'd been watching proceedings with a keen eye.

I probably alleviated their boredom for a while, I suppose.

"Aye, sir!"

A loud clunk thundered from the huge solid steel gate, followed immediately by a persistent rattle and the entrance began to yawn open inch upon slow inch.

"That'll do!" Blue Cloak roared, then stood aside and gestured Blake onward. "Through you go, sir."

Blake returned the guard commander's salute with a sloppy rendition then walked through the opening, ducking slightly. He strode along the road, towards the palace, ignoring one soldier whom came to a halt and saluted. He jumped as a mighty explosion echoed out over the city behind him, the vibration resonating through the ground upon which he stood. He turned to see the gate had been allowed to drop closed under its own weight. Dust, thrown up from the steel gate slamming back onto the ground, drifted around the entrance.

Four gate guards jogged to him and came to a halt in a tight square, one saluting. "Sir, allow us to escort you into the palace."

He shrugged. "Of course."

Two guards moved in front him, side by side, the remaining pair marching behind him.

Now this is more like it! I could get used to this.

He was aware of soldiers and civilians alike stopping in the street to watch the small procession proceed towards the palace.

They advanced beyond the guards standing abreast of the long flight of stairs leading up to the palace. They marched past royal soldiers, who stepped aside and held open mighty wooden doors for them to pass. They saluted Blake, or offered respectful greetings. He ignored them all. As the tiny group moved deeper into the palace, the guards looked less complacent and more able to deal immediate and lethal violence at a moment's notice. Blake clenched his jaw and hoped his face portrayed a look of confidence.

Negotiating an open portcullis guarded by several cruel-eyed, powerful-looking soldiers, he knew they were nearing the throne room.

"Halt!"

The group stopped.

Six royal guardsmen descended a short flight of stairs. "We'll take it from here."

"Good luck sir," said one of the gate guards before they turned away to return to their post.

He sounded nervous.

"You're here to see his majesty, I take it?"

Blake looked into the alert eyes and noted the old, white scars running across his cheeks, cutting through his beard and leaving the left side of his mouth in a permanent sneer.

No, I'm here on vacation.

He held the sarcasm at bay. "Yes."

Scar Mouth appraised Blake, but didn't seem impressed. "Before we continue, I require you to show me what it is you carry."

Gods, not again.

Blake unslung the thing he detested and unwrapped it for inspection. The guard seemed to be better prepared than the others, or at least he seemed to hide his revulsion with more effect.

He gestured for him to wrap it back up again and cleared his throat. "And you are?"

Blake stood straighter, although fear began to grip his bowels. "I am Blake, a royal diplomat."

The guard chuckled. "Silver tongue, hey?" Scar Mouth nodded. "You'll come with us and we'll pass you over to the guards who will take you to the royal chamber. If or when his majesty wishes to see you, they'll escort you into the throne room."

If?

"I carry a message, it is imperative I see the king."

Scar Mouth snorted. "You all do. I've already escorted four diplomats into the royal chamber today. What makes you so special?"

"I carry a message from Wendurlund."

Scar Mouth halted and the massive warrior turn

back to him. The guard's eyes glittered. "Do you indeed?"

"Aye, an important one. One that might mean victory for us all forever more."

The guard gestured for his soldiers to continue on. They ascended the stairs to leave Scar Mouth and Blake alone.

"Diplomat, if you're lying in order to gain an attendance with his majesty, I'll hang you with your own entrails." He leaned closer to Blake, his lips peeling back in a cruel snarl, eyes glinting with controlled fury. "Do I make myself clear?"

Blake's head bobbed.

"Good. Then follow us," Scar Mouth gestured towards his soldiers standing in formation nearby. "And we shall take you to see his majesty."

The soldiers led Blake onward. He soon stood within the royal chamber. Blake'd never been this deep inside the palace before. Luxurious silks of every colour adorned the forty-foot stone walls. Hung above the doorway through which he had been escorted, two mighty broadswords crossed one another, above them a kite shield the height of a man was fixed to the wall, the royal colours, black and red, decorating the steel.

He ignored the ache in his neck as he looked at the ceiling high above and the intricate mosaic that stared back at him. The artwork was incredible, the mosaic depicting the death of the beautifully innocent god, Pord. He'd read the saga of the gods when he was a child. Pord's death had always saddened him, but to see the scene depicted in such a stunning visual display was breathtaking. Blake recalled that as Pord closed his eyes for the last time, all trust and hope in the world would depart and a thunderstorm would wreak havoc upon the lands without break for two years. The world would flood. Blake allowed his eyes to sweep the mosaic, stopping and appraising each smallest detail. Several gods fought one another, waste deep in the waters of what would, in time, become The Frost River. The mighty form of Neath, god of the underworld was strangling his brother, Pord. Jasp, goddess of the hunt, stood nearby, her fury-filled face lending a hint of the power behind her fist about to slam into Neath's face. Gulgon stood in the near distance, watching the altercation with fear filled eyes, hands held before him and mouth open as if about to plead for his siblings to cease their fighting. Behind the gods was a dark, angry sky, lightning spearing through thunderclouds, hinting at the terrible storm about to settle upon the world.

Blinking out of the reverie, he rubbed his neck and became aware of the room around him. It seemed there were quite a few people waiting in hope of an audience with the king.

Important message or no, I'll have to wait like everyone else.

An elderly man holding a pile of ancient looking scrolls, sat closest the tall doors leading into the throne room beyond. The doors, however, remained closed and heavily guarded. Perched on a bench seat close to Blake was a man who looked like a farmer.

Smells like one, too.

Beside him were a couple of women, hands close to their noses, probably to alleviate the pungent smell drifting from the farmer. In one shadowed corner of the room stood a cloaked, hooded man. Blake was not oblivious to the empty sheaths hanging from his belt. One in which a sword would have rested and the other where his hunting knife would have resided. Both weapons would be safely in the hands of the guards outside the palace. No one other than royal guardsmen could be armed in the presence of his majesty.

Even though the hood hid the man's face in darkness, Blake could not help but feel like the man stared back at him. A chill ran down his spine and he looked away.

The doors to the throne room creaked open and guards appeared, escorting an elderly woman out. She rubbed tears away from red-rimmed eyes.

"My son is innocent, sire. I beg you!" she shrieked.

"Shut your trap," growled one guard as they brushed past Blake, leading the woman away.

"Royal diplomat!"

Blake turned back to the doorway and noticed a tall, blue-cloaked guard standing in the open entrance.

"Is there a royal diplomat here?"

Blake stepped forward. "Yes, right here."

He held out a hand and gestured the diplomat to him. "King Fillip will see you now."

"Have you been in attendance of his majesty before?"

He stopped before the tall soldier. "No."

"I shall walk behind you, I ask that you kneel before his excellency and not to speak until he speaks to you. It's all fairly straight forward practice. Think you can manage that?"

"Of course, yes."

The soldier clapped him on the shoulder. "Good man." He looked Blake up and down. "Looks like you've travelled a long way and have spared no time in coming straight to the palace. Must be an important message." He paused. "What is *that?*" he pointed at the long, thin parcel nestled upon Blake's back.

He held out his hands. "It's already been checked,

several times, and all I can say is it's no weapon."

The guard nodded. "Very well. But hand it to me and I shall carry it in." He held out an open hand towards him.

Blake pulled the strap over his head and handed the package over, relief washing over him. *Bloody take it.*

The guard snatched it from him. "Very well, let's proceed. Guards!"

Blake noticed the troops who'd escorted the old lady away had returned and bustled forth to form up in front of him, facing the entrance to the throne room. The tall soldier whispered a command and the formation began marching forward. He felt a firm jab in the back. "You follow behind them."

Did he just jab me in the back with the fucking spider's leg?

With a few quick paces, he'd caught up to the guards and slowed to their pace. Looking around the huge open area, he realised the word 'room' was unfitting. It was more like a hall than a room. Several twenty-foot pillars adorned with intricate carvings from Huronian mythology stretched from floor to ceiling. His eyes locked onto the distant king sitting upon the large throne carved from pure ivory, the arm rests encrusted with gold. He was vaguely aware of a bearskin hanging on the wall behind the king beneath a beautiful square piece of silk bearing the royal colours. As the distance between he and the monarch closed, the hall seemed to constrict so that only he, the guards and King Fillip seemed to exist. Standing amongst a cheering crowd of thousands some years before, he'd seen King Fillip from a distance and then only for a few seconds before he disappeared into the palace.

The guards came to a halt in front of him and then the formation split down the centre, half the guards marching to the left, the others to the right.

"Kneel." The whispered word came from behind him.

Blake recalled what was required and he dropped to his knees and bowed his head.

"I take it you have a message for me, son?"

Blake looked up at King Fillip. Steely blue eyes stared at him, and although the monarch's bare forearms were criss-crossed with old scars where knives, swords or arrows had scored the flesh, his face remained free from such marks.

Not just a warrior king, but a skilful one.

"Aye, my liege."

The king leaned forward, unblinking eyes boring into Blake. "Well, what's the message?"

"Forgive me my lord, I forget myself." Blake took a deep breath and then began recounting the tale of recent events at Lisfort and the number of guards, King's Own and civilians who'd lost their lives to the onslaught of spiders and wolves.

King Fillip leaned back, passing a hand through his long, dark beard. "I've heard old stories about The Waning Wood. I've listened to men who stated they'd been there, sole survivors of scouting parties. I thought them to be mind hurt. But perhaps not." He took a deep breath and let it out slowly, all the while, piercing eyes boring into Blake. "Perhaps not. And if this is to be believed, what would you expect me to do, other than rejoice?" He grinned.

"I do not pretend to know the will of my liege."

"What would you do diplomat, were you in my place?"

Blake forced himself to look into those flint hard eyes. "Me sire?" he cleared his throat, nervous tension clenching his entrails. "I'd invade."

King Fillip's eyes narrowed. "*Would* you?"

"Aye, sire."

"I like how you think, diplomat. How long did you spend in Wendurlund territory?"

"Five summers, sire."

The king stood and descended the few stairs to stand before Blake. "If you've spent so long in enemy territory, how do I know you're not now an agent for them? How do I know you're not organising some ambush where my forces will be caught out in the open mid-march and destroyed?"

How could he even question my loyalty? I would bleed for Huron.

"I am loyal to Huron, my lord, now and always. You have my word. But if that's not enough for you, your guard commander carries proof of my word."

When King Fillip turned to the guard commander, the man placed the package on the ground at the feet of the monarch, unbound the ties and unwrapped it, before leaning back.

King Fillip squatted in front of the opened parcel. "Fascinating."

"It is part of the leg of one of the giant spiders."

The guard commander leaned further back, although his eyes remained fixed upon the long, black object, thick as a grown man's leg.

The king looked up at the commander and chuckled. He waved a hand at him. "Stand easy, Garx."

The commander scrambled to his feet and stepped away from the arachnid's leg, disgust etched upon his face. "Thank you my lord."

Blake had been careful to amputate the limb to include one of the joints.

King Fillip slammed both hands onto the amputated leg and held it up for close inspection. As he turned it, the lower half bent at the joint and Blake flinched away.

The monarch burst into laughter. "Nothing to fear diplomat. It cannot hurt you." When he'd finished looking at the limb, he dropped it.

"Thank you for bringing it to me. Now I do believe your word." He returned his piercing glare to Blake. "But I don't trust you."

Blake held out his hands. "What must I do to win your trust, my liege?"

"Nothing. Guards! Take him into the town square and behead him."

What felt like a red-hot spike stabbed through his guts as realisation dawned on him. "My liege?" rough hands slammed onto Blake's shoulders and he felt himself being dragged to his feet. "My liege! Please, I am loyal to you, now and always!"

"You spent five years in enemy territory convincing my enemy of your loyalty to them, and to remain there for such time, you must have done a good job." King Fillip ascended the dais and sat upon the throne. His piercing glare came to rest upon Blake once more. The guards holding him in place must have been aware of the muscles in his legs and arms quivering. "If you could do to them what you have done today, what is to stop you from doing the same thing to me and my kingdom?"

"Sire." Blake licked dry lips with a parched tongue. "Sire...I...I, just give me a cha –"

Fillip gestured to the guards. "Take him away. Give him a swift death."

Warm liquid soaked Blake's pants and ran down

his legs, the pungent aroma of piss reaching his nose moments later. With leg muscles refusing to bear his weight, the guards dragged him out of the throne room.

"Please Gods, no! I beg you!"

He was unaware of the curious stares of those waiting to seek attendance with the king as he was half-carried through the royal chamber. Blake was oblivious as he was guided in silence down the street towards the portcullis. He pleaded with the guards, tears, saliva and snot dripping from his chin onto his shirt.

"Please Gods. Help me!" he screamed, spittle exploding from his lips. "Help me!"

Before he knew it, he was forced to his knees in the centre of a large square, where passers-by stopped to stare. The last words he'd ever hear were muttered from somewhere behind him.

"I'm sorry diplomat," and then, "make it quick."

He heard a sword drawn, followed by a faint, metallic whistle as blade cut air. Then all went black.

* * *

Fillip relaxed upon the throne and tapped an armrest, staring down at the motionless, amputated limb of the spider.

The beast must have been massive in life! Imagine facing that in battle.

The door to the throne room groaned open and the guards marched in, one of them splattered in fresh blood. Fillip smiled.

That didn't take long at all!

"Garx!"

The guard commander came to a halt before him. "Yes sir?"

"Dismiss all others waiting to see me. Gather my senior officers and have them meet me here inside the hour."

"Sir, at once."

Garx turned and with a few whispered words of command, had his troop marching back out the way they had entered.

Fillip's eyes returned to the amputated limb.

Tomorrow, we march for Lisfort.

X

Vyder lay upon the soft blanket, hands behind his head. He watched patches of night sky through the forest canopy high above. The stars seemed to duck and weave as a soft breeze teased branches and brushed against leaves. The side of his body closest the campfire was soaked with warmth.

He closed his eyes and listened to a tiny, distant drum beating at an incredible pace. The soft noise seemed to be drifting down from the trees.

You hear that, too Vyder?

He nodded.

It is the heartbeat of a sparrow. She is nestled on a branch up there. She will sleep there tonight.

He felt one arm move, seemingly of its own accord and he opened his eyes to see his finger point into the blackness above him. It was a strange feeling.

Can you see her?

"No," he whispered.

Your night vision will improve the longer I remain with you, I think. Give it time.

A soft hiss streaked through the treetops nearby.

Close your eyes, Vyder, I want to show you something.

The flickering, yellow shrubs and bushes closest the fire disappeared behind his eyelids. He felt light, like he was floating and then his stomach lurched into his throat as he felt himself rushing upward. Then he was soaring, his arms outstretched either side of him, controlling his glide.

Now open your eyes.

The forest came into view below him. He glanced

to one side and flinched as he saw a feathered wing where an arm should have been.

Have you ever been an owl before?

"No." At least he intended to speak the word, but no sound followed other than the hiss of air rolling past his ears.

I thought not. Only your most powerful wiccans are capable of this skill.

Vyder felt elation as the forest slid by beneath them. He found he could focus upon areas of leaf littered ground, even from the great height they found themselves. He watched insects flitting from leaf to leaf and sensed a rabbit hidden amongst the safe confines of a small shrub. He twisted and attempted to make the bird bank to the right, but the predator continued flying straight.

You cannot control him, Vyder. Think of it as we are with the owl, not in control of him. We can see what he sees, but that is all. He still decides where he does or does not travel.

The owl banked one way, changed direction just as rapidly and then tucked its wings in and plummeted towards the ground. Vyder panicked as he watched trees rush past and then noticed the rat upon which the bird swooped.

Time to leave before we travel too far from your body.

Vyder felt himself ripped sideways and then flying through the night sky faster than he thought even possible. He jerked awake and sucked in a deep breath. Sitting up, heart racing, he looked around and noticed Endessa nearby, her back to him as she tended the fire.

"Having fun?" she asked without turning.

He moved to her, legs feeling weak and sluggish and sat beside her. He watched her throw a log onto the fire and use a long thin stick to push it further into the heart of the blaze.

"Gorgoroth said powerful Wiccans can travel with animals as well."

She shrugged and nodded.

"Can you?"

"It's known as shape shifting. People who don't know any better think that we turn into the form of a beast, but that's not entirely true."

"So you *can?*"

Endessa turned to him, her cheek closest the fire flickering orange, the other half of her face hidden by darkness. "You sound surprised, Vyder."

"Not at all." He fell silent and watched the flames darting around the fresh log, the underside beginning to blacken.

"You should get some rest, Vyder. You will be tired after your night flight. It takes a lot out of you in the beginning."

Only if you're human.

"The thing I don't understand, is it would be much more handy if I could control the animal. Say if, oh I don't know, let's say for argument's sake I was hunting for the King's son who'd been taken prisoner by the enemy. It'd make my mission much easier."

Endessa returned her attention to the fire and grinned, her teeth flashing in the dull light.

"Oh you can."

Shutup Wiccan!

"But Gorgoroth may not want you to, for fear of injuring the animal. He may allow you to later, but for now listen to him. He may allow you to take control of the animal in question once your understanding has progressed beyond the rudimentary knowledge of shape shifting."

"Hang on! Didn't Gorgoroth use thousands of animals to besiege Lisfort? I imagine hundreds upon hundreds of them were killed in the process? Not to mention the number of people slaughtered in the process. And he's concerned I'll hurt *one* animal?"

Wiping out evil, especially an evil threatening my children is no bad thing.

"You must understand the way of Gorgoroth. He loves the animals of The Waning Wood, or his children as he calls them, above all else. Using them to remove a direct threat to them, perceived or real, is satisfactory in his mind."

She knows me too well.

"If you've killed Miriam, this entire mission ends tonight."

Relax little man. My children barely made it past the walls. The horse warriors they faced were exceptional. I grew to like those soldiers in the end. They'd die to protect one another, their loved ones and the city they held so sacred. An ideal I understand.

"Not all humans are evil, Gorgoroth," Vyder said, flicking a stick into the fire, sending several sparks toward the night sky.

I am beginning to see that, human.

"He seems much calmer." Endessa turned back to him. "Gorgoroth I mean."

Vyder felt himself speaking with no ability to control it. "We have come to an understanding." It was an odd feeling to hear the deep, resonant voice devoid of the Highland accent with which he'd spoken since he was a bairn.

"I'm not sure if I'm needed here much longer. My only concern's will you go back to your old ways the next village we happen upon? Will you use the creatures of the forest to wipe the villagers from existence?"

Vyder felt anger flash through him, unbidden, then his lips began moving again. "I am tempted, Wiccan, I'll not lie to you. But as you have been saying since the first day, not all of you monkeys are evil."

"And what or who changed your mind, Gorgoroth?"

Vyder relaxed and allowed the nature spirit to speak.

"It might sound strange, Wiccan." Vyder felt his shoulders move up and down in a shrug. "But the soldiers who fought to defend their city against my children."

"The Wendurlund Army?"

"I don't know. All I know is they fought from horseback mostly and were near unstoppable."

Endessa chuckled and nodded. "Ah." She stared into the fire, her eyes twinkling a faint orange. "The King's Own. The elite warriors tasked with protecting the king's life." She prodded the fire again, sparks crackling to life, drifting skyward in gentle tumbles. "Some call them the Horse Lords. No matter their name, arrayed in battle, the enemy centre will avoid closing with them at all costs."

"I can see why."

"They are only a small unit, but most agree that even though they are few in number, they are the finest soldiers in the world."

Vyder remained silent, intrigued by the conversation between Gorgoroth and Endessa.

"But it was not just their skill in battle, but the revered way in which they treated their dead. As if they were their own family. I've never seen that before, Endessa. It gave me pause."

"I'll say it now and I'll say it until I'm blue in the

face, Gorgoroth. Not –"

"Not all people are evil," he finished. "I know Endessa, I was hearing you say that earlier, but I wasn't listening. Now I understand what you mean. You have my word, Wiccan. I shall not harm another human that does not deserve death's call. Is that fair?"

Endessa nodded. "That is fair, nature spirit."

Vyder felt Gorgoroth drift from the fore and feeling returned to him, his arms and legs tingling. He cleared his throat and coughed.

Endessa smiled. "Back with us I see, Vyder?"

"Aye, it'd appear so."

"I keep forgetting how thick your Highland accent is until I hear Gorgoroth speak."

"Some people find it hard to understand me."

"Show's how poorly travelled some are. My first husband was a Highlander."

Vyder looked at her and noticed the distant look in her eyes as she gazed at the burning log.

"I'm sorry to hear that. Was he young when he died?"

She blinked, dragged in a deep breath and looked at him. "No, not at all. Death claimed him just shy of his eightieth summer."

"How many times have you been wed?"

She cleared her throat, leaned to one side and spat into the dark forest. "Five times. All dead now. All claimed by Father Time." She watched sparks spiralling upward. "He is a harsh bastard that one," she whispered.

Vyder was not good at numbers, never had been, but he was astute enough to know that the sums didn't add up.

"Wait. How old are you?"

She smiled, but chose to ignore the question.

Older than she looks little human, that much I can tell you.

"Time for me to sleep, Vyder. Get some rest, you'll need it in the coming days and weeks."

He lay back, and stared up at the few stars he could see beyond the forest canopy.

There is a fox nearby, assassin. Have you ever run fast as a bolt of lightning through a forest in the dark of night?

Vyder smiled and closed his eyes. "No."

Would you like to?

"Why not?"

* * *

As morning sunlight lanced through the canopy, they broke their fast in silence. Vyder chewed on salted meat, staring with nonchalance into the forest's depths. Movement broke his reverie and he watched Endessa hurl a chicken bone away, before standing and kicking dirt onto the already deceased fire.

"Time for me to go. The comfort of my cave calls for me."

He stuffed the last of the food into his mouth and stood, watching her pack away what little belongings she owned.

The Wiccan moved fast. She'd already rolled up her sleeping blanket and placed it away in a saddle bag. She saddled her horse and mounted, looking down at the highlander.

"I bid you farewell, Vyder."

He stepped forward. "Thank you, Endessa, for all you've done."

She nodded and swung the horse away, but paused. She looked over her shoulder at him. "Your promise is still solid, Gorgoroth?"

Vyder felt a strange floating feeling and his body went numb. He spoke without meaning to, Gorgoroth's deep, gravel voice issuing from his mouth. "My word is my bond, Wiccan, it is solid until beyond the end of time."

"Good."

"But if a human deserves death's visit, I promise I will arrange the meeting." Vyder felt his lips widen into a smile. "However, I will not take the life of another innocent monkey."

Endessa nodded, looked away and pushed her horse into a canter. She was gone in moments, the staccato clatter of hooves drifting into the distance and then into silence.

His arms and legs tingled and Vyder felt a tickle in his throat. He coughed, cleared his throat and picked up his saddle. Walking to Storm, he saddled the horse and stepped up into the saddle. He felt alone without Endessa. She'd been with him since Gorgoroth had joined him.

"Dare I say it, but I miss her."

He patted Storm's neck.

I don't.

"Don't lie, Gorgoroth, I know you'll miss her too."

Vyder pushed the horse on. "Time to be moving, my lad. There's a prince who needs saving."

✳ ✳ ✳

Henry sat in the Huronian cell like an abandoned dog. The cold stone seeped into his bones. He drew his legs up and rested his head against his knees. Long, dirty, matted hair draped around his face. He heard the rhythmic thump of boots growing louder.

What do those bastards want?

He looked up, ignored the pain in his neck and counted the scratches he'd made in one of the stones making the wall that entombed him in the tiny prison cell.

I'm not due to eat until tomorrow.

Henry rested his forehead against his knees once more, the sharp pain in his neck disappearing at once.

So what the bloody hell do they want?

A keychain rattled and the sound of metal sliding upon metal seemed deafening as a key was pushed into the lock of the door holding him prisoner. A loud click followed, then a groan of hinges and light flooded the cramped space. He squinted against the assault.

"Get up, we're going on a little journey."

Henry ignored the voice, squeezed shut his eyes and hoped whoever beckoned him would depart. But it was a frivolous hope and he knew it.

"Oi!" he grunted as a booted foot kicked him in the ribs. "I said get the fuck up! Now!"

Henry raised his head, fury soaking his body as he looked up through slitted eyes at the man who'd kicked him. The bright light caused his eyes to leak and ache. Other than the silhouettes of two men standing before him, he was unable to focus on their faces.

"I aint gonna ask you again, boy!"

Ignoring the pain issuing from his joints, Henry pushed himself to his feet to tower over the pair of guards. He'd lost weight since being taken prisoner all those long months ago.

Months? It could have been years now. Who'd know? There's been many days I've forgotten or couldn't be bothered to mark the stone.

He guessed he was less than half the weight he'd

been before capture.

"Get out here, runt!"

The silhouetted man on the right pointed at the narrow stone hallway behind him.

Runt? There was a time I'd have cut you in half with one blow.

He stepped forward, fixing his eyes upon the man on the right and noticed the guard take a tiny step back.

And you know it, don't you?

Henry refrained from smiling. He stepped out of his cell and the light thrown by torches lining the hallway in both directions became even brighter. He squeezed shut his eyes and rubbed them, ignoring the tears sliding down his cheeks.

"Give me your hands, boy!"

He felt a firm grip latch onto a wrist and dragged his hand away from his face. Within moments, both hands were behind his back and clapped in metal cuffs that bit into the skin. But he ignored the pain and remained silent.

He stumbled forward as someone shoved him from behind.

"Get your arse moving!"

He walked along the hallway, his legs beginning to burn with strain. This was the furthest he'd walked since being taken prisoner and the muscles of his legs began to mutiny. But onward he walked. He clamped his teeth together and disengaged his mind from the pain.

"Where are we going?" he asked through clenched teeth.

A hand grabbed his long hair and he felt his head dragged backward.

"Did I ask you a fucking question?" a voice yelled inches from his ear. "No I didn't, runt, so keep your dirt hole shut! When I want you to speak, you'll fucking know."

The hand released his hair and pushed his head away.

"Oh you'll know alright, boy."

"Enjoying this, aren't you Steef?" the second guard asked.

"Shut up numb nuts! No names, thick skull!"

Steef, eh? If I ever escape, Steef, you and I are going to have ourselves a serious disagreement.

"Sorry, Steef."

"Fuck you're dumb."

Henry attempted to ignore the blistering agony emanating through his legs, but failed. He stumbled as he lost his footing and fell onto a knee.

"Get up, dog!"

Rough hands grabbed him under his arms and hauled him back to a standing positon.

"Now get on your way."

Another shove in the back.

He advanced once again, reducing his stride length so he was almost shuffling. It helped alleviate the strain on his leg muscles.

"What's wrong with you? Hurry up!"

"He hasn't walked for a long time, Stee –"

"No bloody names! How many times do I have to tell you?" Steef's voice blasted around the hallway, making Henry's ears ring.

The corridor ended and Henry stood before a closed, locked door which led out of the dungeon and up towards freedom.

Finally, after all this time, I'm to be executed.

Steef brushed past him, unhooked the countless keys from his belt and thumbed through them until he found the one he wanted. Unlocking the door, he pushed it open.

"On you go."

He grasped a firm grip of Henry's shoulder and pushed him forward towards the stairs.

As he moved forward, he looked directly into the guard's face, noted the shoulder length brown hair, streaked with the silver of age, the dark eyes, bags bulging from the skin beneath them and the stubble adorning his pudgy face. Steef's eyes widened for a moment, then the man regained control of himself and the worried glint disappeared.

I have your measure, weakling.

He pushed past the guard and took the first step.

If walking hurt, this is going to be sheer hell.

Then the second.

But it has to be done.

The third.

Death will be a welcome freedom from this prison.

He stopped on the fourth step, his legs on the verge of surrender.

"Hurry up, runt!"

The familiar shove in the back sent him off balance and Henry crashed face first to the stone stairs, pain lancing his nose. The acrid metallic taste of blood oozed beyond his lips and began to fill his mouth. He spat the blood out and felt hands drag him back to his feet.

"His majesty wants him uninjured! You might have just signed our death warrants!"

"A little touch up won't hurt him. Nice of you not to use my fucking name for once in your stinking life."

Uninjured?

"Up you go, dog, we ain't got all day neither, so best you get a hop along."

Henry worked an already loose tooth free with his tongue and spat it out. "Best I get a move on then."

He took the steps as fast as he was able, ignoring the pain in his legs, gulping in great gasps of air as he rapidly became short of breath, sweat beading upon his forehead before dripping clear, or splashing into his eyes. He blinked against the stinging.

"Alright, alright, stop and take a breath. It's no good to us if you turn up dead."

Henry heaved in the air, focusing on the stairs yet to be defeated and ignored his legs screaming their protest.

Another several efforts similar in fashion and they'd reached the top of the stairs where another door, closed and locked, barred their way. After Steef unlocked and opened it, he pushed Henry on through. With countless rest stops, they made their way down long hallways, up another two flights of stairs before they came out of a steel gate leading out onto a cobbled street.

Exhaustion racked Henry's body and if it were not for the firm hand, which dragged him backward, the horse and wagon would have run him down.

"Look where you're goin' next time dolt!" the driver roared as the wagon rumbled past them.

Henry didn't even have the energy to look up. He stood, watching the ground near his feet, hair hanging limp either side of his face as he slowly began regaining his breath, all the while ignoring the burning from his legs.

"Ready?"

Before Henry could reply, he felt a prod in his back. "Of course you're ready, get on with it *your majesty!*" Steef mocked.

The guards laughed.

"Don't look like royalty does he?"

"Wendurlund royalty don't count, weak as piss those bastards. Isn't that right *your grace?*"

He felt the familiar shove in his back and stumbled, but was able to regain his balance. Their laughter intensified. "Been walking long, *sire?*"

He was pushed from behind once more and the toe of one of his shoes caught in a small crevice of the cobbled street. He fell to his knees, pain lancing through his legs. He clenched his teeth together and refrained from crying out.

That'd give them even more pleasure.

"You're so clumsy, can't even walk in a straight line without falling over. Get up!"

Hands pulled him back to his feet and drove him forward again where he nearly lost his footing for a second time. He felt warm liquid leaking from his knees, travelled down his shins tickling the skin of his ankles as the rivulets soaked into his decrepit shoes.

Another few wagons thundered past in both directions, but Henry was careful to keep his eyes down cast. He saw people trot past on horseback, occasionally greeting the guards. One of them spat at Henry, but the globule missed him and splattered upon the street nearby.

A much larger wagon rumbled alongside them and slowed.

"Where you taking this abomination?" the driver called down.

"To the western gate and outside, sir," Steef replied.

Old Steef sounds nervous. I wonder who this man is?

"They're formed up already and ready to march, so

get your arses in gear!"

"Aye sir, going as fast as we can," the less intelligent of the pair spoke.

"Shut up, idiot!" Steef's voice was barely audible.

"It aint nearly fast enough boy, now get your prisoner moving, your king is waiting on you. If you don't want to lose your fucking heads before noon than I suggest you heed my advice."

"Yes sir, of course."

Henry watched in his peripheral vision as the driver flicked the rumps of the two horses drawing the wagon and clicked his tongue to encourage them. The wagon rumbled past, and when it was well in front of him, only then did Henry look up. The wagon was huge, stacked to overflowing with bales of hay covered in massive oiled sheets of canvas.

Supplies for the cavalry. The Huronian Army is about to march. Are they at war with us again?

"You heard him, dog." A hand shoved him from behind. "Get a move on, I aint dying today because of you, you piece of shit."

They made their way along the streets, keeping to the side as much as possible to allow supply wagons ferrying supplies to the army to roll past, or empty ones rattling back in the other direction, where no doubt, they'd then be loaded in a similar fashion. Henry clenched his teeth against the agony and thought of his father, King George, instead.

An army will march and ultimately win any battle by logistical prowess as much as martial skill. Always remember that, boy. His father's voice spoke into his mind from some long lost memory. *Starving soldiers and unfed horses do not win battles. They die in them.*

As hard as his father had been on him growing up,

he missed the man. He reflected on the day he'd told his father he'd started training as an officer in The King's Own.

You're not a bloody soldier! You're my son, the prince and heir to my throne. The days of the warrior kings of old are gone!

Henry glared up through his matted hair hanging limp around his face and noticed the western gate approaching. "Not if I can help it!" he muttered. The same words he'd spoken in reply to his father that day all those years ago.

He felt a jab in his back. "You say something, dog?"

Henry ignored the jeers of the guards standing at the western gate. He didn't acknowledge their mocking chants, the globs of phlegm, which caught and dripped in strands from his hair, or slid down the skin of his neck. Anger was his friend, hatred his comfort, fury his driving force. Before he knew it, they were out of the gate and headed towards an open field upon which stood the incredible might of the Huronian Army. Tens of thousands of soldiers and thousands of cavalry. In the centre, King Fillip sat upon a black warhorse surrounded by his personal guard who'd formed a tight square around him. Henry's eyes swept the small square of elite cavalry warriors entrusted with guarding their king.

You might be better than average, but you aren't any match for The King's Own. You'll learn that when you meet them upon the field of battle.

He spat bloody phlegm upon the ground and kept his thoughts to himself. A faint shout echoed out across the plain and Henry looked up through his filthy locks to hear King Fillip shouting some mockery towards him of which he could not make out. His personal guard began laughing and jeering as Henry approached. Curious as to what was happening, the members of the rest of the Huronian Army took some time to realise whom their monarch mocked. Then they started to join in. Only a few pockets of soldiers to begin with and then the noise grew in volume as others lent their voices to the taunting. The air itself seemed as if it would soon be torn asunder as the ruckus increased into a wall of thunder created by human voices.

"Aren't we popular, dog?" Steef slammed a fist into Henry's spine almost knocking him to the ground. "See that wagon near the King's Guard?"

Henry tried not to wince against the noise, but it was near impossible. His ears had been used to the silence of the dungeon for so long that the clamour seemed to pierce his skull. He spotted the wagon of which Steef spoke and saw it was a prison cart.

"That's where we're headed." The guard chuckled. "Well, that's where *you're* headed."

As they tramped across the open field, he ignored the shouts of abuse, refused to flinch when they past close to a formation of infantry, many of who broke formation to spit at the Wendurlund prince. But, the phlegm hit the guards as often as they splattered upon Henry. Steef and his off-sider began shouting and attempted to stave off the soldiers. For the most part, they were successful. Two soldiers, more rowdy than the others pushed Steef to the ground and then advanced on Henry. He could see the murder glistening in their eyes. They were clubbed from behind by their non-commissioned officers and dragged back into formation, where their unconscious bodies were dumped upon the ground.

"Fucking maggots!" Steef roared.

Henry allowed a slight smile to crease his mouth as

he heard the guard grunt as he climbed back to his feet. He dared not turn around to see for himself, though.

"You alright?" Steef asked.

"I think they broke my nose, Steef."

"You'll be okay, just a bit of blood. Your nose looks fine."

"I'll see the flesh flogged clear of their spine."

As he walked, Henry saw in his peripheral vision the two soldiers still lying motionless in the near distance.

If they awaken at all.

He began to desensitise to the dull roar of the Huronian Army. He felt less intimidated, especially after the guards who escorted him had suffered injury at the hands of their own comrades. Although he was careful to keep his head dipped to stare at the ground a few metres in front of him. Looking too confident or cocky would not end well for him. King Fillip was a ruthless, cruel and spontaneous king who'd been known to order someone's death purely because he disliked their features. If he allowed his confidence to show, the enemy king might well take it as a sign of disregard to his authority.

He'd order me beheaded on the spot. Keep a level head, Henry.

They reached the prison wagon and he climbed up the several rudimentary stairs and onto the level tray. The thick wooden gate slammed closed behind him and locked. The prison cart was open for all to see in, but it allowed him to observe his surroundings as well. The bars lining the perimetre of the prison wagon were the height of a man, built close to together and were thick as a man's wrist.

The Huronian Army continued its taunting,

individual words lost amongst the storm of noise so that the shouts of abuse seemed to take on its own, indistinguishable voice. He turned to the door so recently locked and scrambled towards it. Holding onto the bars he pushed his face through the bars. He was barely able to squeeze his head through the gap, but he managed.

"Steef!" he shouted.

Fresh waves of anger began to warm him and he snarled as the guard turned back towards him, an amused look on his face.

"What do you want, *your majesty*?" he allowed a slight, mocking bow.

Amongst the roars of the army, pockets of laughter peeled out across the plain.

"I'm going to escape from here, and soon." He glared at Steef, allowing the hatred to take over. "And when I do, I'm going to find you. And I'm going to fucking kill you." Henry's eyes adjusted to stare at Steef's offsider standing just behind. "And you'll watch me kill him. Then I'll take your life too."

Henry grinned, white-hot fury spreading throughout his being. Then he began to laugh.

The amused expression on Steef's face disappeared to be replaced with fear. He tried to mask it, but the eyes didn't lie.

"You'll never find me, *sire!*" Steef bowed again, but his voice was higher-pitched and his movements more wooden than before.

The second guard's face lost all its colour.

"I'm trained as a member of The King's Own," he felt his eyes widen as he spoke. "I know how to track a prey, and I know how to kill. We're the finest soldiers to ever walk the earth, you think you can hide from me?"

He stood, so that he towered far above the two guards standing on the ground beneath him. "You think you can hide from me? I *will* kill you!" he roared.

"Shut up and sit down scum!" A new voice shouted from the opposite side of the wagon.

Pain exploded across the back of his calves and his legs gave way. He clenched his teeth and pushed himself into a sitting position. Standing on the other side of the wagon, a soldier holding a wooden club withdrew the weapon between the bars.

"You'll be quiet or I'll stave in your skull next time. Are we clear?"

Henry nodded.

Don't forget yourself Henry, you're now the prisoner of the Huronian Army, not some frumpy, lazy dungeon guards.

The soldier remained, glaring at the Wendurlund prince before turning and walking to the rear of the wagon, where Henry noticed four or five others stood in a tight formation.

Anger warmed him again, but he kept it in check.

What will I do if I did escape? I can hardly walk, I'm starved, weak, exhausted. Just walking out here took all of my effort and will power.

He hugged his legs to his chest and rested his head against his knees. Guilt washed over him.

And I'm a liar. I trained with The King's Own for less than three weeks. Many of them are trackers beyond compare, but I'm not one of them. I wouldn't know how to track if my life depended upon it.

He raised his head and watched the distant departing pair of guards who'd marched him out here.

Let the bastards think otherwise.

He lurched sideways and placed a hand upon the floor beside him to maintain his balance. The wagon's wheels rolled across the ground and the Huronian Army was underway towards Henry's homeland to conquer their enemy.

On the upside, at least I'm going home.

His forehead touched his knees once more and he smiled.

At last, I'm going home.

* * *

Vyder prodded the fire with a stick, mixing the coals back to crackling life before throwing a fresh log on. The rabbit, dressed skinned and washed, skewered with a thick branch was cooking well, the smell making the assassin's belly grumble. He turned the rabbit over, ensuring it cooked evenly.

"Are you sure there're no hard feelings?"

We must eat to survive, Vyder. This child of mine.

Vyder felt his hand gesture towards the cooking rabbit.

He gave his life to feed us and the important part is he died instantly and experienced no suffering.

Vyder nodded.

We have company, brother.

"Let's eat first before we go flying or running through the forest."

You misunderstand me.

Vyder felt his legs moving beneath him and he stood.

There are five men in total. Two in front of you, one to either side and another behind. They are still a little way off, but they have seen and smelled your fire. They mean to advance from all sides.

Vyder closed his eyes and parted his lips. He'd

always found opening his mouth slightly helped increase the sensitivity of his ears, particularly at night. A branch snapped off to the right, a rustle of leaf litter to the left.

"These men are professionals, Gorgoroth, I had no idea they were even here."

Vyder felt himself chuckle.

I bet they haven't met a nature spirit before.

"Probably not," he whispered.

You understand we may have to kill several or all of them?

"I had no doubt, they will kill us for the food and the horse. Fighting is the only way. But let us see what they have to say first."

Are you sure that's wise, human?

"Good evening, stranger," a tall man pushed clear of a shrub before Vyder.

The assassin, still on his feet, relaxed and smiled.

"Well met." He held out a hand. "Welcome to my fire. Have you eaten?"

"Can't say I have." The newcomer's eyes flicked to Vyder's saddlebags nearby.

A gentle creak from behind them and Vyder was immediately on guard again.

The sound of a bow being drawn. We have a bowman behind ready to put an arrow into us.

"Has your bowman eaten?" Vyder jerked a thumb over his shoulder.

The newcomer chuckled. "You're observant, my friend." His eyes hardened, the slight grin vanishing from his face. "Yert, let him have it!" he shouted.

Time to move.

Vyder felt his legs bunch beneath him and he sailed through the air, rolled on his shoulder and came up running. A dull hiss cut the air behind him.

"Take him down boys!"

Vyder darted around a tree, leapt over a small bush and suddenly felt himself change direction as Gorgoroth assisted.

Other side of that tree.

Vyder saw the trunk of the mighty oak, sidestepped around it and grabbed a fistful of the archer's shirt. The man had another arrow knocked, but was facing away from the assassin. He threw the bowman to the ground, pushed aside the bow and ignored the arrow he loosed, the tiny missile streaking up towards the forest canopy.

Allow me.

"I don't die so easy, little man." Gorgoroth's voice spoke through Vyder.

He punched the man's throat so hard Vyder heard and felt the windpipe crushed beneath his fist. The bowman made strangled, choking sounds, his bow long forgotten as he clasped both hands to his throat, eyes wide with terror.

Gorgoroth leaned forward to look directly into the dying man's eyes and spoke again, "but you do."

Then the assassin was sprinting through the forest again. Vyder felt as if his night vision was somehow enhanced, he ducked, jumped and dodged while at full sprint. As he concentrated he became aware of the presence of another bandit hidden in a bush nearby.

Now you're starting to get the knack of this, Vyder. Good.

The assassin launched himself through the air directly at the bush and shoulder barged the assailant clear, where he landed on his stomach, groaning. Vyder leaned over him, clasped a handful of hair, dragged the man's head back and with his other hand gripped his jaw and snapped his neck with a sickening, wet crack.

"You lot, come forward to the campfire. Now!" the fear in the newcomer's voice was evident.

Vyder grinned, adrenaline fuelling his body. He ran towards the fire, jumped into the small clearing, dived for his saddlebags and came back up with his knife in hand. He darted forward and stabbed the newcomer in the guts, cutting upward until the blade ground to a halt against the bone of the man's chest plate. He pushed the newcomer away, who sat on his arse, a look of bewilderment passing across his face, bright blood beginning to soak into the dirt around him.

Vyder held his arms hands out parallel either side of him. "A fine idea! Yes, come forward to the campfire," he yelled.

The one to your left is fleeing.

"You can run!" Vyder's laugh boomed through the forest. "Or at least you can try. But I will find you. Come, let us finish this here and now."

The other one is running away now.

The assassin ran to the left enjoying the rush of moving through the dark forest at such speed, like some hunting wolf. He sensed the man creeping through the darkness nearby. Vyder stopped, turned slightly and threw his dagger, the weapon flipping through the night air with a dull flutter followed by a deep *thwuck* and soft groan.

He strode in the direction he'd thrown his knife and came upon the dead body of the former fleeing bandit, his knife buried up to the hilt in the side of the man's throat. Blood still gently pumped from the wound. The knife came free easily enough and within a few moments the last of the man's life blood had slid from his open throat to splattered against the leaf litter beneath him.

One more to go, my friend. Shall we?

Vyder launched into full sprint, branches whipping

mere inches from his face. The slow footfalls of his prey became louder with each passing moment. Jumping onto a boulder and clambering to the top, he took deep breaths, wiping the sweat from his brow.

"You may as well face me," he shouted at the night sky. "You had the chance at peace and neglected to take it. I would have even shared my rabbit with you."

When he began regaining his breath, he jumped clear of the boulder and landed lightly, before jogging in the direction of the fleeing man.

Just ahead there and a little to your right, he's about to climb down into a dry riverbed.

The assassin increased his pace, dodged several shrubs, ducked under a low hanging branch. Vyder launched himself off the side of the riverbank into mid-air. He landed on the bandit's back and slammed his knife into his neck, severing the spine. He was dead before they slammed onto the dry sand together.

A job well done, Vyder. You're a fast learner. I think we will work well together.

Vyder retrieved his blade and stood, gulping in air. He didn't reply, he simply nodded.

"Should we bury them?"

The children of this forest need to eat, too. If you bury these robbers you deny my children that chance.

His breathing slowed. "Hadn't thought about it like that before."

Come now, gather yourself, it is time to return to the fire. Speaking of food that rabbit will be starting to burn and I'm hungry.

Vyder smiled. "That makes two of us."

XI

Henry lay on his back, hard wooden boards of the floor digging into him. Each bump or divot the wagon rolled over sent a jarring shudder through his body. But he ignored the pain, instead staring through the gaps in the bars at the blue sky, watching a distant bird soaring high above them.

An eagle?

It was the most free he'd been in however long he'd been locked away in the dungeon. The shadows cast by the bars offered some protection from the sun's assault, but the exposed skin of his arms, legs and face burned. The pain was a comfort. He touched a cheek and winced as the pain lanced his face.

I'm still alive.

He focused upon the sky once more and scanned the endless blue until he spotted the tiny speck once again. The dot continued to soar in great circles.

I wonder if it waits for me to die?

The bird changed direction mid-flight and began circling in the opposite direction. It seemed directly above the marching army. Anger flickered within him and he smiled.

You'll be waiting a while my old lad. I won't be dying any time soon.

Pushing an elbow beneath him, he half sat and looked around. Nothing had changed. Behind him marched the small formation tasked with guarding the wagon, which kept him prisoner. Beyond them, he rested his gaze upon the endless, rolling formations of Huronian infantry, light glinted across their mighty ranks as sunlight shone intermittently from spear tips, swords or armour, like the sun reflected from the surface of the ocean. The distant drum that echoed out across the plains upon which they marched ensured they remained in step. He twisted to look at the head of the mighty columns and winced as the bone of his elbow dug into the unforgiving hardwood. The tight square of elite cavalry remained around King Fillip, but behind them walked the auxiliary cavalry. He'd been pretending to sleep, but had listened to the mutterings of the soldiers directly behind the wagon. As far as he understood, the auxiliary cavalry were simply mercenaries.

And if what I heard is accurate, good ones too.

He watched the mercenary cavalry. Although they wore no uniform, they seemed well equipped, carrying muskets, spears and swords. Their horses were well-tended, muscles glinting through healthy coats as their hooves clopped upon the dry ground. He lay back and rubbed his elbow.

Looks can be deceiving. Let's see if they have what it takes when it really counts. Show ponies look amazing in fair weather. When the chips are thrown to the wind and it's life or death, more often than not, their guts will turn to water.

Henry watched the sky reduce in size so it was no more than a horizontal slit, than disappeared altogether as his eyelids met.

Time will tell.

The bouncing and rocking of the wagon combined with the heat of the sun brought on slumber faster than he expected. The quiet mutterings of the soldiers behind him and the gentle squeak of the wagon's wheels faded into the background, replaced with heavy silence.

* * *

The Huronian soldiers were all around the beleaguered King's Own force. The King's Own had conducted a fighting withdrawal in the rain uphill through thick forest to reach the apex of the small mountain. Henry stood amongst the ranks standing shoulder-to-shoulder facing out in a semi-circle defending their commanding officer and his bugler, both positioned behind them. It was here they'd make their last stand.

He looked over his shoulder at Tork, watching the officer reload his musket with blistering speed, while issuing a command to the bugler. The man brought the instrument to his lips and the sound seemed distant, muffled. He flinched as the semi-circle around him opened fire with blunderbuss, the roar deafening. He faced front, unslung his blunderbuss, pulled the buttstock into his shoulder, stared down the rudimentary sights at a Huronian soldier sprinting straight for him and pulled the trigger. The stock bucked his shoulder backward and the enemy soldier disappeared behind a grey cloud of spent gunpowder.

"Sire. Fall back!"

He looked over his shoulder at Tork to see the commander beckoning him to his side. "Sire, it's for your own safety."

Henry looked away, placed the buttstock upon the ground so the open maw of the blunderbuss's barrel stared up at him and started reloading. Fast as he tried to move, those around him brought their weapons up and fired another volley. By the time he'd finished reloading, the men of The King's Own had reloaded for a third time, brought their blunderbusses to bear and fired at the same time as Henry.

Still the Huronian soldiers came, screaming their foreign war cries as they ran uphill through the forest towards them.

"It seems we die today, lads," a voice said to his left. There was no fear there, though. The words were delivered in a matter of fact way born of stoic determination.

"Not without a fight," another shouted from the far side of the semi-circle.

"Aye , not without a fight."

He'd never served alongside soldiers like these before. Henry had trained with the general infantry from time to time as a younger man, but working with The King's Own and deploying with this tiny force deep into enemy territory had opened his eyes to true fearlessness.

The clash of steel on steel rang out from the right flank and Henry turned to see Huronian soldiers break through the ranks and charge towards Tork. The commander unslung his blunderbuss and fired, the single remaining Huronian not cut down by the bloody swathe disappeared into the cloud of gunpowder, sword raised over his head, shouting a string of words he could not understand.

Henry dropped his blunderbuss then, the heavy weapon coming to rest upon the forest floor with a dull thud. He drew his sword as those around him opened fire once more. The scene decelerated into slow motion. Glancing over his shoulder one last time, the cloud of gunpowder had dispersed. Tork was wrestling with the enemy soldier, before gaining an advantage and pressing him to the floor beneath him, hands choking the life from the Huronian. The enemy soldier was as good as dead. Tork swivelled to look back at his soldiers and for a moment Henry locked eyes with him.

"Protect the prince!" Tork roared.

Henry turned away, gripped his sword and snarled.

"Protect the prince!"

A hand grabbed his shoulder, but he shrugged it off and charged straight into the midst of the enemy. His sword cut the life from the first man, the blade slicing clean through his neck. The second crumpled when Henry's sword slammed into his midriff, the point of the weapon exiting near his spine. He turned to meet another attack and the side of his face exploded with pain. The ground came up to meet him. He rolled onto his back and watched a Huronian step over him, a wicked grin upon his face and a small wooden club in his hand. He held the club up over his head and brought it down with force towards Henry. Everything went black.

* * *

A prod in his ribs awoke him, his eyelids peeling apart to reveal darkness and in the distance around them in a mighty circle spaced out with military perfection, huge campfires.

"It's time to eat, prisoner."

Henry could not make out the face of the man who'd spoken, but the dark figure thrust a wooden platter through the bars at him. "Here!"

He took the wooden platter in silence and the smell of the food made his mouth water.

It can't be.

He brought the flat piece of wood to his nose and inhaled the aroma of cooked beef.

It is!

He grasped hold of the meat, ignored the heat and took a bite.

"Don't want a knife and fork?"

The darkened figure held the implements through the bars towards him.

"No," he managed through a mouthful of juicy steak.

"Don't give him a knife and fork." Another figure stopped beside the first. "What's wrong with you? He's the fucking enemy. You don't think he'd try and cut your throat if the opportunity raised its head?"

The first soldier scoffed. "He's half starved, weak, probably dying. You think he's any kind of threat, Braif?"

"Of course, idiot! Don't forget, he's also King's Own. All he'd need is a butter knife and he'd kill you dead. Don't ever underestimate a prisoner, especially a soldier of the King's Own, starving or otherwise. Got it?"

"Alright, Braif, alright, don't get your pants in a twist. I get it!"

"Good."

The figure withdrew his hand from the bars and moments later held a wooden cup towards Henry.

"What about some water?"

Henry placed the meat carefully upon the platter and snatched the cup, downing the cool liquid in several swift gulps.

"Is there any more water?"

"Of course." The figure took back the cup and turned away.

"Don't give him too much."

Henry heard the pained sigh from the first man. "And why not, Braif?"

"Because...he's...a...prisoner!"

"Maybe so, but we're not barbarians. Not like those dungeon keepers. Bunch of bastards they are. Do not forget he is still the son of a monarch, Braif."

"Just don't give him too much, alright? And stop saying my name."

"Whatever you say, Braif."

Henry grinned.

The dark silhouette, barely distinguishable from the darkness around him returned to the wagon. "Here you are." He passed the cup through the bars.

Henry took it and drank it slower this time.

"Thank you."

He drained half the water and placed the cup down upon the floor. He was full and felt bloated, but also knew he'd not eaten much. Henry decided to wait until he felt hungry again before he finished his meal. If he forced himself to eat, he knew he'd vomit, denying his body of essential sustenance.

Braif, eh? Your name's now on my kill list.

He stared out into the darkness, focusing on one of the distant campfire's around which sat Huronian soldiers.

I'm going to kill you dead.

* * *

Vyder watched flames dancing as they fed upon the blackening logs he'd recently thrown onto the fire. He relaxed. Ever since he was a child wandering the Shadolian Highlands, fire always possessed the power to take away his tension and stress. He could sit for hours, simply feeding a campfire and watching it burn. When the odd thought crossed his mind, it moved in slow motion as if it had become stuck in some deep, muddy bog.

You know what that is little brother?

"What are you talking about?"

Over yonder, on the far side of the fire, you see that tree?

The assassin squinted through the flames and saw a tall tree straight enough to use as a ship's mast, the trunk white as a ghost. Rising heat from the fire caused the upper branches to seem like they were blurry one moment and in focus the next.

"I see it. Never seen one before."

It's a Ghost Oak. And there's a good reason you've never seen one. They only grow in Huronian forests. The temperature is slightly warmer here than in Wendurlund.

"So we crossed the border into enemy territory." Vyder smiled. "Finally."

No more night fires from here on in. Too easy to spot, not to mention, smell.

"Aye, I know. This isn't my first foray into dangerous territory. I've been doing this a long time, Gorgoroth."

Laughter peeled out in his mind and anger lanced Vyder's chest. He clenched his jaw.

A long time eh? You have no idea what a long time is. Remember to whom it is you speak my little human friend.

"Oh fear not, I know laddie."

But we may need the help of my brother before our mission is at an end. Is that not correct, brother?

"I don't know what you mean?"

I do not speak to you, Vyder. Agoth, are you here?

Soft wind greeted them, brushing the skin of his cheek and caressing his hair. Vyder looked at the mighty upper branches of the Ghost Oak, the leaves emitted a dull glitter as they reflected the orange glow of the campfire far below.

Agoth?

He leaned across and grasped another fresh log he'd gathered before the sun departed below the horizon hours earlier. He flicked it onto the fire.

"Doesn't look hopeful, Gorgoroth."

Patience, my friend. Patience.

Vyder felt his mouth open and Gorgoroth's voice began singing a gentle melody, almost inaudible over the slight breeze. He'd heard Endessa hum the tune before. Was it some kind of song for summoning?

Very good. That's exactly what it is.

A sudden gust of wind threw sparks across the

ground and displaced one of the logs, the blackened, glowing piece of timber almost rolling clear of the campfire. But, the gust vanished as fast as it appeared. Gorgoroth's voice increased in volume. Vyder felt his arms raise parallel with the ground, his hands opening, palms facing the fire.

An explosion rang out from the fire and the log Vyder had so recently placed upon the blaze went spinning away from them into the forest's darkness. Vyder's arms dropped back to his sides and feeling returned to them. He swallowed and coughed.

The centre of the fire seemed to take form, flames curling and intensifying to create a deep orange face. It was the same face he'd seen Endessa speaking with. Horns adorned the temples, tusks protruding from each corner of its mouth.

"Hello Agoth."

The face turned to him, glowing red eyes appraising him. "Vyder, greetings to you." Fangs lined the mouth as the fire spirit spoke. "Well met, my friend."

This time, Vyder could hear Agoth's voice. It was deep, gravelly and didn't sound so much a voice as it did if the noise of a wildfire could be formed into words.

We need to speak, brother.

"Ah, Gorgoroth, I supposed as much, seeing as you summoned me here to this forest of Huron."

Fire will be used sparingly from now on. Can you be summoned without fire?

"I can be summoned through the power of a single spark."

I understand, my second question of course is, are you deaf?

The fang-lined mouth opened, head titled back and laughter filled the forest.

Because, you may be needed at short notice and if tonight is example of the length of time required to summon you, it may be too late.

Silence returned to the small clearing although Vyder could still hear a gentle chuckle. The fire exploded with a thunderous *boom*. Vyder leapt to his feet, knife clutched in his hand as he backed away into the shadows. A red-hot coal, the size of a man's palm tumbled through the air and came to rest on the ground at Vyder's feet with a *thud*. He watched it for a moment as the dry leaf litter surrounding it began to blacken and smoulder. Returning his attention to the fire, he saw that although it was diminished from what it'd been, it continued to burn, and Agoth still resided in its depths.

"Relax, Vyder. There's no threat here. That is a summoning token. It'll bring me to you within moments, as long as there is at least a spark of fire present."

Thank you brother.

"But use it sparingly, it can be used but one time before all power is faded from the token."

* * *

Ahitika crouched upon an upper bow of a Ghost Oak looking upon the camp below. The man who sat near the fire was crazy. That much she knew. But, when the fire erupted and the face of an evil spirit resided within the fire, she rubbed her eyes and wondered if it was she who was the crazy one.

She touched the breastplate, made from long thin beads created from animal bone. Medicine men had imbued the breastplate with the power of The Great Spirit, protecting her from evil. She stood and with lithe agility walked to the outer edges of the branches so that she stood directly above the campfire.

When the evil spirit in the fire spoke, she ducked into a crouch, fear spreading through her. Ahitika touched the breastplate and held onto it this time. Long enough for the fear to dissipate.

I am Ahitika, warrior of the Kalote people. And I am not afraid.

The evil spirit in the fire seemed to be talking to itself, because the man sitting nearby remained silent. As the one way conversation continued, she lowered herself into a sitting position, so her legs dangled over the edge of the branch. As time passed, she grew accustomed to the face in the fire and listened to the words. It was speaking in the language of Wendurlund. She could pick out some words, but for the most part, it spoke too quickly for her to keep up. Outside of Kalote, she'd heard Huronian spoken so often that she'd almost forgotten the Wendurlund language.

She focused upon the back of the head of the seated man.

So you are a man of Wendurlund. I hate you less, then. I might not take your scalp. Although the scalp of a Witch Doctor would see my initiation at an end.

Her lips stretched into a smile as she watched the man far beneath her.

I may take your scalp, yet.

When the fire exploded with a thunderous noise, her moccasin enshrouded feet were beneath her and she stood once more, backing away. She padded backward on the branch, her balance instinctive while her eyes bored into the man, who himself was on his feet and retreating from the fire. Like she, he'd moved in an instant blur and backed away into the shadows.

So, you too are a warrior.

A piece of red hot coal bounced against the branch

upon which she stood and fell to earth, coming to rest upon the ground with a soft *thud*.

She crouched again, watching. Her brow creased, eyes narrowing as the fire regathered itself into the face of the evil spirit.

What is happening here?

The warrior man returned to the fire and knelt beside the piece of hot coal. Although he was wise enough not to touch it. Ahitika sat upon the branch once more legs dangling over the edge to be caressed by cool evening air. Soon the evil spirit faded from the campfire, the flames simply flickering and wobbling in the gentle breeze exactly as they should.

Ahitika brushed a hand against her breastplate once more, drawing strength from it. If the evil spirit had departed the fire, then it was free to roam where it pleased. Would it come for her? She clutched firmly onto her breastplate, feeling the power of The Great Spirit wash over her.

No!

As the dull white orb of Finkam The Hunter ascended higher into the night sky, Ahitika held a fist to her mouth and supressed a yawn. When the Witch Doctor warrior lay upon the ground near the dying campfire, she stood and stretched. Padding along the mighty branch she came to the tree trunk of the colossal Ghost Oak. She leapt, swung and dropped from branch to branch, until she landed lithely upon the ground. Ahitika knelt and touched the earth, taking a handful of leaf litter and brought it to her nose. She closed her eyes and breathed in the scent. Splaying her fingers, the dead leaves drifted back to the ground.

With fluid movement she was on her feet and striding to a nearby tree against which was leant her longbow, quiver and set of scalps. She tied the quiver and scalps to her belt next to her hunting knife and slung the bow. Pushing past a sapling, she crept through the forest, past vine-enshrouded trees. Ahitika brushed a hand across a fern's broad, soft leaf as she moved in silence. The forest was like her second home, she was no stranger to the wild woodlands of Huron or Kalote. She'd once heard of a merchant becoming lost in some distant part of a Huronian forest. They'd found his body days later, although his horse had broken free of its tethers. The story amused her at the time.

How soft have the Huronian people become that a man can no longer sustain himself within this huge home the woodlands provide?

She looked through the canopy high above at the dull glow provided by Finkam The Hunter, the light filtering through the branches to cast random patterns upon the ground.

Here there is food, water and shelter. The Huronians are so weak. How did the Huronian soldiers drive our people off this land in the days of my fore fathers? Our *land.*

She clenched her teeth and her jaw bulged. She touched the scalps tied to her belt, the soft hair soothing against her fingers. Ahitika smiled.

All from Huronian warriors.

Her lips morphed from a smile into a snarl.

All dead.

Returning her attention to the dark forest in front of her, she saw what remained of the campfire, a dull red glow hidden away amongst the foliage before her.

Three more scalps and my initiation as a warrior is at an end.

Ahitika walked on with care, her soft moccasins almost inaudible as a soft breeze whispered through the forest. Her smile returned.

Or the scalp of one Witch Doctor warrior.

As Ahitika advanced past trees, shrubs, stumps left over from ancient trunks that, in life, would have dwarfed all the forest, she came upon the campfire. She crouched, brow creasing as her eyes swept the small clearing. The Witch Doctor was nowhere to be seen. She remained silent, her focus gliding more carefully across the glade, but the man who'd been there so recently was gone. It was as if he'd never existed at all. A horse stood in the flickering shadows, tied loosely to a tree and munching with content upon the pick growing through the leaf litter.

A fern nearby moved seemingly of its own volition, sending a shock of fear spearing through her. She shot a look in that direction and saw the silhouette of a man, barely distinguishable from the darkness around him, kneeling nearby staring at the campfire.

"Who are we looking for little monkey?"

It is the Witch Doctor warrior!

The man turned to face her, one bright blue orb where an eye should have been, illuminating his face in the soft colour of the ocean. His teeth shone from the depths of a wide smile. He slammed a hand onto his chest with a *thump*.

"Or is it *me* you're looking for?"

She made to speak, but the words caught in her throat.

"Because if it's me for whom you look." He exploded into motion, leaping through the air to come to rest in a crouch inches away from her. "I can help you."

Ahitika stared into the eyes of madness, her fingers curled around the deer horn hilt of her hunting knife. The Witch Doctor continued to hold her gaze, the grin spread across his face unwavering.

"Are you sure you want to do that, little one?"

Her grip tightened upon the weapon and she tensed her arm ready to draw it and strike a killing blow, something she could carry out in the blink of an eye. But, a cold sensation spread from her chest to her gut, causing hesitation to win supreme. The feeling was foreign to her and after a moment's pause, she realised it was doubt. She relaxed her hand and allowed it to slide free from the knife.

"A wise choice."

She made to retort, but the dull glint of Finkham The Hunter's light reflected upon metal caught her eye and she looked down to see the Witch Doctor holding a knife, which looked more like a small sword, less than a finger's breadth from her gut.

"You are warrior," her lips struggled to form the words of the Wendurlund language. Ahitika had not spoken the language in so many years.

The Witch Doctor stood and sheathed the knife. "I am many things."

"What is Wendurlund Witch doing here in enemy territory?" she couldn't remember the Wendurlund word for doctor.

The tall man chuckled. "I could ask you, a Kalote woman, the very same thing. Let us return to the fire." He walked away, but cast a glance over his shoulder at her. "And I'm no witch. I'll leave that to Endessa."

Her brow creased.

Endessa?

She stood and followed, watching the Witch Doctor throw a log onto the glowing coals. Clearly, he held no fear of her.

I'll not scalp this one. Safer to scalp another few Huronian warriors.

Sparks were cast skyward, drifting through the air in random patterns. Soon small flames were flickering up around the outer edges of the fresh wood as the campfire began to return to life.

"Me," she touched her breastplate, drawing strength from it, "Ahitika."

The Witch Doctor sat cross-legged, watching her, that glowing blue eye boring into her soul. "I am Vyder."

Ahitika took a pace backward, her hand snaking to catch a hold of her breastplate.

"Your voice…different."

The Witch Doctor's voice had become somehow deeper and held an accent. Struggle as she might with recalling the Wendurlund language, she was sure the accent was one of the highlanders of Shadolia.

"I'll not hurt you lass."

Ahitika walked closer, but stopped at a safe distance. She sat upon the forest floor. "You are witch dotoc…dotocor?"

"A witch doctor?" Vyder's laugh boomed throughout the forest. "I'm not entirely normal, but I'll tell you in time. For now, think of me as a man with a split personality, but I'm no witch doctor."

"What is split personality?"

Vyder reached with a long, thick stick and poked the log, rolling it over. Flames leapt higher. "It means there are two people living in one body."

She shifted and pointed at him. "Insane?"

"No, not me," he smiled. "The other one though?" Vyder nodded. "Very possibly. But he likes you I think. I doubt he'll harm you."

"You not sure though?"

The shoulders of the big highlander rose and fell.

"Add more spice to life," Ahitika pushed herself to her feet and crept closer to the fire.

Vyder laughed.

If the crazy one attacks, I'll kill him. Then scalp him.

She smiled.

She gestured towards the man. "You speak Wendurlund, but with different accent?"

He nodded and looked away from her, returning his attention to the fire. He poked the fire again before the odd coloured eyes returned to drill into her being. "I'm a Shadolian Highlander."

As I thought.

"I met a Wendurlund woman on a short trip across the Shadolian Sea to Wendurlund, many years ago now. Her father was a merchant who travelled often between Shadolia and Wendurlund."

Silence drifted once more across the camp.

"She bound herself to you?"

His brow creased then relaxed just as fast. "Yes, we were married."

"Where she now?"

"Dead."

"Killed by crazy one?" she pointed a twig in his direction. "Killed by blue-eyed split personality?"

Vyder's eyes returned to the fire, his chest expanded and then contracted rapidly. "No."

She almost misheard him his voice was so soft.

"We lived in a cabin in the Likane Forest on the eastern most border of Wendurlund."

"East?"

"The direction from which the sun rises."

She nodded. "You lived near the border with Huron?"

"Aye, lass."

"Huronian soldiers killed her?"

The bump in Vyder's throat rose and fell. "Huronian hunters."

"Now you kill Huron?"

He held his palms out towards her. "Too many questions."

Vyder stood and walked away. She watched his departing back before he was consumed by shadow at the far edges of the campfire.

We are not so dissimilar. The Huronians killed my people, used them as slaves, poisoned them, spread disease. They would have annihilated us as a people had my ancestors not chosen to flee north.

She clenched her jaw and snapped the twig between her fingers, throwing the pieces into the fire.

"We are same, you and I," she called into the darkness.

Silence greeted her words.

Even if the crazy one attacks, I'll not kill this one. I'll run away.

She heard a branch snap underfoot and saw movement amongst the shadows. A moment later Vyder's form appeared in the flickering light offered by the campfire. She drew herself up into a crouch, legs bunched beneath her as those mismatched eyes bored into her. She glanced over her shoulder and saw a small gap between a thick shrub and tall tree.

That's my line of escape if the crazy one is back.

Snapping her focus back to the approaching man, she noticed he still glared at her. He stopped on the far side of the fire and sat.

"I'm about to rescue a prince of Wendurlund." It was Vyder's voice.

She relaxed.

Prince.

She thought about the word. It was unfamiliar. Although the Wendurlund language was solidifying in her mind the more she spoke and listened to it, that one word caused her pause.

"The son of a war chief," he added.

"You kill Huron to rescue this warrior?"

The hint of a smile teased the corner of Vyder's lips. "I suppose so, yes."

Ahitika touched her breastplate, the power emanating through her. "Then I come with you."

* * *

Captain Rone sat upon his warhorse in the centre of the King's Own column, wending its way back towards Wendurlund territory. Their scouting mission at an end, it would be up to another King's Own unit to ride out into the wildlands of Huron. As with every other unit that had returned from such trips deep into enemy territory, his men were unkempt, their mouths hidden beneath thick beards, long hair touching shoulders. Dust and dried mud smeared their armour, although their weapons remained pristine.

They filed through thick forest, which would eventually become the Likane Forest of Eastern Wendurlund. He had chosen not to patrol along the road paralleling them somewhere in the distance of the thick forest. Rone had been an officer of the King's Own for close to a decade and grim experience had taught him walking along a road was recipe for an ambush.

A staccato of dull thumps made him turn in the saddle. He watched one of the rear scouts cantering through the forest towards him.

Where's the other scout?

He'd sent two soldiers forward of the column to give them early warning were they to be riding into an ambush or particularly rough terrain. The other pair of scouts he'd ordered to remain behind the column and watch their route of departure for an enemy force that may have discovered them and were following. The scout reigned in his destrier beside Rone.

He strained to hear the scout's voice. "You need to see this, sir."

Rone cleared his throat as quiet as possible. "Where's the second scout?" he whispered.

"Still in position."

He nodded. "We have an enemy force tailing us?"

The scout paused for a moment. He shifted in his saddle. "Not quite, sir, no. But you need to see it all the same."

"Wait here."

Rone turned to Baras, his bugler. "With me, Baras."

He pushed his heels against the flank of the horse and the animal responded instantly, accelerating into a canter, the hessian sacks tied around each hoof dampening the thuds. He allowed the destrier to pick its way around trees as he moved towards the head of the column of King's Own. Twice he was forced to lay flat upon the animal's neck as low hanging boughs swept mere inches overhead. Horse after horse passed them by. He pulled gently upon the reins so he was walking beside Dreas, his most senior subunit commander, leading the column.

"Sir?"

"Hold this course, Dreas, I'm heading back to our rear scouts."

Dreas's eyes narrowed. "Enemy follow up?"

"Apparently not. I shouldn't be long."

Dreas touched his temple with an index finger. "Right you are, sir."

He nodded, looked at Baras, then jerked his head in the direction in which they'd just come. Baras turned and cantered away, Rone following suit. As he passed along the column, Rone spotted the scout and signalled the soldier to him. The scout broke formation and within moments was cantering in front of Rone, heading back the way the column had travelled.

After several miles, the scout slowed and nudged his mount down a small embankment into a small, open space in the forest. Rone noticed the second scout's horse tied to a tree, grazing in silence. Rone leaned down and checked the hessian sacks were still secured around his boots. When he was satisfied, he withdrew his musket and dismounted. The sacks over the boots of his soldiers greatly diminished their sound as they patrolled, but also thwarted the task of tracking them. A set of clear boot prints gave a tracker a vast array of information about his quarry. Size, weight, boot prints may distinguish the soldiers of a particular army, and even a unit within that army. A shortened pace on one stride may indicate a limp and therefore the possibility of injury. The hessian sack tied around each boot was rudimentary, but made tracking just that little more difficult. He led his warhorse across the leaf litter past a campfire. He paused and kicked the charcoal.

Relatively fresh, may a day or two old.

He caught the scout's eye, who held up two fingers before gesturing towards the campfire at his feet.

Two day's old.

He moved on. Passing an open palm along the

neck of his horse, he tied the reins loosely around a nearby branch and ensured the horse had enough free rein that it could drop its head to graze upon the pick. He held the musket across his body, index finger touching the trigger guard. Baras finished tying his horse before joining them. Rone gestured for the scout to lead the way. He paused, watching the soldier's departing back, allowing the scout to gain distance from them. Maintaining a good distance made it more difficult for the enemy were they to walk into an ambush where a musket volley would decimate a group of soldiers bunched together.

He began walking, careful where he placed his feet, avoiding dead branches, or saplings, where pushing past them would cause unnecessary extra noise and movement. The trio moved in near silence. Several birds fluttered in the branches high above them, calling between one another. But, another noise, distant to begin with, pervaded the forest. As they advanced, the familiar noise grew in volume. Rone's eyebrows drew together and he clenched his jaw.

Military drums.

The beats fell in a precise, repeating pattern.

Sounding the beat for marching soldiers. Gods.

The scout swung around to him as he walked. Rone was not oblivious to the concern in the soldier's eyes, before he turned away again, leading the way up a small hill that would give them a good visual of the open plain Rone knew would roll out in the distance below them.

I'm not sure I want to see what will be upon the plain.

He passed between two trees and stopped in front of a sapling barring his advance. Touching the thin trunk, Rone pushed it aside slowly, side stepped around it and then guided the trunk back into place. When the upper branches of the sapling stopped moving, he removed his hand and continued to follow his scout.

Light invaded the forest as the trees thinned out and blue sky drifted in through the gaps in the canopy. Rone noticed the scout crouch beside a thick shrub. He came to a stop and knelt beside his scout.

"Morning sir," the shrub whispered.

Rone flinched and turned and caught the stern glare of his second scout hidden within the shrub.

"We got a problem."

The loud drum beats brought him back and he looked out upon the plain below them. A cold wave swept across his chest and down into his guts as his eyes drifted across the endless ranks of Huronian infantry, line after line, unit after unit. Cavalry, auxiliary cavalry and the small square of household horsemen dedicated to protecting their king. He did a rapid calculation in his mind.

"At least thirty thousand, sir." Rone could barely make out the soft words.

If not more. Two things to note, they're marching west, towards Wendurlund and their king is with them. So definitely not some training exercise then.

"Seems we are at war, sir."

"It would seem so gentlemen."

The first scout touched Rone's shoulder. "There's something else, sir. Look to the centre of the Army."

He watched the massive formation, almost a mighty beast in its own right from this distance. Flashes of sunlight glanced from steel as armoured men marched, like light reflected from a babbling river.

"In the centre, sir. The wagon," the second scout's whispered voice pitched in.

Then he saw it, a small, wooden prison wagon rolling along between vast squares of infantry. He squinted and could make out the tiny figure of a man sat on the floor.

"What of it?"

"It's him, sir."

He frowned. "Speak plainly man, who?"

"It is Prince Henry, sir."

Another shard of ice lanced through his body, his lips parting, eyes widening. He licked his lips. "Are you sure?"

"They call me Eagle Eye for a reason, sir. I'm sure. It's the prince."

Rone's lips peeled apart and his teeth flashed from the depths of his beard as he snarled. He turned to the first scout and clenched a hold of his shoulder. "You lad, ride back to the column, halt them and bring them back here. Fast and quiet."

Rone released the man who brushed past him without a word and made his way back the way they'd travelled so recently. He looked out at the seemingly infinite army marching on the plain beneath them.

"We have work to do."

XII

Crouched behind a shrub, Vyder swept his gaze across the campfires that dotted the night enshrouded plain in a mighty circle. The sheer number of them gave some indication to the mighty army that were at harbour for the night. After the Army moved out into its position for the evening, parties were sent out in all directions into the forest to gather wood. The incessant *clop* of axes rang out all around Vyder as he and Ahitika remained hidden. One roving party had come within visual distance of him, but they remained ignorant of the assassin in their midst. He'd waited until nightfall before moving forward to a closer position. The ring created by the campfires was more than five miles across, at least. Occasionally, Vyder heard distant singing or laughter drift to his ears as the breeze changed direction. Around the closest campfire were several hundred soldiers. Some sat in groups, talking, others stood in idle gatherings, while some slept. Shifting his position to alleviate the ache in one foot, he saw all either had their personal weapons carried with them, or on the ground within arm's reach. That spoke of discipline and training.

What are we waiting for brother?

"Give me a moment, Gorgoroth," Vyder whispered. "We can't just walk in without a plan."

Why? You have me now, remember? You're more than sure it was the king's son locked up in that prison wagon. So we need to get in there one way or another. No time like the present.

He felt a soft touch on his elbow. "You talk to crazy one?"

The assassin looked at the young Kalote woman

beside him. Her head was cocked, eyes wide and he knew she was ready to flee at the hint of Gorgoroth's presence.

"You're safe Ahitika."

She relaxed and returned her attention to the army arrayed in the darkness before them, her black hair and olive skin making her almost invisible in the darkness. "What we wait for?"

See? The woman is all for strolling in as well! I'm beginning to like her.

He allowed air to fill his lungs before he let it out in a sharp exhalation. Although there might have been a massive army arrayed before him, infiltrating their ranks was far easier than gaining entry to a castle. Huge numbers of soldiers mixed with the dark of night could work in their favour. If things turned sour, confusion would reign supreme, giving him the upper hand.

"We wait for a moment Ahitika, there're probably soldiers watching the perimetre of the encampment, hidden in the darkness. I need to work out where they're most likely to be before we just wander on in."

There's no way to know for sure without *wandering on in.*

"How you know without walking forward?"

Vyder gritted his teeth, sat in silence and listened to the laughter peeling out in his mind.

I like her. Yes, I like her.

"I thought you hated all humans?" he whispered.

Not any more, brother. Shall we?

"Stay low and quiet, Ahitika. We move at a snail's pace."

He stood, withdrew his knife with one smooth, slow movement and stepped forward into the night, mindful of his footing. Although Vyder didn't check to see if Ahitika followed, he heard the soft pad of her moccasins behind him. Glaring at the campfire in the near distance, he watched for rapid movement or sudden calls of warning to suggest they were alerted to his presence.

The soldiers illuminated orange by the dancing flames of the fire remained in position, oblivious to what was happening outside of their circle of light. The air was cool, a refreshing change from the oppressive heat of the day. His shin slammed into a fallen branch and he winced, coming to a stop. Taking a pace back, he raised one foot and stepped over the obstacle with methodical lack of speed. Ahitika was crouched beside a tree, her face glowing in the soft light thrown by the fire in the near distance. She was looking back at him, waiting for him to catch up.

She is at home in the darkness.

Negotiating over a much smaller branch, he knelt beside her. She tapped his arm and gestured in front of them. Leaning towards him, she placed a cupped hand against his ear.

"Two soldiers sitting in grass, facing outward watching on other side of this tree."

He nodded. "Are you sure?"

She raised one eyebrow and glared at him.

"Do they know we're here?"

Her shoulders rose and fell in rapid motion, then finally her eyebrow fell into line with the other and she turned away.

Vyder stood, the crack of his knee seemed deafening in the night.

You're getting old.

Vyder felt suddenly numb, a heaviness creeping into his arms and legs.

Allow me, brother.

Gorgoroth dodged the tree and inside four strides was at full sprint. He leapt high, flying over the heads of the seated guards and landed lightly behind them. Swivelling around, he faced the backs of the soldiers. Before they could cry a warning, the first died with the hunting knife embedded in his neck at the base of the skull. Gorgoroth ripped the blade free and as the second soldier was half way to his feet, slammed it into the same area of his neck. The man was dead before his body thudded onto the ground.

Vyder clenched and opened his hands as feeling returned to his body. He covered his mouth and supressed a cough. Kneeling beside the taller of the two sentries, he unbuckled the deceased man's armour.

"What you do?"

He looked up at the Kalote woman standing over him.

"Get changed," he whispered. "If we come across any soldiers, it'll be easier to blend in if we're wearing their uniforms." He gestured towards the dead men at his feet.

She shrugged. "We come across soldiers, we kill them."

Vyder ignored the roar of laughter peeling through his mind.

"Not when there're tens of thousands of them. You don't know the Huronians. We'll be dead or worse if they find out who we are."

Ahitika moved in a blur and before he knew it, she was staring into his face. Her teeth bared, eyes wide, the flames in the near distance glinting from them, lending power to her fury.

"Don't tell me I not know these people. This *our* land! *Kalote* land!" she swept her hand out to encompass their surroundings. "I know Huron, my people know Huron. They are enemy. I kill Huron warriors where I find them." She tapped the scalps hung from her belt. "And if they strong warrior, I take scalp."

Vyder took a deep breath and let it out slow. "I'm sorry, Ahitika. I meant nothing by it."

She spoke rapid words in the Kalote language, spat on the ground, then turned away. She began to unbuckle the armour of the second sentry. Vyder dragged the armour clear, placed it on and began buckling it up. He was immediately aware of the weight, but knew his body would adjust. He flicked the cloak off his shoulder and felt it billow out behind him, touching the back of his trousers, then stooped to drag clear the armour leggings of the dead guard. The weight of the chest armour tipped him off balance and Vyder nearly fell as he was pulling on the leggings. They fit well over his trousers. Unclipping the strap beneath the cooling skin of the guard's chin, he lifted clear the open-faced helmet and lowered it onto his head. Tightening the strap, beneath his jaw, he locked it into place.

He turned to the Kalote woman. "Nearly finished?"

She stood before him, the chest armour several sizes too large, armoured leggings barely fitting and the helmet sitting so low on her head it hid the top of her eyes. Vyder supressed a laugh.

"Comfortable?" he couldn't help the smile that creased his lips.

Narrowed, partially hidden eyes glared up at him from beneath the helmet. "Let us get it done."

Vyder strode through the knee-length grass in the direction of the prison wagon. He'd burned the direction of the wagon into his mind prior to the dying sun slipping below the horizon. Confidence reasserted itself. Were they to be seen, they'd just look like another couple of guards.

Until you get stopped and questioned.

"Shutup," Vyder whispered.

Doubt crept into the back of his mind. The only words he knew of the Huronian language were 'yes' and 'no'.

Lucky for you brother, you have me. I speak Huronian fluently.

The doubt evaporated.

"If they question us, just don't get us killed."

Where's the trust my human friend?

Vyder listened to the chuckle boom in his mind. "You talk?"

Vyder glanced over his shoulder at Ahitika. "Everything is good. No need to worry."

"Ah, you talk to crazy one."

He returned his attention to his direction of travel and smiled. "Yes, I talk to crazy one."

The closest campfire was now at his right shoulder and would soon be behind them. At a guess, they'd need to cross another two miles of terrain before they reached their destination. He kicked something soft, lost his balance and found himself sailing through the air. Hard ground met his face and air erupted from his mouth in a rush. He groaned. A shouted sentence in the Huronian language exploded from behind him.

Let me help, brother.

Heaviness swept around his body and Vyder allowed the nature spirit to take control.

"You hear me, idiot? Who the hell was that?"

Gorgoroth grinned, leapt to his feet, turned around and knelt beside the Huronian soldier lying on the ground near him.

"I'm sorry boy, my mistake."

"Damn fuckin' right it's your mistake, why the hell are you walking through this area of the camp anyway?"

"It seemed like a good idea. Besides, I need the exercise." The nature spirit slapped the armour plate covering his stomach.

"Stick to the track. There's even rope marking it out over that way, closer to the fire. For the sake of the gods, just go away before I report you to my superior."

Gorgoroth's hand dropped to caress the hilt of the knife at his belt.

No, Gorgoroth! Just walk away.

His smiled widened, fingers clenching a hold of the weapon.

Gorgoroth! Trust me, we don't know who else is close by. If we break our disguise, we're done for.

The nature spirit clenched his jaw. "It won't happen again."

"See that it doesn't, or it'll be the skin of your back feeling the scourge of the whip come sunup."

Gorgoroth stood, tapped Ahitika on the arm and walked away.

"Should have slit his stinking throat," Gorgoroth whispered through clenched teeth.

Just walk!

The nature spirit stopped. "I've had enough for now brother, here you take the reins, or I'll end up killing the next person I come across."

Numbness flooded Vyder's arms and legs. He locked his knees to prevent himself collapsing to the ground.

Ahitika prodded him in the back and something in Huronian. He clutched a hand to his mouth and stopped himself from coughing, clearing his throat instead.

He glanced over his shoulder. "It is I."

The Kalote woman switched back to Wendurlund. "Ah, I see. You not speak Huronian anymore. You crazier than cut snake."

Vyder stifled a chuckle. When he was sure the muscles of his legs would support his weight, he walked on towards the fire. The flickering light cast by the flames illuminated the ground, aiding their vision. Three times, Vyder narrowly avoided stepping into the middle of clusters of sleeping soldiers. While the camp fires dotted around the vast open ground gave light to warriors sitting or standing around the tall stacks of burning wood, it was only a fraction of the Huronian army. The majority of the enemy soldiers were hidden in the shadows sleeping, or talking with one another in hushed tones.

From out of the darkness appeared a faint, white horizontal line, growing more distinctive with each step. Vyder reached out and clamped a hand onto the rope. The campfire was close, close enough for him to hear the voices of the soldiers cast in hues of flickering orange. He turned away from the campfire, released his grip on the rope and began walking, keeping the white line signifying the track on his right side. Ahitika's soft steps fell in behind him. The position of the prison wagon, still etched in his mind was in front of them and to the left. It would be a long walk in, but if the rescue was successful, an even longer stroll out.

If unsuccessful, we don't walk out at all.

He grunted in agreement. They walked in silence for some time before he heard movement ahead of them. The gentle thud of boots grew louder and out of the darkness appeared the silhouette of a tall Huronian solider heading straight for him. The Huronian rattled off a sentence in an aggressive tone of voice, Vyder stepped out of the way and then the soldier had passed them by.

Ahitika stopped beside him. "He said move over. We stick to left of track."

"He say anything else?"

"Yes, don't know word, though. I think he liken you to stupid animal."

Vyder smiled and moved on. "Fair enough."

Several times they strode past small clusters of Huronian soldiers moving in the opposite direction, probably on their way to relieve soldiers standing watch. Vyder had heard many tales of how weak and unprofessional the Huronian army was, but he realised none of it were true. A cold chill swept down his spine. If the Huronian continued their march into Wendurlund territory, King George's army would be facing a first class enemy.

***

Ahitika clenched a grip on the helmet and pushed it back up, so she could see properly. The heavy steel dome continued to slip down her forehead hindering her line of sight.

How did the Huronian soldiers fight weighed down with all of this rubbish?

Her legs and neck ached under the weight of the chest armour and helmet. With a curse, she adjusted the helmet once more. The thud of boots upon the ground was muffled from within the enclosure of steel and moments later the silhouettes of another group of

Huronian soldiers trudged past. She glared at them as they swept by, willing them to stop and question her. One of them might be worthy of scalping, but she doubted it. The Huronian warriors, however, remained silent, minded their business and disappeared into the night behind her.

She returned her focus to the wide back of the tall highlander walking in front of her. Ahitika could barely see him in the blackness, other than a figure slightly darker than the night itself. He paused and she narrowly missed barging into him.

"We're almost there, little human. Are you ready to fight?" The crazy one spoke in fluent Huronian. The pale flash of teeth gave a hint of the grin widening his mouth from within the depths of the open-faced helm.

She adjusted the steel dome upward and stared at the single gently glowing blue eye that appraised her. "Always. How have the Huronian soldiers not noticed your eye, though?"

"I close it each time we walk past a group. Vyder's vision is enough for me until the enemy have departed."

The tall assassin changed direction and headed off the track. She dropped a hand and touched the steel of the chest armour. She could feel her breastplate wedged against her breasts beneath the Huronian steel and wanted, *needed* to run her fingers across it. She wanted to feel the power of The Great Spirit. But, the cold, lifeless armour hanging from her shoulders formed a barrier stopping her from gaining comfort from the Kalote breastplate. For now, the Great Spirit and the soft voices of her ancestors were separated from her. She cursed and followed the tall crazy man. They travelled in silence for what felt like an age, the ache in her legs and neck growing. Soon she would cast the helmet and armour aside. Damn the consequences!

I'd rather die with the wind in my hair, than entrapped in a heavy metal cage like some animal.

"I seem to have lost my way!"

Ahitika was about to tell him to shut his mouth, when she heard a new voice.

"Aye, you certainly have, boy. You need to go back the way you come from. The main track is a fair way off. How the hell did you get this lost?"

She stepped alongside the assassin and the scene came into view. She slammed a hand onto the helmet and pushed it away from her field of vision. The dull glow of a single torch attached to the prison wagon gave limited light to the area.

"There's two of you!"

Oh, you can count Huronian! Good for you.

The muscles of her face contorted, pulling her mouth into a snarl.

The dim, flickering light provided by the torch fought back the darkness blanketing the wagon. Her eyes narrowed and in the gloom she could just make out the figure of a man sat on the floor, knees drawn up to his chest, arms hugging his legs and head resting on one arm.

"That second one, looks like he's got the build of a twelve year old."

A chortle broke the silence and another Huronian soldier appeared to stand beside the first. "You're not wrong," the newcomer's voice was deeper and for some reason Ahitika thought she heard a hint of cruelty in his voice.

Ever come across a Huronian that wasn't cruel?

Her jaw bulged.

"How old are you lad?"

"He's mute. Tongue cut out before he joined up," Gorgoroth spoke, cutting off Ahitika as she made ready to reply.

She shuffled forward a step as Gorgoroth slapped a hand onto her back, the metallic ring echoing out over the immediate vicinity. "Bloody terrible. He'll see his nineteenth year this coming Summer."

Gorgoroth slammed another hand against her back and she lurched forward, although regained her balance before she was forced forward another step. "Won't you boy?"

She snarled, pushed the helmet out of her vision and glared up at the crazy one beside her.

Is he doing this deliberately? I'll cut his stinking throat.

Ahitika strode forward, felt Gorgoroth's hand clamp onto her shoulder but shrugged it away. Her fingers snaked around the haft of the torch and she pulled it clear of the bracket holding it in place.

One of the guards stepped forward. "The hell you doing boy?"

Ahitika ignored him and shoved the torch in between the bars of the prison wagon. The light illuminated the prisoner.

He's skinnier than a starving dog on its last legs! And this is a prince? Pathetic.

"Good idea boy," Gorgoroth stopped alongside her. "We may as well see the prisoner while we're here before we head off. No harm is that is there?"

"I suppose not."

Ahitika felt Gorgoroth lean forward, pressing his forehead against the bars. "Exactly as I thought," he spoke softly.

It is confirmed then. This is the man we came here for.

The Kalote warrior withdrew the torch, moved

around the crazy one and dropped the torch back into its bracket. Her hand dropped to her waist and came up holding her hunting knife. She lunged forward and buried it into the throat of the first guard, the weapon's advance only halting when the hilt slammed against the skin of his neck. Hot blood flooded across her fingers and trickled up her arm, dripping from her elbow to the ground. She ripped the weapon clear and stepped away as the wide-eyed guard clutched at the wound from which his life-blood pulsed. He tried to speak, but blood bubbled from his mouth and slid down his chin.

As she prepared to attack the second guard, the tall crazy one had beat her to it and was already lowering the dead guard to the ground, his knife buried in the back of the Huronian's neck at the base of the skull. The Wendurlund assassin had moved with lightning speed.

He turned to her and bent down to look her in the face, that pale blue eye lancing through her. "What the hell are you doing?"

"We're here to free the prince are we not?" she spoke through clenched teeth. "We can't really do that with these pieces of scum wandering around can we?" she prodded the body before her with a boot.

"And how do you expect we gain entry to the prison wagon? Hm?" Gorgoroth cocked his head, teeth flashing as his mouth widened in a death's head grin. "Any thoughts?"

Ahitika glanced at the wagon, focusing between the bars at the statue-still prisoner who was now watching them with interest. She cast a look back at the crazy one. "Hadn't thought that far."

"Fantastic! What an incredible plan." He clapped a hand to his forehead. "I hadn't even *considered* that line of thought." The assassin straightened to look over her head at the wagon behind her and switched to the Wendurlund language. "And what of you, prince, any thoughts?"

She turned back to see the prisoner had scuttled closer to them, he sat hands clasping the bars, head pressed between them, like some rabid dog eager for freedom. "One of them carries a key."

Ahitika kicked one of the bodies and after a moment's pause to gather her thoughts, also changed to the tongue of Wendurlund. "One of these has key?"

"No, not those. There is a guard by the name of Braif, he has the keys." The skin covered skeleton pointed on the far side of the prison wagon. "He's sleeping over there somewhere." The prince looked at the sky. "But hurry. We don't have much time."

Ahitika followed his line of sight and noticed that the eastern horizon was turning a hue of gunmetal grey, a stark contrast to the black blanket cast over the rest of the sky. Dawn was coming.

* * *

Gorgoroth cursed. He tapped Ahitika on the shoulder. "Little one, you stay here, I'll summon this Braif."

Get moving Gorgoroth!

"You don't say, brother?" he muttered, striding away from the prison wagon.

Once he'd negotiated around the far side of the wagon, he crouched beside the first sleeping figure he saw. Grasping a hold of the sleeping man's shoulder, he shook it. "Braif?" he asked in the Huronian language.

The sleeping man took a deep breath and groaned. Gorgoroth shook harder. "Braif!"

"I'm not Braif, he's sleeping two down from me idiot. I've already done my watch tonight. Go away!"

Gorgoroth chuckled and patted the man's cheek. "Sorry to bother you."

"Piss off and leave me alone!"

He stood, stepped over the sleeping figure, ignored the next two sleeping guards and knelt beside the fourth man. He clamped a hand onto the man's arm and felt it tense beneath his grip. "What is it?" the man whispered.

"Braif?"

"Yeah, what the fuck is it?"

"We have a problem."

A groan, a stretch and Braif sat up, yawning softly. "Gods, I was having a good dream too. This better be life threatening!"

"You have your keys on you?"

A metallic tapping followed as Gorgoroth realised the dark figure must have been patting a hand against the key ring at his waist. "Always."

"Then yes, it's life threatening."

Gorgoroth reached down with both hands and snapped Braif's neck with the sound of a sodden branch breaking. He lowered the body to the floor slowly, before patting his hands down the man's flanks until his fingers touched the keys. He detached them from the guard's belt and stood, moving back the way he'd come with the same care.

He reached the prison wagon, found the small, locked door and chose a key at random. Too small. He flicked through them. Too large, wrong shape. Each one he tried, failed. Distant shouts broke out on the edge of the encampment. There were several voices, with others adding to the cacophony with each passing moment. Although he could not make out the words, the tone of voice gave a hint to the urgency.

He turned to Ahitika standing nearby, watching him struggle with the keys. "They've found the bodies of the guards we killed earlier!" he hissed.

She chuckled.

Then an ear piercing horn shred the still air asunder. "The enemy are amongst us!"

Gorgoroth paused. There was no denying the words shouted by the deep pitched voice. The horn blew again. "The enemy are amongst us! To arms!"

Let me try Gorgoroth, you have no clue.

"Fine!"

Vyder coughed, locked his knees against the numbness sweeping his legs, clenched his fingers into fists to fend off pins and needles sweeping his hands, squeezed shut his eyes, then forced them open again a moment later to focus upon the ring of keys. He clasped the torch out of its bracket and brought it close to the prison wagon's door. The lock was long and thin. He shoved the torch closer and leaned in so he was looking into the depths of the lock, ignoring the heat cast from the torch next to his face.

"It's a wooden lock, not metal." He opened the hand containing the keys and flicked through them. Finally he found a short, stubby wooden key hidden in the midst of the keys. Clasping a hold of it, he slid it into the lock and turned it gently. There was a click. He pulled on the door and it groaned open.

"Just what the bloody hell is going on here!" a guard appeared on the far side, rubbing sleep from his eyes. Another appeared behind him and a third stopped beside the pair. Bleary-eyed as they were, their focus soon became keen as they watched their prisoner step clear of the prison wagon and jump onto the ground.

"Here!" one of the guards screamed. "They're here!"

A protracted scream exploded from beside Vyder, sending a shudder up his spine and something pushed past him. He watched Ahitika sprint forward and with lightning speed was amongst the trio, her knife rising and falling. She moved around and through them with lithe agility and even as he withdrew his knife from its sheath and he prepared to help the Kalote warrior, the last guard fell to the ground, his wide, dead eyes staring up at the eastern sky, now hewn with streaks of deep purple and faded pink.

She ripped the metal helmet clear of her head and dropped it to the ground, long, black hair streaking down around her face, light glinting from fury-filled eyes hidden beneath strands of thick hair. She spoke a sentence in Huronian and spat upon the grass.

Vyder sheathed his knife. "It's me, Vyder."

Ahitika knelt beside one of the bodies. "I said," she wiped the knife clean upon one of their robes. "None of these worthy of scalping. Weak men."

He returned his attention to Prince Henry. The royal moved slow and it was obvious the man was struggling to walk. With more than two miles to travel out of the area and through forewarned throngs of enemy soldiers, a slow stumble would not do. He grasped hold of a forearm, drew Henry to him, ducked down and lifted the man over one shoulder. He straightened and turned in the direction from which they'd originally advanced. Although the prince was almost as tall as Vyder, he was skin and bones and lighter than a child.

"Time to leave."

Ahitika sheathed her knife. "Lead way, I watch our

backs. We may not live, but it is good day to die."

Vyder looked at the soft light flooding the eastern horizon and inhaled a refreshing breath of cool air. "Yes it is. I haven't seen Verone in so long."

"Verone? What you talking about?"

He let the air out in a rush and strode forward. "Never mind."

* * *

A blanket of mist covered the ground, hiding the hooves of walking horses from view. Dawn was fast approaching and already the sky was beginning to lighten. Captain Rone cast a look to his right, then his left. He was flanked by fifty soldiers on each side. The warhorse beneath him stumbled and Rone leaned back in his saddle to assist the animal in regaining its footing. The steep descent was perilous, made even more so by the thick forest through which they negotiated. It was near impossible to maintain any kind of formal formation given the terrain, so Rone was happy for his soldiers to array themselves in a ragged extended line, until the descent was at an end.

Horn blasts rent the air in the distance from the valley floor below, exactly where they intended to ride. More horns, then a hoarse shout. Rone was not completely fluent in the Huronian language, but he knew enough for the words to cause cold dread to sink into the depths of his guts.

Baras, seated on a destrier beside him, cleared his throat. "Enemy have breached their perimetre."

Rone grunted and tightened his grip on the reins. "So it seems. It may work in our favour, however."

The horses of the King's Own skidded, slipped and

carefully picked their way down the slope towards the valley depths awaiting them. The mist thickened as they progressed, hiding many of the horses from view so that it looked as if the soldiers were seated upon the mist itself in some magic feat. Gradually the angle of the incline became less treacherous and they were once again walking upon near flat ground. Rone cantered forward of the formation, swung his horse around, held his hand high above his head and signalled, 'halt'. Swivelling in his saddle, he repeated the command to those soldiers on the opposite flank. When he was sure all his soldiers had brought their destriers to a stop, he turned back towards the open plain waiting behind what little remained of the forest and urged his mount forward.

He walked his warhorse around several large trees and the plain opened up before him. He stopped beside a large bush and looked out upon the mighty army before him. A stick snapped beside him and Baras came to a halt nearby.

"Some sight, sir."

Rone nodded. "Our one hundred against their thirty thousand." He looked at his bugler and grinned. "What could go wrong?"

"Seems fair odds to me, sir. We'll have them surrounded by sunup."

The plain narrowed as Rone's eyelids drew closer together, cold focus returning to him. His smile faded. "They won't stand a chance," he muttered.

Shouts erupted from all over the camp. Now on lower ground, it was more difficult to see into the centre of the encampment. There was still a small descent to negotiate before the King's Own were on the plain proper and the slightly elevated position offered moderate view into the enemy formation. Rone swept the mighty army with slow, methodical progress, eyes stopping to analyse individual pockets of troops. Most were milling around, awoken suddenly from slumber, they were packing away blankets, or standing in confused blobs, probably trying to work out what was going on. Now, while confusion reigned amongst the Huronians, was the time to strike. But, Rone needed to know where to hit them in order to affect the retrieval of their prince.

"There, sir!" Baras's arm came up and he pointed towards the slight right of centre of the massive army before them.

Rone looked across at his bugler and followed the direction to which he pointed. There, stood almost hidden from view behind masses of troops awakening from sleep stood the prison wagon. His field of vision narrowed further as his eyelids drew even closer together. "It's empty Baras! The wagon's fucking empty. Where's Prince Henry?"

"Look three knuckles to the right of the wagon, sir."

Rone held his right arm out horizontal to the ground, clenched closed his hand and aimed his fist so the knuckle of his index finger sat just below the wagon. Counting three knuckles to the right, he saw a giant of a man and a small figure beside him. They were moving fast.

He dropped his hand back to rest on his thigh with a *slap*. "What of them?"

"They have Prince Henry, sir. Look closer, they're carrying him."

Rone released the reins and stood in the stirrups and refocused upon the pair. "By the Gods." He sat back down in the saddle. "So they do." He noticed on the furthest side of the Huronian encampment stood a mighty Ghost Oak, dwarfing all the forest. The tiny figures carrying the prince were in line with the tall tree. That would be his point of aim when the charge began. Once the last descent onto the plain below was made, the pair would disappear from view, hidden behind thousands of soldiers, on their feet trying to work out for themselves exactly what was taking place.

Rone turned the warhorse away and cantered back to his waiting soldiers. Halting before the extended line, he stood in the stirrups and held both hands above his head. Looking down the line of soldiers, he ensured all eyes were turned towards him. Then he began to use slow hand signals.

Arrow head formation. Form on me. I am the centre. No sound. No war cry. Follow my lead. Understood?

He shifted focus from one soldier to the next, ensuring each was nodding. When he'd made sure every single man understood what was required, he unclipped the full-faced war helm from his saddle and pushed it onto his head. The sounds of the forest immediately became a dull muffle as the cold steel covered his ears, the bottom edge of the helmet coming to rest against his chest armour. The visor was pivoted up out of his field of vision. He watched as his soldiers replicated him. It was not often the King's Own wore the full-faced battle helmets. By default, their work was usually conducted in the shadows, without their enemy ever knowing about their presence. But, the fight about to happen was overt. The exception was Baras, who wore an open-faced helm so that he could use the bugle when required. When the last man had unclipped and settled his helmet into place, Rone lifted a hand, grasped a hold of the visor and slammed it down over his face, his view immediately reducing to a horizontal slit the width of two fingers. A metal staccato echoed down the line of King's Own as his soldiers followed suit. He swung his warhorse away and pushed the animal into a fast walk. War spirit flooded his being, his heart thundering within his chest.

Leaning back in his saddle, Rone allowed the warhorse to work its way down the small descent, past trees, bushes and saplings. The branches of one thick shrub brushed his thigh and then the plain opened out before them. Looking over the heads of the distant enemy, he spotted the Ghost Oak on the opposing side of the open ground. Steering the destrier towards the tree, he pushed the animal into a trot. Twisting in his saddle, he watched the right flank fan out at an angle behind him. Baras, the closest soldier on his right side, lined his horse up so the animal's head was adjacent to the rump of Rone's warhorse. Turning to the opposite side, the man on the left flank did the same and within moments the arrowhead formation was in place and progressing at the trot. He returned his attention to the front and pushed the warhorse into a canter.

Thousands of soldiers in the near distance were on their feet, milling around in groups. Their attention, however, remained fixated towards the centre of the encampment. They were still trying to work out where exactly the threat lay. As far as Rone could see, none of the enemy had noticed the charge fast approaching their position. Turning in his saddle, he rechecked the left and right flanks. Both were exactly where they should be, progressing at the canter. Patting the horse's neck, he readjusted his position in the saddle. He pushed the beast into a gallop, raised his arm above his head and then brought it forward in a blur of movement, so his outstretched arm was horizontal to the ground pointing directly at the Huronian mass before them. The destrier's hooves drummed against the earth, knee length grass blurring by beneath Rone. A loud snort just to his right rear indicated Baras was with him. He cast a glance over his left shoulder and saw the left flank was arrayed out at an angle behind him, matching his gallop. Specks of earth flung up into the air behind some of the animals as their hooves thundered against the ground. He returned his attention to the enemy soldiers before him.

Rone ignored the weapons in the large holster attached to the saddle just forward of his right knee. The initial section of the charge would rely on the speed and weight of the destriers to carry them through the enemy ranks. Weapons wouldn't play a part. Becoming bogged down and losing momentum, especially when so badly outnumbered, would spell the doom of his tiny force.

If we can force our way through to the prince before the Huronians know what's going on, we might have a chance at fighting our way back out.

He looked at the huge Ghost Oak in the distance and made a slight adjustment to his direction. Rone saw a boulder half hidden amongst the grass directly in front of his warhorse's path of advance.

Oh shit!

The warhorse's mighty muscles bunch beneath him and the animal sailed over the boulder, hooves slamming onto the ground on the other side of the obstacle. As the Huronian soldiers filled his field of vision, one of them turned towards him, his eyes widened, mouth dropping open. Before he could shout a warning, the horse slammed into the soldier, the Huronian disappearing beneath a blur of hooves.

Rone tilted forward in the saddle as the warhorse brought both hind legs off the ground to launch a powerful double-barrelled kick. The dull crack that followed was muffled by the helmet as was the pain-filled screech of the injured enemy solider. Onwards the formation pushed, barging soldiers out of their way as they hammered towards the centre of the enemy camp. The lucky soldiers were forced aside, the ones unfortunate enough to come in contact with the galloping warhorses were left bloody and broken upon the earth, those that survived shouting or screaming their agony to the sky.

Rone's warhorse, ears flat back to its skull, clenched the face of one Huronian soldier between his teeth and with a jerk of his powerful neck, sent the enemy warrior sailing through the air. Then the destrier battered through the ranks standing behind the man.

Apart from the thunderous cacophony of the warhorses, the soldiers of the King's Own remained silent. Gradually, the drum of the destriers' hooves were drowned out by the shouting of the Huronian army. Eventually the noise from thirty thousand throats rolled out across the plain hiding all other sound. The roar filled Rone's helmet, ringing in his ears.

Clenching his teeth and keeping a firm grip on the reins, he looked over his left shoulder. The left flank was still with him, belting their way through rank after rank of enemy soldiers.

Excellent!

Shooting a look to his right side, the right flank was still intact. He flinched as he saw something brown advancing between Baras and he. He tried to focus between the thin, horizontal gap the slit in the helmet provided, but the thing had moved beyond him with lightning speed. He felt sharp pain shoot from his knee and up his thigh as something barged past him, crushing his right leg against the saddle. Turning to face front again, he saw the riderless horse accelerate past him.

One of my soldiers is down.

His face creased into a snarl, fury spreading through him. Focusing at the horizon, Rone raked the distant forest until he found that for which he searched. They were still heading towards the Ghost Oak. When they'd slammed through the next rank of Huronian soldiers, a section of open ground welcomed them before another mass of enemy ranks began. Urging his destrier onward, the animal slammed clean through the lines of enemy soldiers. Some of the Huronians were scrabbling for their muskets. They were still panicked, unsure, confused.

Won't be long before they're organised and start putting musket volleys down upon us.

The horses of the tiny unit of the King's Own barged, kicked and bit their way through the Huronian army like a hot knife through butter. With one final effort, Rone's warhorse broke through the ranks of the Huronian soldiers. Another small section of open ground greeted him at the centre of which was the trio for who they'd come. The tall man assisted the prince onto the destrier, which had so recently barged past Rone, the small man, skin the colour of smoke, leaping up behind the monarch's son with lithe agility. He turned to look at the approaching King's Own and Rone realised it was a woman.

Rone clasped a hand onto his visor and rotated it up and out of his field of view. He looked back at his bugler as they galloped.

"Baras! Reverse arrowhead, all round defence, outward face, blunderbuss."

"Yes, sir!"

The piercing scream of the bugle cut through the

roar of the mighty Huronian army, declaring each order with sharp precision.

Rone slowed to a canter, the left and right flanks streaming past him, Baras now sitting at his front right, the rest of the right flank arrayed in front of the bugler at a perfect angle. The left emanated the move and although Rone was still the centre of the arrowhead, from a bird's eye view, the arrowhead formation was reversed. The distant soldiers riding at the front of each flank changed direction towards each other once they'd ridden beyond the prince and his miniscule entourage, encircling the group.

The circle ensnared the mounted prince in rapid efficiency, warriors bringing their destriers to a skidding halt, turning them outward to face the Huronian army besieging them on all sides. Rone pushed beyond the circle and cantered towards the trio in the centre. The blunderbusses spoke with a unison *boom* from all around him, temporarily drowning out the roars of the enemy. The tall warrior held a hand to the warhorse's forehead as if soothing it.

How the bloody hell did he capture a King's Own destrier? It should have shredded his face to pieces by now.

Rone leaned forward, grasped a hold of the spear haft and ripped the weapon clear of the sheath. Holding the reins in one hand he gave them one gentle tug and his mount halted beside the horse which had once belonged to his fallen soldier. He held the spear down at the man, the polished spear tip hovering just beneath his chin. One firm thrust and it would skewer him. Rone didn't need to look around to know that Baras was covering the woman seated behind the prince.

"Who the fuck are you?"

The tall warrior turned from the horse and held up

both hands, palms open. "I am Vyder Ironstone, sent by King George to rescue the prince."

One of his eyes seemed to shine a bright blue, giving him a strange look.

A highlander.

"And what does a highlander want with our prince?"

The man dropped his hands by his side. Rone thrust the spear forward but refrained from following through, the spear tip touching the skin of the highlander's throat. "Hands where I can see them."

Boom, another volley of blunderbuss echoed out, cutting Huronian soldiers down.

He raised his hands again. "The king offered a handsome price."

"Running out of time," the woman spoke with a thick Kalote accent.

She's right. No time for more questions. He looked at the prince. Sunken eyes stared back at him from a gaunt face. *Gods he looks half-dead. At least they're helping him.*

Rone sheathed the spear and gestured at Vyder. *If that's even his name.* "Climb up behind me, but if you try anything, Baras here will put a spear through you. Am I clear?"

Boom.

The highlander nodded and leapt up onto the warhorse behind the King's Own officer. He leaned over and clasped the reins of the horse upon which sat Prince Henry. He pulled the horse closer and glared at the prince.

"My lord, we are taking you out of here. It's going to be messy and we may not all survive. I need you to hang onto this horse with all your strength and no matter what happens, or how many of my men fall, keep riding for Lisfort."

The long, dirty locks hanging limp around the prince's head swayed back and forth as he nodded. "Let us go home," the king's son muttered.

Rone released the reins. "Baras, call cease fire, swine array, full charge, direction of advance."

"Sir."

They should have reloaded their blunderbusses by now.

The King's Own warriors moved with practised speed, melding into the swine array facing the direction from which they'd arrived. Making sure the prince was by his side in the protected centre of the formation, he caught the royal's eye, gave a nod then looked away to focus on the front ranks. The soldiers at the head urged their warhorses from the walk straight into the gallop.

Rone stood in his stirrups, but was unable to see the enemy formations in front of his small unit.

We will be upon them in moments.

Taking his seat, the warhorse lurched into a gallop beneath him, along with those warriors surrounding him. The noise of the Huronian army diminished to a dull roar as the thunder of hooves took over.

"Baras!" he shouted. The bugler looked at him. "Front rank blunderbuss, then spears."

The bugle blasts peeled out followed almost immediately by the *boom* of several blunderbuss carried by those warriors at the spear point of the charge. The screaming of dying enemy became louder as the swine array punched through the Huronian ranks.

Rone looked across at the prince. He held on tight, as advised. Turning in his saddle, he managed to see through the ranks of his soldiers to either side. They were surrounded by enemy soldiers, continuing to charge through the Huronian ranks.

"Baras! Left and right flank, blunderbuss, then spears."

The soldiers on each extreme flank were reaching for their blunderbusses even as the bugle was still sounding. *Boom.* The lethal weapons spoke point-blank into the enemy ranks either side of the fast moving swine array. The weapons were replaced with spears and sunlight flashed against the sharp, polished steel as spear tips were thrust down into enemy soldiers.

The crackle of return fire started. Musket shot zipped over their heads. Rone was always intrigued why rushed and panicked enemy soldiers almost always fired high, missing their targets. By the time that section of enemy had reloaded, Rone's unit would be long gone.

Another barrage of muskets fired from the left. Point blank. Straight into Rone's troops. The sickening scream of a horse pierced the air. He shot a look in that direction. None of his soldiers had fallen. One horse was slowing, but several King's Own warriors had rallied around the horse and rider, providing protection.

"Baras! Battle at will."

Those nursing the injured horse withdrew muskets and provided covering fire for their comrade.

He glanced across at the prince. He was still holding on tight, his face determined.

Still fight in him yet.

As fast as it'd started, the swine array punched through the enemy ranks and sped for the tree line from which they'd charged.

"Baras! Rear rank, protect rear, blunderbuss."

Rone didn't need to look behind him to know that those forming the rear rank had swung their warhorses around to face the enemy, withdrawn their blunderbusses and *boom*.

303

Even as the noise of the weapons faded, trees whipped by them and the swine array was consumed by the forest.

"At the walk, loose formation, no sound."

The bugle spoke the commands and within moments, the formation of King's Own had slowed and broken formation, the soft thud of hooves and horses struggling to regain their breath the only sounds pervading the forest.

Rone cantered to the front of the formation, stood in his stirrups and used hand signals above his head. *Follow me!*

* * *

"Did we just do that?" hissed a soldier nearby. "We just charged against thirty thousand enemy soldiers!" his teeth flashed, mouth widening into a grin.

"Something to tell my children's children many decades from now," another spoke.

"We were probably only successful because of the sheer size of the enemy," the officer seated in front of Vyder said.

"How does that work, sir?"

The officer's shoulders rose and fell. "We struck fast and were amongst them before they knew what was going on. Their lines of communication were a mess. Aside from those standing directly in the path of our charge, no one else knew what was happening. Had we attacked a force of one thousand, they could have rallied much faster and brought fire upon us before we even reached our target."

Vyder released his grip on the King's Own officer. The charge was over and it was easier to maintain his balance while the horse was walking. The officer pulled clear the steel helmet and clipped it onto his saddle.

Vyder leaned forward in the saddle. "Do you think we could get a hurry on?"

The officer whirled on him, wet, sweaty hair slapping against Vyder's face. "Watch your tone!" the man hissed.

He wiped his face with a hand. "In case you'd forgotten, the Huronian Army are on our heels. You think they're just going to let us go without at least trying to recapture the prince?"

"Keep your bloody voice down, highlander! We're resting the horses. Once they've regained their breath, they'll pick up the pace again. Until that time keep your teeth together and sit there. Understood?"

Bossy little monkey isn't he, brother?

Vyder answered the officer and Gorgoroth with a single word. "Yes." The words the officer used gnawed at him, though. "What do you mean *they'll* pick up the pace?"

"I'll explain soon."

Cares for his horses, though. That is something at least.

A keening sound started somewhere on the left, gaining Vyder's attention. Several mounted soldiers were bunched around a comrade, who had dismounted. In unison, the entire formation slowed to a halt. The horse was injured, copious amounts of blood sliding from a wound on its rump, to drip to the forest floor. It had raised one of its hind legs off the ground, no longer able to weight bear on the hoof.

They unsaddled the animal, the soldier stroking the animal's face, speaking soft words. When he'd finished comforting his horse, the soldier wiped his eyes with the back of his hand, stepped back, brought musket to bear and fired a shot. The horse was dead before it collapsed to the floor. Passing the musket to a comrade, the man knelt by the dead destrier, resting his forehead against his horse's face, his shoulders shuddering.

"They really do care for their horses," Vyder whispered.

Aye brother. Even Gorgoroth's voice sounded subdued. *They do. I like these horse warriors.*

"You'll need to switch horses, highlander."

"Why is that?"

The officer turned to look at him over one shoulder. "Because I have one of my men lying dead back there. Now the horses are rested, I'm returning to retrieve my soldier. Dismount and mount up with Baras."

Vyder did at he was bid.

"Baras, you have control of the formation. Ride for Lisfort. Inform the king of the threat approaching."

"Sir, I'll come with you, you may need help."

A group of soldiers urged their mounts closer, ready to join their commander in retrieving their fallen brother in arms.

Yes, that way I can kill some more little monkeys.

Vyder could even hear the smile in Gorgoroth's voice as he spoke from the safety of his mind.

"No! I'll work better on my own this time. It'll be harder for the enemy to detect one man. Get going, Baras. Take the soldiers home, they've done well today. Get the prince to safety. I'll not be far behind you."

"Yes, sir."

The officer pointed at Vyder. "And you, highlander."

He held the piercing gaze of the officer, waiting for him to speak.

"Thank you for your help. Had you not already freed the prince from his cage, we may well have failed today. You have my thanks." He turned to Ahitika. "You too, young lady."

Ahitika nodded. "Welcome."

Vyder didn't know the officer's name. He raised a hand. "Take it easy out there, King's Own."

The officer turned his destrier and cantered away.

Brother?

Vyder grunted.

Shall we go home?

* * *

The distraught soldier was pulled away from his dead horse. He mounted behind a comrade and then the tiny force were underway, negotiating the forest at a steady trot. Towards Lisfort. Towards their home. To their families eagerly waiting their return. But advancing behind them marched the Huronian Army.

In front of that mighty force were several hundred cavalry heading for the forests into which the King's Own had disappeared so recently. They were galloping.

<u>Novels by Keith McArdle</u>

<u>The Unforeseen Series</u>

The Reckoning: The Day Australia Fell
The Unforeseen Series Book One

Australia has been invaded.

While the outnumbered Australian Defence Force fights on the ground, in the air and at sea, this quickly becomes a war involving ordinary people.

Ben, an IT consultant has never fought a day in his life. Will he survive?

Grant, a security guard at Sydney's International Airport, finds himself captured and living in the filth and squalor of one of the concentration camps dotted around Australia. Knowing death awaits him if he stays, he plans a daring escape.

This is a dark day in Australia's history. This is terror, loneliness, starvation and adrenaline all mixed together in a sour cocktail. This is the day Australia fell.

Aftermath

The Unforeseen Series Book Two

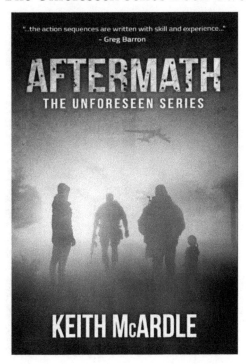

Mick and his family have returned home to the farm following Indonesia's withdrawal. But thousands of battle-hardened enemy soldiers remain hidden in the forests and hills, ready to strike when they are least expected. This fight will take Mick to the limit, and protecting his family will require all his strength and determination.

Jimmy and Spud lead a platoon through the Australian scrub on relentless guerrilla strikes. But when they find themselves outnumbered and outgunned, it might have all been for nothing.

A new Australia will rise again ... or will it?

Havoc

The Unforeseen Series Book Three

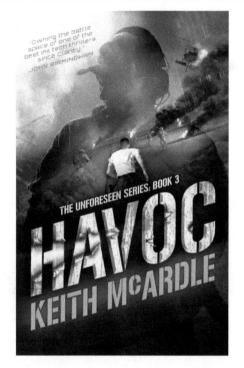

Australia has survived invasion.

Now the people of Brisbane must face a new, fearsome threat. At the same time, Ethan and his small team of specialist soldiers are tasked with a mission deep within the heart of Indonesia. When the mission goes horribly wrong, they have to fight their way out of a situation that may be their end.

Hiding is no longer an option.

Stand Alone Novels

Tour To Midgard

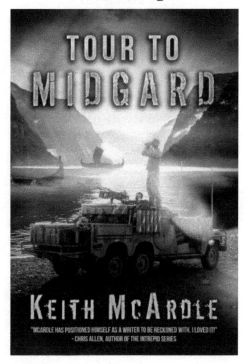

Tasked with a mission in Iraq, an Australian SAS patrol deploy deep behind enemy lines. But when they activate a time portal, the soldiers find themselves in 10th century Viking Denmark, a place far more dangerous and lawless than modern Iraq. The soldiers have no way back. Join the SAS patrol on this action adventure and journey into the depths of a hostile land, far from the support of the Allied front line. Step into another world...another time.

Short Stories by Keith McArdle

Assassin

Vyder Ironstone is an assassin with a troubled past. At the order of his king, Vyder must undertake his most dangerous mission yet. A mission from which he may never return. If he is successful, it might just be enough to alleviate war tearing the kingdom apart. The prospect of failure is not worth considering.

Against The Odds

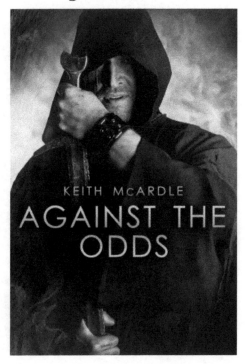

Three veteran hunters are on the trail of a supernatural creature. It is a simple tracking mission, promising easy money. But things go horribly wrong and the mercenaries realise too late that they are facing one of the deadliest creatures known to man. Embroiled in a desperate fight for survival, their doom may well await them.

Ground Zero

Generations after a bloody nuclear civil war, the United States is not as we know it. The inhabitants of the Northern states live as normal, but the South, after being decimated during the Second Civil War, are a changed people. Nuclear fallout has stolen any vestige of humanity. When the aircraft carrying the President of the Northern United States takes an erroneous detour, it is shot down somewhere over the south.

Now Brek and his small team of Delta Force soldiers must infiltrate enemy territory to save the president. But outnumbered and with time rapidly running out, they will be hard pressed to fight off the onslaught about to surround them. Can they survive?